PENGUIN METRO READS

WISH I COULD TELL YOU

Durjoy Datta was born in New Delhi, and completed a degree in engineering and business management before embarking on a writing career. His first book—*Of Course I Love You . . .*—was published when he was twenty-one years old and was an instant bestseller. His successive novels—*Now That You're Rich . . .*; *She Broke Up, I Didn't! . . .*; *Oh Yes, I'm Single! . . .*; *You Were My Crush . . .*; *If It's Not Forever . . .*; *Till the Last Breath . . .*; *Someone Like You*; *Hold My Hand*; *When Only Love Remains*; *World's Best Boyfriend*; *The Girl of My Dreams*; *The Boy Who Loved*; *The Boy with the Broken Heart* and *The Perfect Us*—have also found prominence on various bestseller lists, making him one of the highest-selling authors in India.

Durjoy also has to his credit nine television shows and has written over a thousand episodes for television.

He lives in Mumbai. For more updates, you can follow him on Facebook (www.facebook.com/durjoydatta1) or Twitter (@durjoydatta) or mail him at durjoydatta@gmail.com.

WISH I COULD TELL YOU

DURJOY DATTA

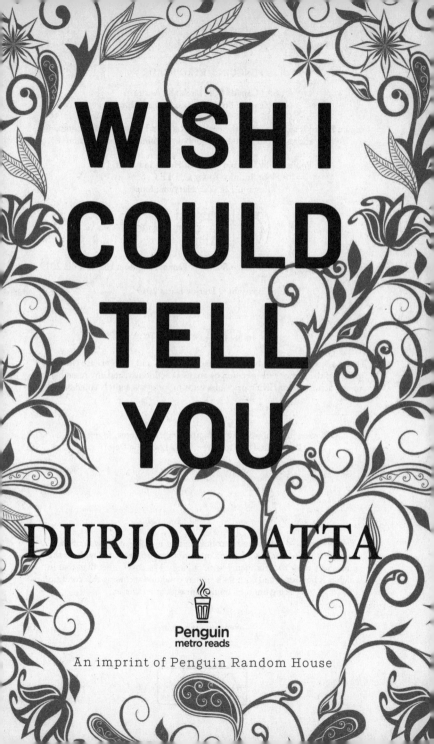

Penguin
metro reads

An imprint of Penguin Random House

PENGUIN METRO READS

USA | Canada | UK | Ireland | Australia
New Zealand | India | South Africa | China

Penguin Metro Reads is part of the Penguin Random House group of companies
whose addresses can be found at global.penguinrandomhouse.com

Published by Penguin Random House India Pvt. Ltd
7th Floor, Infinity Tower C, DLF Cyber City,
Gurgaon 122 002, Haryana, India

First published in Penguin Metro Reads by Penguin Random House India 2019

Copyright © Durjoy Datta 2019

ISBN 9780143448334

Typeset in Bembo STD by Manipal Digital Systems, Manipal
Printed at Thomson Press India Ltd, New Delhi

www.penguin.co.in

To Avantika

Ananth Khatri

'Everyone dresses up for the first day of work, *beta*,' says Papa.

'You will look good, Ananth. At least wear it once and see for yourself. Just once? For us?' says Maa, dangling a blazer in front of me.

'You made me wear a frock, said I would look good and took me to Chachu's wedding. I can't trust your word now, can I?' I grumble.

'You were three,' says Papa. 'And you looked so cute, beta.'

'He looked like a pretty girl,' says Maa.

Papa looks at Maa and both their eyes glaze over. They smile and get lost in the memories of me as a child. My growing up has been hard on them. If they could, they would choose the three-year-old in a white frock over the twenty-three-year-old they are struggling to get into a blazer.

'We should get the album out,' says Papa.

'If I see that album once more, I will burn it!' I tell Papa, who is a nostalgia addict, an obsessive recorder and revisit-er of the past, and he stays put. 'Give me the receipt, I will return the blazer on the way back.'

'I lost it,' says Papa.

'Your papa got it with so much love. Wear it once?' says Maa.

'It's unnecessary. And who asked you get it from Zara?'

Papa gives in and fishes out the receipt from the file he maintains of the quarterly expenses. I knew he hadn't lost the receipt. There's a file for every quarter of our lives. Despite certain sections of our house looking like a government office with tall stacks of files held together by strings gathering dust and cobwebs, sometimes it's exciting to see receipts from grocers, cablewallahs, and other regular expenses from the eighties and the nineties. Every paisa we have spent over those decades has been recorded in those files. The ink is fading from most, so every weekend Papa and I click pictures and upload them to Google Photos.

'Are you sure, beta, that you want to return it?' asks Maa.

'Papa's not getting paid for the overtime he is putting in for the past three months and he's behaving like a child,' I say.

'Fine, fine, I won't spend,' relents Papa.

'If you do feel like spending, buy a new briefcase. Yours is tattered and torn,' I tell him.

'And throw away this lucky briefcase?'

Papa has been a junior engineer in the municipality for the last thirty-three years. The briefcase is the opposite of lucky.

For a second, I wonder what Mohini would think of me in a blazer. She would probably think it's stupid too. I brush away the idea.

Maa serves me a big helping of curd and sugar and doesn't rest till I have scraped the bowl clean. We leave for the Vishnu Mandir after that.

At the neighbourhood temple, Maa–Papa are the only ones chanting out aloud, making a spectacle of their devotion to Vishnu. Papa, 5'4" and Maa, 5'1", take very little space in the world. They let people get ahead in the long queue to the water tank. They talk so softly that one can barely hear them. They sit through the extended lunch hours at the government bank without complaining. But here—in this little neighbourhood temple—they walk around with furrowed eyebrows, arched backs, angry grimaces, like titans, like the moody gods from the Vedas.

Maa–Papa's chants are louder, more fervent than the resident pundit's, who looks around, embarrassed, as if caught in his subterfuge. He tries to match my parents' *shraddha*, devotion, and falls short every time. The quieter devotees stare at my parents' synchronized chanting, impressed. The bells toll urgently in the background, as if swung by the strength of their hymns.

'You are named "Ananth" after the serpent Lord Vishnu rests on,' Maa tells me like every time.

And like every time I watch them here, I imagine an enormous serpent irritably stirred out of sleep, coiling and uncoiling around the earth, by the alarm-clock like hymns of my parents.

Papa puts a *tika* on my head, closes his eyes and says, 'May you be the best member the medical team at WeDonate has ever had.'

'Did you thank Mohini in your prayers? She's why you got this job,' says Maa, thrusting prasad into my palms.

'She's the only reason?' I ask, faking anger.

'I . . .'

I laugh. 'I'm joking, Maa. Of course, I did. Did you think I wouldn't?'

When they leave the temple, Maa–Papa return to their natural, unintimidating selves, burdened with taxes and everyday struggles like potholes, spoilt milk and moulded bread. Papa pulls his trousers right up to his navel because that's where he thinks they should rest. Maa pulls the saree over her head because the sun's too bright. They both accompany me to the bus stop, struggling to keep up with me with their short steps. At 5'10", I'm a giant to them; but they don't forget to remind me how un-cuddle-able I'm now.

'You don't need to come,' I tell them.

They chide me, say I'm careless, that I will trip and come under the wheels of the bus. That shuts me up.

There are other children with their parents at the bus stop too. None of them are over thirteen.

The chartered bus turns around the corner. Maa slams her hand on the side of the bus till it comes to a complete stop.

'I will call the police if you drive an inch before everyone boards,' she uncharacteristically threatens the bus driver who had done nothing wrong.

She makes sure I'm the first to get on.

If there's one thing she hates more than bus and truck drivers, all of them murderers in Maa's eyes, it was Papa's scooter. It was the only topic they argued about. For ten years, Maa had asked Papa to stop driving the scooter and take a bus instead. But he wouldn't budge. He loved his two-stroke grey scooter.

The day I turned eighteen and expressed the desire to drive it to college, Maa—who didn't know how to drive a scooter—dragged it for miles and left it to rot under a flyover. We didn't find the scooter for years after that. She threatened to leave the house if either Papa or I even talked about it. Later when we needed the money, she led Papa to the scooter. It was hidden but clean and well-maintained. She used to wash it twice every week. Maa–Papa still share a good relationship with the ones they sold the scooter to. They live two colonies away from us and Papa drives it sometimes on Sundays.

'Sit behind the driver,' she shouts. 'That's the safest seat in the bus.'

Papa adds, 'Don't throw away the ticket.'

'And don't do *tukur tukur* on your phone too much. Concentrate or else you will miss your stop,' says Maa.

They wait at the bus stop till the bus drives away. A few children on the bus giggle as I take the seat Maa–Papa asked me to. The middle-aged woman sitting there shifts to make space for me.

As the bus turns around the corner, Maa calls me and starts to sob. She tells me it was just yesterday that it was my first day at school. 'How awfully you cried and how heartlessly we pushed you inside the gates of the school! And look at you now, you're happy to leave us behind,' says Maa.

'I will be back by 6 p.m.,' I say.

'Go now, do your job,' says Maa, angrily.

'Dream job, my foot,' says Papa.

'Papa—'

The call's cut.

'Parents, eh?' says the woman sitting next to me. 'I have a thirteen-year-old and he makes the same face you just did.'

'I'm twenty-three. They need to learn to spend a little time without me,' I say.

'First day?' she asks.

I nod.

When I'd told my parents about WeDonate's joining date, their faces had fallen. In another family, that might have been a reason for celebration—not in mine.

My restraint gives away after ten minutes and I send a group text 'will miss you'. And like petulant teenagers, they read my message and don't reply.

Google Maps shows the office is another forty minutes away. I will have to eventually find the right combination of metro and chartered buses to minimize travel time.

I type WeDonate.org in the address bar on my phone. I read up on all the medical campaigns they are running on their website. I take notes on how the stories can be told better.

I share the stories on all my social media profiles, urging people to donate for the medical procedures of people who can't afford it. When I'm done, I update my LinkedIn profile: Ananth Khatri, Campaign Manager, Medical Team, WeDonate. I met most of the team on the day of my interview, so I send them friend requests.

Helmed by Sarita Sharan, WeDonate was one of the first crowdfunding platforms in India. The concept was too simple for it to not exist. People who need money—for medical purposes, for college projects, for creative enterprises—sourcing money from everyday people. An online version of *chanda ikkhatha karna*, collecting donations.

The woman sitting next to me—she works in the HR department of a call centre—is intrigued when I tell her about the organization I'm joining and wants to know more.

'Two weeks ago, they had a case, that of a twelve-year-old girl who needed 15 lakh for a kidney transplant. So someone from the medical team wrote her story and the campaign went live. People shared and re-shared it on social media, thousands of donors read the story, took note and contributed,' I tell her. 'There were young people in colleges and schools parting with pocket money for a girl they didn't know and will never meet.'

'Anyone can contribute?'

'Yes, not only that. If you can't contribute, just share the story with others on social media. It might reach someone who can. The girls' parents got the money in ten days. Can you imagine? Everyone who gave a little was a hero!'

'And you're joining this team?' she asks.

'Absolutely, bang in the middle of all the action, like in a whirlpool of good karma. Matching people who need money the most to these heroes.'

She takes my number before alighting at her stop and wishes me luck. I might have made my first office-commute friend.

*

WeDonate is on the fifth floor of an old building in Paschim Vihar. It's an unlikely place for a start-up. Sarita Sharan, the pied piper of the crowdfunding industry, wanted to keep the costs down and pump every available resource into scaling the business.

Vishwas ji, at the guard's post, looks up from his cell phone and waves at me as I walk out of the elevator.

'*Stud lag rahe ho* (you're looking like a stud),' he says.

'*Aap se kam* (less than you),' I answer.

Vishwas ji smiles. He would have been quite a stud, middle-aged no doubt, with his bright smiling eyes and the dimpled cheeks had his teeth not rotted with gutkha. But I don't tell him that.

Last week, Vishwas ji chatted me up when I was waiting for my interview. He told me how WeDonate had crowdfunded 5 lakh for his daughter's engineering studies when he had given all up as lost; she's now in second year, mechanical engineering. We shared my lunch after the interview.

'Did you get the books I couriered?' I ask.

'Haan ji. My daughter told me there are notes on the margin too—that's really helpful.'

'If she needs anything else, will you tell me?'

'Of course,' says Vishwas ji. '*Aur bhabhiji kaisi hai* (how is the sister-in-law)?'

I tell him she's fine. Mohini and I aren't married but I don't correct him. *Girlfriend kaisi hai* wouldn't have the same ring to it.

Twenty pairs of eyes look up from the laptops and phone screens, flash the briefest of smiles, synchronized more tightly than the Olympic swimming teams, and get back to work. The medical team sits in a far corner of the room. That's where I will be sitting from today. My hands are clammy from nervousness.

Nimesh Arora from IT is scratching his head, making dandruff flecks rain on his keyboard when I find him.

'Don't mind him,' says Nikhat Shaikh.

'Been there, done that,' I say and Nimesh flashes me a thumbs-up.

I had mistaken Nimesh and Nikhat for siblings. They are dating—I found out when Karunesh had made me meet the team after my interview. Nikhat and Nimesh are older than I am, but with their small round faces, big, surprised eyes, turtle shell eye glasses perched a centimetre too low on their tiny noses, and big ears jutting out from their faces, they look childlike. The only difference between the two is that Nimesh towers over Nikhat. At 6'4" he's the tallest boy I have ever met, while Nikhat is diminutive at 5'1".

These two—graduates from NIT Surathkal—are amongst the dozens of employees who had responded to Sarita Sharan's call for applications to join WeDonate, and make a real difference.

Nikhat makes me sign a form and hands me my work laptop. Nimesh and Nikhat handle the back-end of the website. Legend has it that they haven't left the office in two years.

I feel the weight of the ThinkPad in my hands.

'Always wanted to have one of these. This one has a great keyboard,' I say.

'Finally, someone recognizes that!' says Nimesh and looks up. Both their specky eyes light up.

'They do, Ananth, they do,' says Nikhat.

'I have to tell you guys this. You two look great together. You guys are custom built for each other—just revoltingly, unbelievably cute,' I say.

They smile and retreat shyly into their shells. I want to keep them in a little glass box in my house.

'Go see Sarita first. She's expecting you. It's regarding your department. There has been some change,' says Nimesh.

'You and Mohini look great too,' says Nikhat as I'm leaving.

It is my turn to smile shyly.

*

Sarita Sharan's laughably small cabin is a mess. There are papers and boxes of her protein supplement, Glutamine, BCAAs strewn all over, and there's a strong stench of cheap perfume. She doesn't look up when I enter her cabin.

'I'm glad to be here. Thank you for giving—'

Sarita cuts me with a smile. 'I'm assuming Nimesh and Nikhat have already set you up with the laptop. I know you wanted to be a part of the medical team but as it turns out, the management feels it's best if you start off with something lighter.'

'Lighter?' I ask.

'I am putting you under someone from the entertainment division. You will be trying to get music albums and movies funded . . . that sort of thing. Karunesh will tell you more. It's our fastest growing vertical.'

The words don't register; this is unacceptable.

'It will be a good start for you,' she says.

'But Sarita, I was told—'

'It's what the company has decided,' she says.

'Can you please put me in medical? There's nothing more I have wanted—'

'The decision is final. You can talk to HR but I don't think that will help,' she says and gets up.

She thrusts her hand out and I see no option but to shake it. As my hand disappears into hers, my metacarpal bones crumble to dust.

'Best of luck,' she says.

'Thanks.'

The finality and the tenor in her voice, the broadness of her shoulders, keep me from saying anything more. By the time I reach my desk, my new mail ID already has a bunch of Excel sheets with the list of all the entertainment-related, successful and unsuccessful, crowdfunding projects. I feel nauseous; this is a mistake.

When I find Karunesh who heads my team, he has industrial strength headphones covering his ears and is bobbing his head to someone's demo. Some say he rejected an offer from Google to work here.

'Hey?'

'Hey! Welcome to the team,' Karunesh says brightly.

'I watched the last one you produced. It was phenomenal. I loved it!' I lie.

I haven't seen what he's made, but creative people lap up any encouragement. He's smiling like a labrador after lunch, glowing like the sun. He seems like a nice guy.

'So now we can—'

I cut him.

'About that, Karunesh. I wanted to be in the medical team. so if you can talk to Sarita and make that happen, it would be great.'

It takes a few seconds for him to register what I have said.

'Ummm . . . Ananth, that's either her or the HR's decision, not mine. And don't worry, you will be fine!' he says. 'Look, why don't you start off by watching a few things we have done in the past. Maybe you will warm up to it?'

I realize the futility of the conversation. I turn and go back to my seat.

With every music video, with every short film that I watch produced on crowdfunded money by WeDonate, it becomes clearer to me that this division should shut down. The money for these projects should be diverted to people who really need it; the entire team should be dissolved.

Why are people paying to get these made? Just last month WeDonate had collected 1 crore for entertainment projects and it was the second fastest rising category in crowdfunding.

I drop in a mail to Ganesh Acharya in HR for a meeting. He doesn't reply till the evening when it is time for me to leave the office.

Once home, Maa notices my sour mood. Maa–Papa sit me down for one of our family discussions. It started when my father read a self-help book a few years ago written by a Western writer. It said that a family should sit and talk, peeling off the layers of the problem to its bare bones to solve an issue. It's not the Indian way. We do not discuss issues but let them build up over years, over decades, take it to our deathbeds, even.

They grill me till I spill everything.

In a bid to be fatherly, Papa tries to relate his own experience to mine.

'It's like when Sharma ji wanted the Shalimar Bagh road to be repaired, but Mandal bhai sahab wanted the funds to get more machines to replace manual scavenging.'

'More or less,' I say.

'Sharma ji had a lot of support. He lives in AP Block. You should see the road in front of his house,' he says.

It's not the sixth standard. Maa–Papa don't have to revise reverse-angle-bisector-theorem just because I have an exam, and yet they spend the entire night watching the short movies and the videos WeDonate has helped make. Through the paper-thin wall I can hear them in the living room, watching and discussing every video. It's not a wall really. It's an MDF board erected in the middle of the room to make a one-room kitchen into a one-bedroom house. Our landlord—Jasveen Makhija—on her monthly inspections calls the house a one-bedroom apartment to justify the higher rent she charges. She lives in Chandigarh and comes every month to shop at Emporio and collect the rent from six of her houses in Delhi.

Every month after paying the rent, Papa talks like he has savings, a fat PPF somewhere, an LIC policy about to mature, and talks about moving from this rented house.

'The plots in Najafgarh are cheap,' he says.

Papa—the youngest of four siblings—who had been swindled out of his ancestral property, of his office lunches by colleagues, of his scooter by his own wife, is a perfect target for conmen. Sometimes, he comes home with brochures of infrastructure projects in Greater Noida. 'It says the handover is in 2025 but I'm sure we will get the possession earlier,' he says.

Maa and I let him indulge in these fantasies. At his age, we couldn't have rewired him to think differently.

But Maa and I know we are not leaving this house in a hurry. Anyway, I like it here. I like sleeping to the murmurs of their voices. I like knowing what Maa's cooking seconds after the oil starts to splutter. I like that I can give Papa a handkerchief within the minute of his first sneeze. It's the house where Mohini and I started our relationship. Where she met me and my parents for the first time. How can it be someone else's?

This isn't Jasveen Makhija's house, it's ours.

'The movies are bad,' Maa says in the morning.

'You were right,' says Papa.

'I'm talking to Ganesh from HR. He has said he might be able to help me out.'

I take my bag and turn to leave.

'Where do you think you're going?' asks Maa.

'We are coming to the metro station with you,' says Papa.

Anusha Sardana

There was no reception area at the bare-bones office of WeDonate. Just a desk where the disinterested guard made me write down my name, the time of visit and purpose.

'Vishwas ji, I have been waiting for two hours now,' I said to the guard who was glued to his phone.

'*Monday busy hota hai* (Mondays are busy),' he said.

Vishwas ji didn't look up from his phone. I'm sure if I were a man he would engage me in a conversation. He seemed the type who would look at the girls working at WeDonate and grumble inwardly about their presence outside their homes. Pretty sure he went back home and beat up his daughter or wife, or both.

I thought of reporting his excessive phone usage during work hours to his security guard agency but assumed this behaviour was long-standing and tolerated.

WeDonate.org managed to beat other crowdfunding companies and raise 250 crore and yet they couldn't schedule an interview on time? I wouldn't be surprised if Sarita Sharan is caught siphoning money two years from now. Why would an IIM Ahmedabad graduate with six years of consulting experience work here?

When Mumma called I told her I was still waiting for the interview. She thought I was lying.

'Did you get rejected?' she queried.

'No, not rejected yet. Arre? Why would I lie?'

'You tell me why you would lie? How am I supposed to know that?' she said.

14

Mothers have a way of getting under your skin.

'I will talk to you later,' I said and disconnected the call.

This was my fourth job interview that week. After every rejection Mumma would go on like a broken record asking me to do a post-graduation instead. When I would ask her where the money would come from, she would mutter incoherently about education loans. Who takes a loan to learn writing? What course can possibly teach someone to write?

'Your Poonam chachi keeps telling me about prospective grooms. How long do you think I can hold them off?' she would tell me.

Poonam chachi, that pockmarked pig, would like nothing better than to get me—an only child—married, change my surname, forsake the house we lived in. Mumma never took my suggestions of checking Surinder chachu's phone history seriously. If she had, she would find a viewing history of a multitude of *jawaan devar–bhabhi* (young brother-in-law– sister-in-law) sex videos.

I waited for another two hours rehearsing for the interview before I was summoned in by Karunesh Talwar.

'Hi!' said Karunesh Talwar and thrust out his hand.

When he shook my hand, it felt like I had dipped my hand in a tub of Vaseline. Karunesh Talwar was more nervous than I was. He looked the kind of awkward man-boy who shares fat girl memes, and prefers skinny, fair girls with big breasts. Do I have any proof? No. Do I still firmly believe in that? A 100 per cent. People are the worst.

He walked oddly with his legs splayed apart—rashes from thighs rubbing together, I guessed.

The cramped open-plan office had around thirty people sitting on long desks, eyes on their computer screens. There were a few boys prancing about in their shorts. The girls were better dressed but I'm sure these boys in shorts would harass them if they too came wearing shorts to office. It's a universal truth—men are the fucking worst! Women are a close second.

In my white shirt and a solid dark pair of jeans—I was more sharply dressed than anyone around me—I looked like I was there to take an interview, maybe audit their books, restructure their debts. My relatives often told me my face didn't match the rest of my body. I was big-boned like Baba, but my face was a mismatch. Sparrow-like and fleshy; Mumma told me I looked like Durga. Not the high-jawboned, fierce Durga of the northerners, but the soft, grandma-like, duskier Durga of eastern India.

Karunesh led me to the interview room and kept turning back to check if I was following him.

'There's not much to get lost around here,' I said.

We took our seats in the allotted interview room. I remembered my mother's words. *At least pretend to like your interviewer.*

'Good morning,' he said. 'So, you're Anusha Sardana.'

I smiled as widely as my cheeks allowed me. 'Good morning, and yes, as it says on the résumé.'

'You know what we do here at WeDonate?'

'It's a crowdfunding company. WeDonate collects money for people who can't afford certain things—medical emergencies, indie film projects, college start-ups and the like. Last year you raised 250 crores and beat out the competition by a margin.'

'Hmmm. What made you apply here?' he said, squinting at his phone. For someone who had prepared for the interview I found his questions quite basic.

'I want to be a writer,' I said. 'And being in the entertainment vertical will help me be a better writer.'

'What do you want to write?' he asked.

'I believe medium is irrelevant. Books, scripts, plays, they are all interchangeable if the story and the characters are in place. I just like to write, be it anything.'

'They say the best way to learn writing is to just start writing. Why haven't you started doing that till now?' he asked as if he had himself been awarded critical acclaim for what he had written. At best, what WeDonate has produced till now is average.

'I have tried more times than I can remember. I will go back home and write about this interaction too, how my day went, etc., just to practice. But I don't have an interesting character to write about yet. I figured I need to live a little more, see a little more, experience a little more. And while I do that, I need to learn the craft of writing.'

'Why didn't you join a film school then?' asked Karunesh.

'I don't have the money,' I said.

Karunesh Talwar, the head of the entertainment division, kept asking hackneyed, obvious questions and swiftly ran out of even those. *So much for being creative, eh?*

The interview went infinitely better than the ones I had given earlier at publishing houses, newspapers and streaming platforms.

When Karunesh was done with his questions, Ganesh Acharya from HR joined us. He introduced himself, sat right across from me and did what HR people do best, indulge in split-second judgements. Like every HR person, he exuded a false confidence. I guess it helps them hold on to the delusion that their jobs are important.

He looked at my résumé, squinting and grimacing and smiling, trying to throw me off my game. I would wrap up this life, move to the hills the day I let an HR person outsmart me.

Ganesh made a dramatic gesture of keeping my CV to the side and said, 'Tell me about yourself? Something that's not on the CV. I have read of all this.'

I could see the pointlessness of this question reflect even on Karunesh's face. Ganesh was asking to be screwed with.

I lowered my voice and said, 'Ganesh, I thought you would never ask. But since we will work together, if we work together, and since WeDonate touts itself more as a family and less as a corporate, I should probably share with you what I wouldn't in any other interview.'

'Go on,' said Ganesh.

'Ganesh, my father's dead. He's been dead for seven years now. My mother and I haven't quite gotten over it. If you ever come to our house, you will feel like he never left. Of course, we don't talk about his departure, or the big hole he left in our lives. We just let it be. Like he was a guest who had to leave sooner than later. We have left it at that. What will we talk about anyway? It's done. We should get over it. What do you suggest we should do about it? Don't tell me we should visit a therapist. We can't afford one. Especially now that their rates have ballooned no thanks to everyone advertising on Instagram that they are going to a therapist. Life's strange, isn't it, Ganesh?'

I watched Ganesh's Adam's apple bob up and down in his throat.

'I'm sorry I shouldn't have said that. Do you have any more questions?' I asked.

'That's about it,' said Ganesh. 'Do you have any questions that you have for me?'

'I just wanted to know if ethnic wear is allowed on Fridays,' I asked.

On my way out, Vishwas ji was sleeping.

I was jostling for space with annoying little shits in the bus when they called to tell me that I had been selected and would be needed in office the next week. I was over the fucking moon! In my happiness I even gave up my seat to an old man

who was pretending to be more tired than he was. I regretted
it immediately when he stared at every woman who entered
the bus. Why do I give them the chance to disappoint?

It was a big day.

At night, to celebrate, Mumma and I ordered Chinese.
We put out a plate for Baba. The chowmein on his plate swam
in soya sauce and chilli vinegar. Just like Baba used to like it.
Years of smoking had numbed his taste buds. We watched
Arjun Reddy on cable TV. Baba loved the sharp cuts and rapid-
fire machine-gun storytelling of Telegu movies. He didn't
understand the language and often watched the movies on
mute. Looking back, it seemed like his life was a reflection
of those movies—concentrated moments of happiness, anger,
work and love, and an abrupt departure.

*

I could barely sleep the entire week. I spent my waking hours
watching and re-watching every documentary, music video
and short movie WeDonate had made in the past couple of
years. When the day came, I was one of the first ones at work.
I went straight to Nikhat Shaikh and Nimesh Arora to pick up
my office laptop.

Nikhat and Nimesh were amongst those handful of fools—
including Karunesh who's a bigger fool given that he was an
IITian—who had given up better jobs to be at WeDonate. All
for the *greater good*.

'You're giving me this?' I held up the Lenovo ThinkPad
Nikhat handed over to me, heavy as a boulder, with a design
aesthetic of a brick. 'Is there a password or do I need to sacrifice
a lamb on this slab?'

Then I pretended to drop the ancient sundial they called a
laptop. The faces they made. Classic!

'ANUSHA!'

'Behind you,' said Nimesh.

'That's Sarita Sharan,' said Nikhat.

Sarita Sharan—standing tall over the troops she commanded—was calling me from the other side of the office. I had seen every one of her interviews. She was composed and sharp; the interviewer was the one usually fawning and bumbling. She looked older in person, more intimidating and very attractive. I felt a growing need to impress her, to be friends with her, to go to her house and cook her dinner, be in her good books, call her to my wedding, make sure the paneer's soft for her. I hated to admit it, but I liked her. I still harboured suspicions that she siphoned money from the donations, of course.

'IN MY CABIN,' said Sarita.

I followed her into her cabin which was a mouse hole for someone built like her. At 5'6" I was used to being taller than the average girl around me, but sitting across the table from her, she towered over me. When she rested her elbows on the desk, the veins in her forearms snaked like an intricate, unplanned roadmap. I could make out in incredible detail the place where her shoulder muscle ended, and her biceps began. A stern smile rested on her face, a striking resemblance to the Night King.

'I have some great ideas, Sarita. I was looking through all the filmmakers' works and I was thinking—'

Sarita spoke as if I wasn't in the middle of my sentence.

'You're in the medical emergencies team. I have mailed you the guidelines and cases where we have registered impact. Go through them as soon as possible. I will find you someone to work with. You have to hit the ground running, there's no time to waste,' she said.

What.

'I'm here to work in entertainment. I will be a bad fit in medical.'

'What made you reach that conclusion?' she asked.

'I'm not that type.'

What I really wanted to say was that when I saw their medical campaigns I could only think of fraud. Twelve-year-old girl whose parents don't have a single rupee left needed Rs 15 lakh for a liver transplant. Are you sure about that? Maybe they do have a little tucked away in bank lockers? Where's the wedding jewellery? What if they are trying to cover this expense through donations while they have the money?

That's how I looked at the world. That boy in the school uniform in the metro? Pretty sure he stole money from his father and sniffed glue. The auto driver? Definitely rapes his wife every night. The boy who I shared the lift with to WeDonate? Well, he could damn well be cheating on his fiancé. That's how I saw the world, and in all likelihood that's how the world was.

'Anusha? I'm free the entire day to talk to you about how you think I should do my job,' Sarita said, looking into her computer.

'Sarita.'

'Great, then. Ganesh told me about your father, so you know a good deal about loss,' she said. 'So here's what we do in the medical vertical. We vet the stories of patients, check the estimated costs with the hospitals and then the writers write out the stories. We check the urgency with the hospitals, talk to the doctors and then fast track them. The urgent ones get promoted on our social media channels. Most of our donors are the ones who have donated before. The stories need to be written in a way that even if it doesn't make someone part with their money it will make them share the stories on their profiles,' she droned. 'What you need to do right now is to edit them and iron out the mistakes. We are all looking forward to your contribution here.'

'Sarita, anyone can write these stories. I'm a writer and I think—'

Sarita squinted her eyes and my words dried up.

She said with pursed lips, 'I started here as a writer for the medical team, so when you say "anyone" you're talking about me, Anusha. I have saved more lives here than I would have in a hospital. So don't tell me this is a talentless job. Now get out of the cabin and do the job you have been assigned to.'

Fuck.

I left her cabin.

Within minutes, Sarita sent me no less than fifty write-ups about sick parents, babies, husbands and fathers to edit and upload on the website.

It was grief-porn.

The sadness poured out from the laptop and wrapped itself around my neck.

I started with a story of a seven-year-old child with a failing liver. There was a picture of him with tears streaming down his big, yellowed eyes, his mouth, half-open in mid scream, stared at me.

Mummy, will I live? Please save me, mummy.

Next.

A father—a penniless, auto driver—sat on the ground, holding his crying daughter in his arms. The three-year-old lost both her eyes to retinoblastoma. She needed artificial eyes and two rounds of chemotherapy.

Everyone around me was unhappy I had a girl, but I was the happiest. I wanted her to fly but now I just want her to live.

Next.

Three-year-old bald, wasting boy with a single parent needed money for his cancer treatment. He believed he got cancer because he drew on the wall. His mother loved his hair and now there was none.

Maa, I promise I won't be naughty. Please take me out of this hospital.

The stories were endless. Each more terrible than the last. Why would anyone want to write and re-write these? Drown themselves in this brackish slime of sadness?

*

'We saved three children last week,' Rachita Somani, the de-facto head of the medical team, told me during the coffee break.

She unlocked her phone and showed me post-surgery pictures of the three young girls on her phone. She clutched at my hand like a madwoman and didn't let go. Rachita Somani had been at WeDonate for three years. The job was leaving tell-tale signs on her face. The intricate crow's feet at the corner of her eyes, the huge bags underneath, the despondent look on her face, it was unmissable. She was only two years older than I was but the stamp on her face was of a much older, weather-beaten woman.

During lunch, the medical team sat together quietly and forced food into themselves. They mingled with no one. Their lunch break was the shortest, their faces most haggard, they spoke little, their eyes droopy despite getting in the most money for WeDonate.

Rachita Somani and the others in the medical team feasted on the feeling of being holier than everyone, on their work being more important than anyone else's.

I had planned to eat alone but Nimesh and Nikhat came with bright smiles and sat next to me. Of course they didn't ever leave office. They spent bucket loads of their time socializing with colleagues.

'By the end of the day, you will watch at least one of them cry,' said Nimesh when he caught me staring at the medical team.

'They can't take it. Too much work, too many deaths,' said Nikhat.

'The doctors work twenty-four hour shifts in hospitals as your teammates do here,' said Nimesh.

'I'm going to shift, they are not going to be my teammates for long,' I said.

To willingly be a part of this team is an act of masochism and extreme stupidity. Their jobs are more unrewarding than even the doctors'. Unlike doctors, the medical team doesn't have the luxury of not knowing the patients and their families. The medical team knows *everything* about the person who's on the death bed. The person, their family, their history, their desperation and their bleak future. It's their job to know everything and then to glean out the most heartbreaking details.

'We have a counsellor who comes every week and talks to the team. Sarita had made it compulsory after Karan killed himself,' said Nimesh.

'Karan refused to live in a world that couldn't spare a few thousand to save a child,' said Nikhat.

How are people so naive? How can they not know that people are rotten?

They finish the story I had no interest in listening to. It was two years ago. One of his cases were of twins, a three-year-old boy and girl, both needing bone-marrow transplants, a cruel trick of genetics. Despite all of WeDonate's efforts, they couldn't collect enough money for both. Karan, who got too close to the family, pumped in his savings, even took a small personal loan, and yet it could only cover one child. The parents chose the boy. The cancer metastasized and killed the girl. The girl spent the last few days watching her brother get better. The boy's went into remission. But six months later, the cancer relapsed. Without his sister, the boy couldn't muster up the strength to mount another fight against cancer and he too died. Karan ended his life the day the boy was buried.

The rumour around the office was that Karan and Rachita were dating at the time. It's said she blamed herself for not having worked hard enough on the story. But as more people told the rumour it shifted. By the time it was evening, the story had changed to Rachita was manic about the cases because she had lost a patient she was trying to source money for and had nothing to do with Karan.

In every scenario, Rachita came out at the bottom; and every person in medical had a story like hers.

Fuck the medical team. I didn't want to be a hero.

Later that evening, when I got home, Mumma was pretending to be busy. I could see how much she missed me.

Apart from the minor inconveniences of having a gaping hole in the heart, Baba's absence had also put a considerable dent in our social life. Mumma wanted me to be around her, to save her from the loneliness that consumed her. It took me time to understand that. I was fifteen when I lost my father.

Baba left Mumma utterly and embarrassingly alone. How long can you hold on to his smell in the bedsheets, his half-used shaving cream, his shoes with mud still stuck to the soles, the four hundred rupees in his drawer, the spare spectacles, the inhaler he left behind. What do you do of that four hundred rupees Baba hadn't spent? Where would he have spent those? They tell you that after marriage your husband and your family is everything, neglecting to tell you what to do if one of them is not there one day.

Durjoy Datta

After the aggressive mourning turned into a dull pain, Mumma's attempts at forging friendships around the locality were met with hostility. 'Look at her visiting neighbours; look at her smiling; look at her in the mall; look at her ordering food; look at her eating food', everything that she did was open to discussion and condescension. She was expected to walk with a bent head, talk little to none, never smile, live every day as a burden. She was supposed to hide.

The Sharmas, the Guptas, the Mandals, our friendly neighbours kept us at an arm's distance. We were harbingers of bad luck. It might have been five years, but the stench of being unfortunate women hadn't worn off. The women of our locality clutched at their *suhaag*, their married status, with a sense of pride because what else could they be proud of? Not their husbands, of course! All of them, walking bags of heart disease, disappointment and erectile dysfunction. I had legit reasons to be proud. They were still having sex days before it all ended, and not the married, tranquilized, once-a-month kind of sex, but sex that woke me up in the other room, the kind of sex that made them shy and look away from each other the next morning. None of the women who shunned her like a bad omen could claim that.

Now Surinder chachu and Poonam chachi waited for me to get married so they could make Mumma shift to a tiny flat and sell the house.

Baba's side of the family never once looked back. All the time Baba, Mumma and I, as a family, had stressed about what they would think about my clothes, my marks, my career choices, our investments, our car, our house was a waste. Even both of Mumma's brothers who would travel across the city to get rakhis tied would sparingly answer our calls, fearful that we would ask them for money.

That was our breaking point. We knew that niceness in people was an illusion. Deep inside, everyone is a raging asshole. No one cared.

Being the oldest in my generation, all my cousins—all unsmart and talentless—were still in school. I had decided that I would introduce them to methamphetamines and cocaine the day they turned eighteen. That would be some revenge.

For the longest time, Mumma had tried to hide our ostracism by her friends from me. Every two weeks, she would dress up for her kitty party and leave the house. She would then read newspapers on her own at a Chinese restaurant close to our house and then come back. Once she knew I knew she stopped the charade and we never once discussed it.

'It was bad?' asked Mumma about my day.

'It was very bad.'

'What are they asking you to do?'

'Say I get cancer and you don't have the money—'

'I will slap you right now,' snapped Mumma.

'Say a girl has cancer and her mother doesn't have the money. She can come crying to WeDonate, tell them her sob story, and they will reach out to donors to help the mother out,' I explained.

'That sounds like a good thing to do. Why are you being so condescending about it?' she asked.

'Mumma, I don't want to save anyone.'

'Beta, did you tell your boss that your heart is made out of stone?' said Mumma. 'Did you ask to change your department?'

'I tried but she was scary,' I protested.

'More than you?' she asked.

Just because she was the first woman in her family to get an MA, only one to teach in a polytechnic while her sisters bore petulant boys and insufferable girls, she thought she could act cute with me.

'I'm talking to Ganesh from HR tomorrow. Maybe he can help,' I said.

I was hoping he would have decision-making capabilities and wouldn't just parrot sentences Sarita Sharan asked him to, though my understanding was that he was nothing more than Sarita Sharan's sock puppet.

Ganesh Acharya

Ganesh Acharya had taken a massive pay-cut to join WeDonate. Sarita Sharan was the only reason Ganesh had joined the organization, but on days like this, he hated his job.

Ananth Khatri is sitting in front of him, pissed, and Ganesh knows he can't do anything for him.

Ananth says, 'Ganesh, there are two things. First, I want to be in medical. I thought it was clear during the interview. And second, why are we wasting so many resources at entertainment? We don't make anything good.'

'We understand where you're coming from,' says Ganesh. 'Did you tell Karunesh about what you feel about entertainment?'

'I can't. He works hard at it; he's quite passionate about it.'

'Look, Ananth, today someone donates Rs 200 to a music band with a cute boy singer. Who knows, tomorrow she might pay for someone else's heart surgery. We need to throw a wider net, make people interested in helping other people out,' says Ganesh.

Ganesh knows Ananth doesn't buy it but he nods his head. Ganesh didn't entirely buy it as well.

'But can an exception be made and I be shifted to medical?'

Ganesh wishes he had taken those dramatics classes in school to really pull this off.

'Ananth, I will tell you the best we can do. You stay here at entertainment for a month or two, wrap up a couple of projects, and then we will look for a swap?' says Ganesh.

'But—'

'I'm sorry that's the best we can do right now,' says Ganesh with a sternness he has learned from Sarita.

He sees Ananth's face fall. If his opinion counted, he would have put Ananth in medical. He thought of Ananth as someone with endless empathy, the chief requirement for the team. He was a nice boy who sought and saw niceness in everyone. He remembered Ananth being so polite to everyone in the office on the day of the interview one would think he was a fake. But it was *him*—sincere and loving. You could see that in his eyes. The girls at WeDonate had been whispering about him for days after the interview. Of course, they knew he was dating someone, and yet they talked about his jawline, his eyes that had inhuman percentage of pupil—large black pools of water, his short cropped but lush hair, and his slimness, like they were entities of their own. Only this morning, a girl from the college project vertical wanted to know about Ananth's skin care routine.

The team could do with people who would give it their all. And who better than Ananth? He was prepared for this and yet Sarita thought different.

Ananth thanks Ganesh, gets up and leaves.

Not long after, Sarita calls Ganesh to ask him if it went well.

'Thank you, Ganesh,' says Sarita. 'We have a plan for him or I wouldn't have asked you to do this.'

Saraansh Gupta

Saraansh orders a skinny latte and sits in the far corner of Starbucks. He's nervous but pumped. This meeting is going to be his big break, he can feel it in his bones. He's smiling thinking of the future as he waits for Sarita and Ananth.

A few months ago, fresh out of movie school, Saraansh knocked the doors of WeDonate offering to make a bootstrapped advertisement video for the organization. He had been desperate and was knocking every door, trying out everything. He had gone with the script, the storyboard, the budget, everything one could ask for.

Sarita Sharan had turned Saraansh down despite liking his work, citing budget issues.

'Let me know if something comes up,' he had told Sarita.

Saraansh's parents hadn't wanted him to pursue filmmaking. They had a thriving button business, and they wanted him to follow in the footsteps of his father and elder brother. Maybe rename Gupta Buttons and Buttons to something catchier, call himself an entrepreneur, shift the office from Chawri Bazaar to Connaught Place, but still be in the business.

His family had thought Saraansh's fascination with filmmaking was temporary. But when they got to know it wasn't, they stopped talking to him, cut a huge chunk off his finances and they were now threatening to take away his car and the driver.

It's been months since they have talked to him with a straight face. He had disappointed them by rejecting his family's legacy.

However, a couple of weeks ago, Sarita Sharan reconnected with Saraansh and mailed him a link to a YouTube video. She wrote in the mail that she had a better idea to push WeDonate's name out amongst the people than do a straight advertisement.

He had seen the video Sarita Sharan has sent before. Everyone he knew had seen the video. It had gone majorly viral and all aggregator platforms had done pieces on it. Unlike viral cat videos and embarrassing people videos, this one had more legs on it. People were talking about it fervently, sharing it, making rehashed versions of it till the second month of its release.

It was the video of a girl named Mohini, who was confessing her love for a guy named Ananth, in a self-shot video. The video held the country in a thrall, and everyone cried.

The guy, Ananth, had raked up hundreds of thousands of followers overnight. Across Instagram, Twitter and Facebook, more than a million people followed him in the next few months. He became a micro-celebrity overnight. But unlike other micro-celebrities, he didn't pivot towards becoming an influencer, peddle shampoos and sunglasses and watches.

Last week, Ananth had joined WeDonate. Despite the massive following, stupidly enough, Ananth only shares medical campaigns from WeDonate. It is a waste of influence.

Sarita Sharan now wants to leverage the following he had amassed.

Ananth Khatri is Saraansh's break and he's going to kill it. There's no alternative. Saraansh promised his boyfriend he will move in with him before the end of this year. How is he supposed to do that when his career is in shambles?

As he waits at Starbucks for Sarita and Ananth, he watches the video again. The girl's cute, the things she says are heartfelt, simple, relatable. Saraansh sees why it connected with so many people.

It deserved to go viral.

Ananth Khatri

Sarita and I are in the back of a cab, going to a meeting she's too important to attend. Sarita hand-holding me is a little embarrassing. She's too much of a big shot to be in a meeting with a young director and yet she's here.

'The words are at the back of your throat. Spit them out,' says Sarita when she notices my sullen face.

'With no offence to the entertainment team, the world won't miss anything if there weren't any movies or short films or brilliant directors or screenwriters,' I complain.

'We should save sick people, instead? Is that what you're saying?' she asks me.

I nod.

'People will still go ahead and watch the Salman Khan movie even if you wave pictures of dead, rotting Dalit children at the ticketing counter,' she says with a deadpan expression, like she has said this before to many people who have suggested the same. 'The world doesn't run on moral logic. Hear this guy out. It's a love story. And given your own love story, I think you will be a great judge of it.'

No matter what Sarita says, it still doesn't make it right. The rookie writer–director is sitting in one corner of Starbucks. He gets up as we enter.

'Saraansh,' he says and thrusts his hand out. 'Nice to meet you, bro!'

He shouldn't call me bro.

We shake hands. His boyish eyes twinkle. He asks if we want to order something.

'Their blueberry parfait is mad! You should try it,' he says. 'I would offer you some but I finished mine.'

The fact that he orders an expensive blueberry parfait is worrying.

Neither of us wants to but since we are in a coffee shop we order a coffee each. He has the jumpy energy of a teenager on cocaine.

'Thank you for the opportunity,' he says excitedly.

Saraansh to the best my knowledge, a recent graduate from National School of Filmmaking, is a rich boy. There's something inherently wrong in rich people turning to WeDonate for help. The laptop in front of him is a worn-out MacBook Air. There is an Air Pod's case lying about carelessly on the table. He's about my age, twenty-two according to his LinkedIn profile, but he looks more boyish, smacks of privilege, and smells good.

His last Instagram post was a picture of him in the pool of Leela Kempinski captioned, 'Self-care'. There are other pictures too—pictures of him in a club captioned 'I'm too old for this', a picture of his new Onitsuka Tiger shoes captioned 'Sneakerhead for life'.

He's too thin for his height—at 6 feet, he's tall—yet looks okay in a way that only rich people can.

He has made a few documentaries. I watched all of them yesterday. I will admit his student films are better than the ones Karunesh has helped make. His Instagram-rich-kid-feel notwithstanding, there's an unmistakable intensity he exudes in the videos where he's talking about his movies. Which is sharp in contrast with his Instagram profile that looks like it belongs to a brat.

'So let's start?' says Sarita once our coffee reaches our table.

'Bro?' he looks at me.

'Of course.'

'So yeah, since it's going to be a short YouTube-only movie, we will need to find different ways to push it out. I have crazy plans on how we can promote it. It's going to be mad fun!' he starts out, seriously but still smiling. His lazy hair flops over his forehead and he keeps moving it out of his eyes.

'That comes later, Saraansh. The only consideration is the story. We would like a narration, or if you could send it to us in writing, even that works for us,' I tell him sternly.

Why do I feel so much older than him?

His eyes light up and he says, 'It's a great story, bro.'

I have a fundamental problem with him calling me 'bro' repeatedly.

'Can we hear it? Or read it? Whatever suits you,' I tell him.

'I haven't written it down yet. I just have a thought but it's a cracker of a story, it's so complete. To proceed, I would need your help,' says Saraansh.

He's looking at me and not Sarita. There was an unnecessary stress on the word *your*.

'I'm sorry? My help?' I ask.

His eyes twinkle. 'It's your story, your love story,' he says, leaning towards me.

'What do you mean it's my story?'

And then it strikes me.

'That's a very bad idea. There's no story there,' I tell him.

'Hear him out, Ananth,' commands Sarita.

'Bro, let's give it some thought. Your story has all the elements for it to make a great web-series. It's so extra, and it's so real. And not to forget, that video Mohini made is #goals. I don't know a teenager who hasn't watched it. We trip over it every time someone around has a heartbreak. It's our guiding light, bro, our pole star,' he says.

'I don't think this is going to work for us. I think you're wasting your time and ours,' I say.

'Why don't you take some time to think about it?' asks Sarita.

What on earth was happening here?

'This is a bad idea,' I say with as much unpleasantness as I can gather.

Saraansh is relentless. With the smile still on his face, he continues and for the first time I see the intensity, the seriousness I have seen in the documentaries about bully-culture and teenager-on-dark-web that he has shot, 'I really want to make this, man. Your story is simple and that's what works. Hear me out, Ananth. We start from both your childhoods, two parallel narratives, till the two of you meet and everything changes. It ends with you joining WeDonate and using your influence to help thousands of others. There will be a nice subtext of how one girl's simple, selfless love ended up helping so many people. That's what you do with the following that you have, don't you bro?'

'I think we are done here.'

I get up. Sarita's face softens and it's weird to watch her trying to smile. Sarita gets up after me and tells Saraansh, 'If he's not on board, we can't proceed.'

For the first time in the meeting, I sense a doubt in Saraansh. He had put his bets on waltzing in with this god-awful idea and getting me on board with a snap of his fingers. Sarita and I walk towards the exit.

'You set this up, didn't you? You knew what he was going to propose,' I say to Sarita once we are outside.

'Ananth, don't tell me you can't see how making this movie can help WeDonate? I'm surprised honestly at your naivety,' says Sarita rudely as if it was I who had conspired to make a short movie on her story and not the other way around.

'Honestly, I don't see how,' I snap.

'You want to save people? This is your best chance! Going viral online is a major component of our business. You know the movie will get traction with the story you have—the virality of Mohini's video, and that you're now working at WeDonate. I will give you complete creative control over the process. Get this made and I will shift you to medical.'

'Are you dangling a carrot?'

'There's a girl who wants to swap too. We can look into it. Please tell me you didn't think we would hire you and not use the following you have built online? That would be very unwise of us. That's wasting an audience of over a million people,' she grumbles.

'But I already share all the campaigns,' I protest.

'Just sharing the medical campaigns on your profiles is not going to cut it. We need to make deeper inroads,' she says.

I reassess why my first reaction was to walk out of there. Was I being possessive about making what we have with each other accessible to all? Peddle a private emotion, sell out? But Sarita's right, a movie like this, does hold promise. If a video reached out to 123 million people, how far and wide will a movie reach? How many more could we end up helping?

Saraansh and Sarita must have known this sequence of events because Saraansh was still sitting there with his laptop open when we re-enter Starbucks. We take our seats again.

'It's not my permission to give, it's Mohini's,' I say.

'So we talk to Mohini?' asks Saraansh brightly.

'And her mother,' I add.

'Her father? He's going to be a part of the story too,' says Sarita.

'If the mother agrees, other things won't be a problem,' I say.

'You're not going to regret this, bro,' says Saraansh and reaches out for my hand. He holds it like he's an old friend. 'We will do nothing to insult what you guys have. It's brilliant and it needs to be out there. More people need to know. It's going to be cray.'

I catch his gaze and in that moment, I believe in him.

Back home, I watch the video again. It has a million more views than the last time I checked. This is a good idea.

Rachita Somani

Rachita Somani had been at WeDonate for three years. She had seen many new joinees struggle and eventually bow out of the medical team within the first week. It was too overwhelming for most. She had almost given up too, when she first joined. But Sarita Sharan had stood behind her, groomed her and made her into what she was today. Rachita's mother would ask her to change her job every day.

'You could have been an actress, look what you have done to your skin,' her mother rued every day.

But Rachita couldn't bear to think of doing anything different. Given her theatre background, there were times she had wanted to laterally shift to the entertainment vertical, but she would eventually dismiss the thought.

The way Anusha Sardana walked around in the office with an angry, hurt face, Rachita had thought Anusha would be one of the first-week casualties too. Rachita observed that Anusha would keep to herself most of the day. She would be gruff and to the point. It seemed like she was making an active effort to not make friends. There were others in the office who had pointed Anusha's behaviour out to Rachita.

'It's not good for the team's morale,' the team members would say.

Rachita was wrong about her analysis of Anusha not lasting very long at WeDonate; she was, in fact, thriving.

Despite not wanting to be in the team, Anusha had been editing medical stories at a breakneck speed. Rachita also noticed that Anusha altered narratives in the stories she edited, making them more effective than earlier.

Rachita would tell everyone that Anusha was doing well at her work and that's all that should matter.

She would find herself telling others about Anusha, 'Her anger is not specifically directed at you, she's angry at everyone.'

'She's a good writer. Maybe she's right in wanting to be in entertainment. Have you given it a thought?' asked Rachita to Sarita that day.

'Test her with the unsuccessful campaigns,' Sarita answered without elaborating further.

When Rachita told Anusha she would be sending her two campaigns that had failed for them, Anusha rolled her eyes and had said, 'Fine.'

The first one was of a rickshaw puller and his wife trying to save their twelve-year-old daughter from cancer. Despite pictures of the crying child, the grieving parents and a heart-wrenching story, it didn't get them the money. The second was of a twenty-three-year-old boy, Gautam, who needed to undergo an urgent brain surgery. Both these campaigns were falling short of over 20+ lakh.

'Do you need help?' Rachita asked her in the evening when she saw her hunched up over the laptop.

Anusha took off her headphones. She said pointing to the screen, 'I'm going to delete the portion where it says this twelve-year-old girl fighting cancer has a younger brother.'

'But he's crying in the picture. It moves people,' suggested Rachita.

'When I see the boy, I don't care if the girl dies or not. First, there's another child in the family. Who cares if one dies? They have a spare. We need to hide the brother. He's killing the sister. And second, it's a girl so funerals are cheaper than marriages. So maybe people are thinking that this is a good thing?'

'These are real people, real lives you are talking about,' said Rachita testing her further.

'We are selling stories, Rachita. If we get the money, who the fuck cares?' said Anusha. 'When the donors donate, they need to feel like they are really helping someone out. A single child dying makes for a better story.'

'What about the girl's family?' asked Rachita.

'They don't matter. We are also catering to the needs of the rich among our donors, are we not? By telling heart-wrenching stories and making people feel good about themselves when they donate,' said Anusha disdainfully.

'Do what you feel best,' said Rachita.

Rachita turned away from her and smiled softly. She was glad to know Anusha Sardana had no illusions about how the world worked. Rachita had come to WeDonate with idealistic notions about people's niceness, about their philanthropic tendencies. Now she knew that people who donated money to medical campaigns did it for another dopamine hit. It's a commodity they buy for themselves—to feel better, superior.

Rachita was looking forward to seeing what Anusha would do with the stories. No one should have to die just because they were poor.

After a while, when Rachita looked over, she found Anusha zooming into a guy's picture. It was the second case. When Anusha saw her, she said, 'This Gautam guy is cute. Too bad he's dying.'

Anusha Sardana

Manoj Kumar now had a new story. I lied through my teeth, exaggerated certain truths, hid a few things and rewrote the story.

I had met them twice before I wrote the story. Once at the hospital, and once at his residence. The paediatric cancer ward with its colourful walls and light pink beds was more cheerful than their roofless home with soot-laden walls. Manoj told me their house had been broken twice by the MCD. There wasn't much to break. They were apologetic about me having to step inside their house. Twelve-year-old Rajni didn't share her parents' desolation.

'I will buy the house where my mother works at after I complete my engineering,' she told me.

She spoke these words in English. Her parents looked at her with chest puffed with pride as if she was speaking an ancient, powerful language capable of turning ash into gold.

But for any of that to happen, Rajni's story needed to be retold, refabricated, bolstered with lies and half-truths.

Manoj Kumar's twelve-year-old daughter, Rajni, was diagnosed six months ago with an aggressive cancer. Rajni has acute lymphoblastic leukemia—a type of blood cancer that affects the white blood cells. Rajni has painful swellings all over her body and runs a high fever.

She requires maintenance chemotherapy for six months.

A rickshaw driver in Delhi, Manoj earns Rs 3000 a month. His handicapped wife, Jaidevi Kumari, works as a house help in a Gurgaon society.

He sold his ancestral land and ran from pillar to post to collect money for his daughter's treatment. He could only manage Rs 1,00,000. He still needs another Rs 18,00,000 to cover multiple rounds of chemotherapy.

Both parents work for eighteen hours a day and then return to the bedside of their dying daughter. Jaidevi Kumari breaks down and says, 'My employers refuse to give me holidays. I can't even be with my daughter when she's in pain.'

Rajni cries alone when her parents are working to save every rupee for her.

Manoj Kumar was thrown out of his village by upper-caste anti-social elements because Rajni did better than the boys in school. Rajni and her mother were beaten up, her books were torn apart. Manoj Kumar had shifted to Delhi so that his daughter could go to school. Rajni wanted to be a doctor and her parents were doing everything to accomplish that. She was a good student. She still asks her parents when she can join her school again. She smiles and tells her parents it's not hurting so she can leave the hospital.

'Is it too much to ask for?' asks Jaidevi Kumari holding Rajni's hand.

'We will have no reason to live if our daughter dies,' says Manoj Kumar.

Help save her. Don't let a disease brutally cut down a promising life.

Of course, I didn't write that their caste was linked to their impoverished state. People don't want to believe that since they know at least one Brahmin who's poor, and at least one from the depressed class who's rich but is still using reservation benefits. We find creative ways to be assholes every day.

A steady stream of donations started coming in for Rajni.

'The story you wrote isn't true,' said Rachita when she read it.

'The medical bits are true. Anyway it doesn't matter if it isn't true, what matters is that it could have been true. Anyway, you can call the parents and cross-check. They will tell you the same thing,' I countered.

'You taught them, didn't you?' said Rachita.

Before I could answer she turned back to her screen. Rachita wasn't as self-righteous as she'd made herself out to be. The way I saw it, she just kept testing me to see how far I would go, how much I would lie to get the donations in. She's the medical head after all, she's not stupid.

Gautam's was another story. The first story that went up was this:

> Gautam, twenty-three, has been diagnosed with an extreme case of meningioma. The tumour is wrapped on the frontal lobe and requires immediate surgery. The surgery is complex, only a few doctors have the expertise to operate. There's a high risk of him slipping into a comatose condition. There's an urgent need for money since both of Gautam's parents are government servants and have already exhausted all their savings. He needs another 26 lakh.

Short, dry, and useless. Even the picture wasn't helping. The boy looked handsome and was smiling straight into the camera. His campaign collected a record low of Rs 16,000.

Severely short on money, Gautam's craniotomy was performed in a small hospital by less than capable doctors. I imagined a half-opened skull and blood spouting and splashing on a confused surgeon's face.

There was an update a couple of months later.

Update: There was a requirement of 26 lakh for Gautam's surgery which couldn't be completed. Gautam couldn't get operated in a hospital of his parent's choice. His parents maintain if the hospital was more competent, he would have not slipped into a coma. His parents' last hope is a DBS brain surgery that might bring him back.

Not only was the first iteration horribly written, the second one didn't make much sense either. Why would someone spend money on an uncertain case? *Might bring him back?* What kind of sentence is that?

Nimesh and Nikhat ordered dosas that day and joined at the table. They always ordered something they assumed I liked and then used that as a pretext to start a conversation.

'Great job on the Manoj Kumar campaign,' said Nimesh.

I wouldn't have been surprised if they had been sent over by Sarita to uplift my morale. She was a shark, and definitely built like one.

'What's next?' asked Nikhat.

I told them about the Gautam campaign, twenty-three-year-old guy, DBS. I saw their faces fall immediately.

'What's the matter?' I asked them.

'Do you know why that campaign didn't work?' asked Nikhat.

'Because it's badly written, that's why,' I answered.

Nimesh shook his head.

'Do you remember the handle @gautam_gabbar? He was also on Instagram and Facebook and such,' said Nimesh.

'Vaguely.'

Once they started to talk, you couldn't really put a stop to them; like a pendulum the conversation shifted from Nikhat to Nimesh to Nikhat to Nimesh, the annoying little rabbits with their bunny smiles.

Nikhat continued, 'Back when his campaign first went live, regular donators threatened they won't use the site if we supported him. They wanted him to die.'

'Even the medical team with all their self-righteousness was hesitant. There was a lot of backlash,' said Nimesh.

'Sarita took a hard stand. She told everyone categorically that she didn't care who the person was, he deserved to live and the story went live,' said Nikhat.

'His donation didn't get traction. He torpedoed his own donation campaign, made fun of people who were contributing to his surgery. He didn't get enough money and his surgery was botched up,' said Nimesh.

'No one at WeDonate felt guilty,' said Nikhat.

Haha. I wanted to laugh at the faces of the WeDonate people. If you can sacrifice one person's life because of your prejudices, you can let all of them die too. I always knew these guys at WeDonate were the garden variety disappointing people, and not saints. I was better than them, my hate didn't discriminate on someone's Twitter behaviour.

I came back to my seat and logged on to Twitter.

Of all the social media platforms, Twitter has the worst rep—it was a septic tank where people were at their worst behaviour. I differed from this weak, half-assed opinion. I thought they are at their best, or at least normal, behaviour on Twitter. Twitter allows people to be their real selves. Everywhere else, they are pretending. If someone is nice on Twitter, for me, that moron is putting up an act.

Some fools say Internet lets people hide so that they can exhibit their worst selves. Nope. Internet lets people be who they really are. It lets people find their community, and their mob.

And people are unkind, cruel, sexist, casteist, xenophobic, and they find others like themselves and form little ecosystems for themselves. That's the norm, not the exception. Assume that and you will never be wrong about people on Twitter.

Case in point, a few months ago I had defended the release of a Sanjay Leela Bhansali movie starring Deepika Padukone. A fringe outfit had threatened to chop off Padukone's beautiful nose—what a gorgeous nose—and threw stones at a school bus. When I tweeted about it, an army of trolls descended on me like a swarm of locusts, which I completely expected of them:

> *@Anusha_Sardana231: Are these men's egos so fragile they can't handle a fictional story of a queen, which may or may not have a dream sequence from the POV of a man?*
>
> \
>
> *@Karaneer: Randi ki aulaad. Teri maa ka rape sequence daalu kya movie mein.*
>
> \
>
> *@Ranjitkhann2: Tu bata kaha rehti hai. Bhen ki lodi, lund de dunga muh mein.*
>
> \
>
> *@Rrtu455: pakistan ki sasti randi gashti saali.*
>
> \
>
> *@ryti455: Tera gala kaat dunga teri maa ke saamne. Fir uski fuddi fad dunga tere baap ke saamne. End mein tum teeno ko jala dunga.*

Anyone who reacted to this with, *oh, I'm ashamed of this behaviour / I'm shaking I didn't know men in India . . . / I was shocked how men . . .* probably lived under a rock or her private palace, shielded from civilization.

These men were being themselves. Most men are like this, so are many women. They might choose better language, or just not say anything but it doesn't change who they are. I wasn't surprised. I did the usual thing of calling them small-dicked and moved on.

I put the handle name @gautam_gabbar in the search bar. The account was blocked.

I wondered what he had done to make me block his account.

Sunita Ji, Mohini's Mother

Sunita ji, as everyone calls Mohini's mother, is about to put some tea to boil when her phone rings. Her face falls. Her daughter's boyfriend, Ananth, is coming home again. Never had she imagined such a time would come that she would have to think out those words in this particular order. But what don't you do for your child, and for the changing times?

She put the tea back. She will drink with Ananth when he gets here. She gets up and puts the house in a bit of order. There are stacks of books lying everywhere and she put them where they belong.

That boy is always on time.

She doesn't like the boy.

He's too perfect, that's what Sunita Sardana doesn't like about him. He's always too nice, too subservient. Time and again, Sunita has put him through the hoops and he jumps through them with a big smile on his face.

No matter how sweet he is though, his presence always irritates and angers her. Mostly because he's enjoying the fruits of her daughter's brilliance, of her good heart, of her kind face, and of her love. It was her daughter's video that gave Ananth a new lease of life.

When Sunita ji had first seen the video made by her daughter, she had thought what Mohini's father would think of it? Once that ebbed, a little embarrassment crept in, and that too didn't last long. What stayed on was the jealousy. She was losing her daughter to a boy. But that ebbed too.

What has remained is the irritation.

The fallout of the video?

As her colleagues in the college have pointed out to her time and again, her daughter's boyfriend, Ananth, has gained hundreds of thousands of followers online since. He now shares medical campaigns of WeDonate from his profile and thinks he's an angel.

Sunita Sardana is hoping he doesn't go on and on about his new job. The last three times they have met, it's all he talks about.

Just then, the bell rings. She reminds herself how much she hates him.

Ananth Khatri

For the past week, I haven't been able to sleep or eat well. Sarita and Saraansh kept asking me when I'm going to seek Aunty's permission and although I have met Aunty and Mohini every day in that time I haven't managed to pose the question to them. It's not that Aunty scares me—okay, she does a little—but I too needed to be convinced if this was a workable idea.

He has insisted on it that we be friends if we have to go on this creative journey. Every day, he has turned up at the office in gleaming white sneakers and freshly shaved cheeks looking like the goddamn sunshine and has unleashed barrages of small talk at me.

Yesterday, Saraansh landed up at work when I told him I thought making a movie about our love story might seem narcissistic. More so, it just seemed unnecessary. Nobody would want to watch it.

'Let's try something out, bro,' he said in his trademark brash, irrational optimism.

'Saraansh, you're my contemporary and yet you use far too colloquial millennial terms. Do you think that's appropriate?' I said in a bid to make him stop calling me bro and make me feel like an old fossil.

Saraansh laughed and said, 'It's appropriate if I do it. Anyway, for just today, post only Mohini and your pictures on your profile. A little sentence about your story here and there in the captions. Let's see if it's *necessary*, let's see if people want to know more about you, bro.'

'Not your bro.'

'Always my bro.' I was confident it would fail until I wasn't.

The five posts—all pictures of Mohini and me with captions of what I felt for her, edited by Saraansh—that we shared, shot the engagement rates on my social media through the roof.

Countless people commented to tell me that it was content like this they were here for, not donation links. I usually lose followers every time I put up a donation link—it's understandable, not everyone wants tragic stories on their timelines—but yesterday I gained a glut of new followers. People were feverishly commenting on the posts. On last count, 2300 people commented, many shared the post on their stories, some shared screenshots on Facebook and Twitter. As a fallout, the video was raking up thousands of new views every hour.

Not only that, the links I uploaded after these posts about Mohini and me, saw more donations.

'Shook, eh?' Saraansh had asked when he had proved his point.

'You need to stop saying that.'

So here I am, outside Mohini's house in Rohini. She lives on the ground floor.

The house demands fresh plaster and a coat of paint. On the ground floor, there's a living room, one bedroom and a small kitchen. The second floor—where tenants live—has an identical layout. It was on Mohini's insistence that her father built the second floor. She wanted a room of her own, away from her parents. It was an audacious request for a family with their means—and a girl of her age. She was eight.

'Don't spoil her. It starts from here,' Aunty had insisted.

Mohini made up her mind that she will have her private space no matter what her parents decided. She made a little tent on the terrace and would spend hours up there under the glaring sun. Uncle gave in when she fell ill.

The construction of Mohini's floor took two years to complete. The cement, the bricks, the iron rods, the wood and the paint, all came from the material leftover at the other building sites Uncle worked at. A *thekedar*, contractor, by profession, Uncle oversaw the work of the labourers at building sites during the day; at night he worked at his own construction site. It was the first house in their colony to have a second floor. The others followed suit like they often do.

When they'd first moved into this plot, Mohini was three. There were all but four walls and a corrugated roof. They had to walk around the block to the nearest restaurant and pay Rs 5 to use the washroom. The neighbours didn't know, they still don't know, that there was no washroom in the house. The first three years they lived there, they invited no one. Uncle had built this house brick by brick, day by day.

'The house was for your mother, the floor's for you,' Uncle would tell Mohini.

As Aunty now tells me, the scar tissues on Uncle reflected the timeline of the construction of the house and of Mohini's floor. He could point at the healed wounds and tell you when the first brick was laid and how it had snapped his index finger, when the first door was put in place, how he nailed his finger instead, the first coat of paint applied and how his leg brushed against the iron grill.

'They were always a team after that. *Unko ek doosre se alag karna impossible tha* (it was impossible to separate the two),' Aunty had once told me about Mohini and her father.

Mohini's room was painted a light pink, the little cupboards were white, and there was a study table custom-made for her.

A small pooja was done and Mohini shifted into the room. The next morning, Mohini's parents woke up in the morning to find Mohini curled on the floor next to their bed. By the time evening came, Mohini shifted back downstairs.

A month later, the second floor was converted to a paying guest accommodation. The extra money was spent in Uncle's frequent visits to the hospital. Over the years, the inhalation of paint fumes, the asbestos had clogged his lungs, sprouted cancerous cells in his airways and worsened his asthma. The houses he had built were threatening to kill him. It came as surprise to them because both Aunty and Mohini saw him as an indestructible demi-god before that and not without reason.

'It's a shame we never used that floor,' Mohini's mother often laments these days. More than once I have seen her mother eyeing her tenants as if she wanted them dead. Houseowners never really let go.

Uncle had built a life from scratch for Aunty and Mohini, provided for them, taught them, built a house for them, protected them, loved them with all his heart. Aunty would have to make up stories and tell her friends in the neighbourhood when they shared their stories of spousal disappointment. Mohini used to love PTAs when the young and old alike would gawk at her handsome father. The teachers would make him sit for half an hour, their chins perched on their knuckles and hear him talk.

Even after a decade into their marriage, Aunty would wash her face, apply sindoor and lipstick, and dress up twice a day. Once before Uncle woke up, and once before he came back home. Uncle would lock the bathroom door to keep his wife from waking up early in the morning and yet she would find a way. No matter how much he reiterated that he loved her, he couldn't make her stop trying to go the extra mile for him. He gave up after a while.

Mohini went a step further. Aunty would often joke that she and her father were twins. If her father fell sick so did Mohini and vice versa. She looked exactly like him. When she was little, and even now, she shared clothes with her father whenever she could. Aunty would often joke to her friends that they couldn't have another child because Uncle didn't want to disappoint Mohini. It wasn't wholly untrue.

'I will smother the baby if you make one. *Mai maar dalungi use, papa kasam* (I would kill it, father promise),' she would tell her father, crying.

Neither of the parents knew if she was serious or not. She must have been serious because every time someone would tell her that she would eventually get married and be off to her husband's place, she would get furious and throw things at the person's face. It used to be quite embarrassing for Aunty to take Mohini out to relative's houses.

When she was little her father's arms would put her to sleep in an instant. For the first three years, she wouldn't fall asleep on a bed; it was her father or nothing else. Aunty still recalls that time her father had to leave the city for three days. I'm not sure if it's an exaggeration but she maintains that Mohini had cried non-stop for those three days. Things didn't change a lot even as she grew up.

I'm thinking about how so many things can fit into a short hour-long movie when I ring the bell.

'Did you get everything?' Mohini's mother asks me irritably.

I did.

'The *bhindi* as well?' she asks.

'How can I forget?'

'Paneer masala.'

'The first thing I got.'

'Dosa batter?'

'I love your dosa, aunty.'

'Chillies.'

'Yes.'

'Dhaniya?'

'A lot and for free.'

She nods and I hand over all the groceries to her. She checks the bill and hands me the exact change. As much I as I try to tell her, she insists on repaying me to the last rupee which invariably means my pockets jangle with one-rupee coins. I think she does it on purpose. But the joke's on her. Where would she be if I didn't get her her grocery? I have made her so dependent on me that she can't make do without me. I played the long game; she will always need me.

'Tea, Ananth?'

'Haanji.'

'Why don't you ever say no?' she says and stomps off to make tea.

I call out Mohini's name and then make my way to her room. She's looking at me when I enter.

'Hi, you look beautiful,' I say.

I can imagine her rolling her eyes hard at my compliment, although she doesn't. She just gives me one of those smiles that only if you're looking very closely can you see. I hold her hand and look over my shoulder to see if Aunty's coming.

'Aunty makes very *bakwas*, tasteless, tea, Mohini,' I say.

She wants to tell me it's intentional because she doesn't like me but stays shut.

Mohini doesn't like it when I'm unkind to her mother. But she sees her mother's unfairness to me all the same. It's been days since Mohini and I have gone on a date. Aunty says she's too recognizable and there are far too many dangerous boys who might say they only want a selfie but who knows . . .

Aunty gets three steaming, underdone cups of tea. I want to taste hers to check if hers is sweeter.

'Pretend I'm not here. You can say whatever you need to,' she says.

She stares into her book. She doesn't flip the page. For the past month, she has been staring into the same book. For someone who buys second-hand books by the kilogram at Daryaganj she's taking her time with this one. And how would she finish this book; she only picks this is up when I'm in the room and she's watching us with her hawk-like eyes. Neither I, nor Mohini, is happy with this but this is what we have to make do with.

I have seen Aunty's younger pictures. Unlike Mohini's childlike face, Aunty seemed like she always had somewhere important to go. An impatient, piercing gaze that judged you. She had the look of someone who had to interview candidates for a senior management position. A cold, hard look, pursed lips. You had to search for what she felt in her eyes, dig for the slightest of blinks. Worrying for her daughter had aged her swiftly; but in a TV show fashion. Her hair seemed it had been intentionally dyed grey to look more imposing.

I begin, 'Baby . . .'

'Don't call her that!' Aunty interrupts.

'I always call her that,' I protest.

Mohini stares both me and her mother down.

I tell Mohini about Saraansh and what he plans to do, and although she maintains a poker face for her mother's benefit, I can feel her excitement. Aunty wiggles restlessly in her chair. I'm only halfway through when her mother butts in.

She slams the book on the table and grumbles, 'How do you have the audacity to suggest something like that? I'm not allowing anything of this sort.'

I try to explain to her that it won't happen without her express approval. With every word that I say, her anger spikes. 'I have given you enough leeway, Ananth. But if you do this, I won't let the two of you meet.'

'Aunty, just listen—'

'You listen to me. I'm serious about this. I don't want that kind of attention directed towards this house,' she snaps.

'That's not your decision, Maa,' I say.

'I'm not your Maa. HOW MANY times have I asked you not to call me that?'

'I felt it best to not keep a count,' I say. This never fails to throw her off.

'I make her decisions. It's better you leave, Ananth.'

She keeps the book on her side and gets up. Mohini's racquet hangs behind the wall. It wouldn't be a surprise if she plans to use it.

I look at her and she stares blankly at me.

'Baby? Mohini?' I ask.

She has no answer for me. I wish she would stand up to her mother occasionally. How long will she keep doing what her mother asks her to do? Was the video she made the only act of courage against her mother? Sometimes I wish she hadn't used up all her rebelliousness in that single act and instead rationed it to spend little chunks of time with me.

'I will ask you again tomorrow.'

I blow a kiss at Mohini to piss Aunty off.

'I love you, baby.'

'*Besharam*, so shameless! *Nikal yaha se* (get out)*!*' Aunty mutters angrily.

I watch Mohini in the mirror of the living room. She's smiling; she loves these little skirmishes between her mother and me. Aunty's still grumbling and complaining to Mohini.

When I get back home and tell Maa what happened, she says what she always does.

'You don't have to let her mother steamroll you just because she's your girlfriend. Tomorrow if you get married, will she dictate terms to me? I won't allow that in my house.'

'Maa, she's twenty-one! She's not getting married right now. Also, zero points for unlearning the patriarchy.'

'Don't start with me,' Maa says. 'You can't fight with your mother-in-law and you're showing all your bravado in front of me.'

'Maa?'

'Was her chai still tasteless?' She doesn't wait for me to finish and says, 'She always does this to us.'

Anusha Sardana

Welcome to my notes, Gautam.

I should thank you, to start off. Maybe these people at WeDonate are geniuses. When I say people, I mean Sarita Sharan, and to an extent, Rachita. Because after all, I found you, Gautam. Life's come a full circle, hasn't it? I had told Karunesh I couldn't start writing because I hadn't found an interesting character to write about. He found me employable but not in the entertainment vertical. Had he not put me in medical, how would I have found you?

You're interesting, aren't you?

You did make it to the 100 most hated people on Twitter in a survey by *India Today* last year. You were at ninety-three but still in top 100.

I remembered why I had blocked you. You were furiously tweeting *Game of Thrones* spoilers and I have no patience for that. Anyway, I unblocked you and there was your timeline—93,500 tweets. You kept yourself quite busy, didn't you?

Everyone was right—you were hated quite universally.

I was scrolling through August 2017 when 26 August caught my attention. There were sixty-eight tweets in a single day. I read them all.

The Supreme Court called for a ban on Triple Talaq and you saw it as an opportunity to gather some hate.

@gautam_gabbar: Why should Muslims have all the fun?
BIG WIN FOR WOMEN? Nahh. Big win for Hindu men
who had been suffering alone. At least ab bhai-bhai.
Retweets: 2501 Likes: 1543

Hindu men flooded your mentions. Most of them were laughing, others were still lying that they were happy for Muslim women. They were fooling no one.

A little later, you tweeted.

@gautam_gabbar: If we can't get rid of our wives easily, you
can't too. Fair game. #saatjanamkarishta
Retweets: 2501 Likes: 1543

The same Hindu men now shat all over your mentions calling you Paki, porki, pseudosecular, libtard, the works. They collectively lost their shit.

You turned your attention in the afternoon to Gurmeet Ram Rahim Singh—a self-styled, gaudy godman who had directed, produced, acted, sung in a movie on himself, castrated his male followers, slept with their wives. The conviction in rape case led to violence by Dera Sacha Sauda's followers in Punjab, Haryana. Thirty-eight died, 300 were injured. You were less than sympathetic to the entire thing.

@gautam_gabbar: If you're following a Godman, you
deserve to die. It's evolution, weeding out of the stupid.
#DeshMeinChutiyoKiKamiNahi #lovecharger
Retweets: 2532 Likes: 3433

The self-righteous people of Twitter united and bemoaned your heartlessness. They wondered how you could be so cruel.

> *@gautam_gabbar: What do you expect if you're walking to a Godman's room when he himself calls it a gufa? #commonsense*
> Retweets: 3501 Likes: 2343

Well, that was in bad taste. Quite understandably, the feminists of the world united and did what's needed the most—take down a troll. While I support that, what was hilarious was all the male feminists—a mythical being to be honest—were there ridiculing you. All actors, charlatans who use feminism as a paddle board in the dating game. If one is being plain ignorant that's pardonable, but these men were only projecting intelligence, performing for an audience and that was rotten.

People who were using your tweets as diving boards into the filth of their own minds found companionship in your thoughts. It was fun to see people finding your tweets resonating with their own thoughts and going, *yes, I think so too.*

You, meanwhile, honourably picked no camps. You tweeted about everyone—liberals, conservatives, men, women, Hindus, Muslims.

Interestingly, some people—mostly the male feminists—who had pilloried you for one tweet, appreciated your other tweets and even liked them. Say what you will about male feminists, they do have a sense of humour. Maybe that's why feminism is a joke to them.

There was a lot of noise to boycott you since you were a troll. But you weren't the usual troll—bad syntax and grammar, unyielding and unhandsome. You never issued rape threats or were violent. You came across as literate, a bit too much at times. You knew pop culture, enjoyed Beyoncé and Nehru and Ambedkar, wrote with a flair in both English and Hindi. Some of your ardent 'followers' deemed your more dangerous because of that.

Late afternoon, you wanted to tweet a bit more and so you did.

> *@gautam_gabbar: Why do you think Hindu men are so insecure about Muslim men marrying their women? Is it a size thing? #sizematters*
> *Retweets: 501 Likes: 343*

You got hammered from both sides for this tweet before the two sides started having a go at each other.

I imagined you sitting in a tall tower, looking down, watching two factions first abusing you, and then when they didn't find you responding, fighting against each other.

I scrolled to other days. You were just relentless.

> *@gautam_gabbar: There's one job more stupid than a female social media influencer cum blogger. A male social media influencer cum blogger. #higuys*

> *@gautam_gabbar: Vegetarians who aren't vegetarians by choice should shut up. You didn't make an ethical choice, you did what your mumma-papa taught you. Shove your moral lecture up your behind.*
> +
> *@gautam_gabbar: To know the state of the country, watch these fools taking to the roads after India wins the WORLD cup in a sport 12 countries play.*

> *@gautam_gabbar: GENUINE QUESTION. Can you convert to Islam, get married thrice to Muslim women, then convert again and get to keep the women? #askingforafriend*

> *@gautam_gabbar: When you say Virat Kohli is the best batsman in the world you mean he's the best out of upper-order 60 batsmen who play international cricket. Right, right, got it.*

@gautam_gabbar: How weak does one have to be to start being obsessed with English Premier League just to make a few friends?

@gautam_gabbar: People from small towns who shift to big towns and can't stop talking about their small town please go back and live a life of penury. #gareebgoback

@gautam_gabbar: Why do all Greater Kailash aunties have the same hard face? Like they haven't been fucked in a while? #botoxnahincelibacy

@gautam_gabbar: People who talk about feminism, please stop saying what everyone has already said, thank you, you're boring. #unoriginal

@gautam_gabbar: Indian teachers aren't underpaid. They are overpaid. #thosewhocantteach

@gautam_gabbar: Obese people who put hashtags and say I love my body are lying. Even people with abs don't love their bodies. #bodynuetrality

@gautam_gabbar: Want someone to tell me what's the talent of a fashion influencer. Kim at least made a sex tape. #makeasextape

@gautam_gabbar: Men who talk about feminism, please stop, you're fooling no one. Please go back to searching 'rough, forced sex' on pornhub.

@gautam_gabbar: Homophobia exists because every heterosexual couple knows that two boys and two girls have much more fun together.

@gautam_gabbar: People who bitch about the professionalism of Ola drivers are the same who take hour-long cigarette breaks.

@gautam_gabbar: Every time a house help is given a different glass to drink water from, she should spit in the food. It should be a law.

@gautam_gabbar: Feminism is dead if we turn to social media influencers for it.

@gautam_gabbar: All babies aren't cute and parents need to realize that. Love can't be 'that' blind.

@gautam_gabbar: Everyone worshipping Priyanka Chopra called her a slut, and thought she was embarrassing when her music video with Pit Bull came out. Most became fans after the whites accepted her. Please lick the soles of white people.

@gautam_gabbar: How can you tell someone is a Brahmin? They will tell you. They will tell you right after they tell you that caste doesn't matter.

@gautam_gabbar: How big of a loser do you have to be for your role model to be a full-time Instagrammer?

@gautam_gabbar: It's okay to be homophobic. Girls fear men's orientation all the time. It's fine if men fear other men's orientation.

@gautam_gabbar: If I lived in the 16th century—an average lifespan of 25 years—and my wife wouldn't keep hungry for a day for my longevity, I would have mixed feelings about sharing my pyre with her. #karwachauth

@gautam_gabbar: If you're depressed, lonely and friendless, and no one checks on you, you probably deserve it.

@gautam_gabbar: Every girl who learned make-up early to hook a suitable catch before 23 is now a social media influencer.

@gautam_gabbar: I am yet to find a social media influencer who wasn't fat and lost a lot of weight and now posts regularly about body positivity.

@gautam_gabbar: Indian parents care about who their children are having sex with because their own sex lives dry up sooner than you think.

@gautam_gabbar: Male influencers. No one wants to know your beard routine. People have real jobs.

@gautam_gabbar: Even the most woke of you will only call a white person a firangi. Everyone else is either Chinese or kaalu or ye to indian hi lagta hai.

@gautam_gabbar: Female influencers. No one loves you.

Then I scrolled to the last tweet from your account.

@gautam_gabbar: Madarchodo, and Baapchodo (not to be sexist or anything), I will see you on the other side. You have 3500 crores for a statue, you can't spare 20 lacs for a human life. Nice work bhosdiwalo.
Retweets: 7000 Likes: 13443

It was your most retweeted tweet.
You never woke up after that.

Amit Modi

Amit Modi woke up to three missed calls on his phone from the creative director of the production house. There were fifteen messages as well hounding him for revisions of the skit he had written. It would be his seventh revision.

'This is not funny. You used to be funny. What happened?' his creative director—the haramzaada was a twenty-one-year old boy, five years younger than Amit Modi—had said in the last meeting.

Others in the room had chimed in. They were fucking eighteen-year-olds—fucking interns—who had not written a single funny thing in their entire lives and now were telling him off in creative meetings. This production house was built by sharing memes on Instagram and then they moved on to making small videos.

Bhenchod, mujhe sikhaenge (they will teach me)?

Amit didn't allow himself to get lost in nostalgia, of the times his comedy shows sold out in little Gurgaon clubs, or how the YouTube sketches he helped write raked in millions of views, how he was on the list of most promising comedians or how his Twitter following had ballooned to 250,000 followers.

Amit Modi opened his laptop. Without even thinking, his fingers typed the website of WeDonate and then Gautam's name in the search bar. He looked at the amount collected. 1.5 lakh/35 lakh. *'Marega chutiya* (you will die, fucker),' he whispered to himself with a sense of relief. It was the only time of the day Amit Modi could manage to smile. Gautam was going to die sooner or later. He closed the tab. He knew he would open it a few more times during the course of the day. He opened Facebook, Twitter and Instagram pages of WeDonate. He checked if they had shared Gautam's campaign there. Nope.

They wouldn't dare.

When the Gautam campaign had first gone live, he had lost his mind. How could someone want to save him? He had made multiple accounts and dropped scores of abusive comments forcing WeDonate to take down the posts. They would still post about him every now and then and he would repeat the same.

Everyone talked about how public memory was short. That people on the Internet moved on. As someone who built his career on the Internet—by first being funny on Twitter—Amit Modi thought that too.

It had been two years since Gautam had destroyed Amit Modi's life and no one had forgotten yet. Everywhere he went and introduced himself, people referred to Gautam's tweets. The little of the life he had left after Gautam's tweet devastated his entire being, was still getting choked out of him.

Amit Modi was only one of the people Gautam tweeted nastily about. He had driven scores of people off Twitter. Amit knew of him before Gautam turned his attention to Amit one morning for a few hours. He thought of Gautam as one of those attention-seeking insects on Twitter.

Gautam's tweets were directed towards many people like him and yet it seemed that they managed to stall only his life. On some weekends, he would comb through the tweets and stalk the others whom he had driven off Twitter. They all seemed to have moved on with their lives. People like Arvind Mohan, whom Amit Modi ascertained to be Gautam's best

Durjoy Datta

friend, was now working at an MNC, unmindful of what happened.

Amit opened the document of the skit again and leaned back into his chair. He stared at it for a long time. He lit another cigarette and stared at the empty bottle of Old Monk. He shouldn't drink, he reminded himself. Who knows when the hipsters—he was one of them—decided that the outrage against him was too boring to follow up on?

He should have quit working with this production house long ago but he needed the money. The little savings he had had dried up and this project was two months' rent.

Though he hated the bastards who employed him, he was thankful they employed him. Even though he saw the pity clearly in their eyes, they hadn't mentioned the tweets from the handle @gautam_gabbar even once. But they had told him explicitly to not mention that he was working with them.

Amit Modi remembered the day his life imploded down to its last minute; he would still get nightmares of the day.

That day he had first woken up at 7 a.m.; he had talked to his girlfriend of three years till 3 in the morning. He had checked his phone; it was choc-a-bloc with texts, and WhatsApp notifications and mails. He had gone back to sleep because everything could wait. How was he supposed to be productive without sleeping well? He had a busy day of writing jokes and scripts in front of him.

Those days Amit Modi used to forget to fill up invoices and losing out money. He didn't mind it. He was just happy doing what he was always meant to do. Writing funny sketches, doing open mics and the occasional corporate show. He woke up at 10 a.m. again and by that time the tweet from @gautam_gabbar had been retweeted 3000 times. His phone kept hanging from all the notifications; it didn't stop ringing for an hour. All notifications in his Inbox were in caps. Every time he tapped on a notification, his phone hung.

He knew something was wrong; his heart pounded, his fingers trembled. It had happened to him before. He had woken one morning and found himself called an anti-national *bhadwa* because of the cow joke he had cracked. Woke twitter—citing freedom of speech—had defended him at the time but he knew they weren't to be trusted. The liberal, secular, progressive Twitter were one of the most traitorous, opportunistic people he knew.

He logged onto Twitter from his laptop. A stream of invectives and abuses welcomed him. The mentions in his feed all said the same thing.

He was cancelled.

He was named the reason why the youth is the way it is, he was the reason holding back India, he was the scourge, he had to be weeded out. All his employers, his friends in comedy, the venues he performed at, were tagged and people called for a complete boycott.

His heart beat out of his chest; his face twitched. It was another panic attack.

He clicked to the tweets that started it all.

@gautam_gabbar: Just saw the new Amit Modi video about feminism and love and intersectionality and other big words.
\
@gautam_gabbar: Quite boring.
\
@gautam_gabbar: His stand-up set from two years ago was much better. It talked about the simplicity of the lives of Indian women—baby making and sex providing factories. Here's a small clip.
Video.mp4
\
@gautam_gabbar: He also talked about how sending dick pictures to women actually benefits women. It's true feminism.

You send nudes, we send dick pics. No double standards.
Here's a small clip I recorded at the time.
Video.mp4

Amit Modi clicked on the video. It was at least four years
old. Maybe more. He said those things. He was young and
he thought them to be funny. People laughed at them too.
He knew now that it wasn't funny but he was young . . . he
was starting out, he hadn't educated himself, he didn't know
better.

By the time it was 12 p.m. there were page-long articles
on Scroll.in, Wire.in, Opindia.in painting him as all what's
wrong about the Indian comedy scene and Amit had been
fired from all his writing projects, all his stand-up slots were
cancelled. There were other comics who were called out of
their sexist comedy routines but there was no visual proof.
Amit Modi would be the sacrificial lamb. He felt the axe on
the back of his neck, slowly pressing down.

People whom he hung out with wrote threads on
his problematic behaviour, about his misconduct, his
casual sexism. Some girls he had dated recounted how he
was always a bit iffy. They recalled him being aggressive
in bed, crossing some boundaries, abusing his power as a
successful comedian. Successful? Power? When did he ever
have that? He was soon called a rapist, a molester, someone
who should be behind bars. There were tweets in which
his parents were named and asked why they didn't use a
condom or get an abortion. His sister was tagged, his sister's
employers were tagged and she was called a rapist's sister
who must have known about his predatory ways. For those
few hours, Twitter forgot about dying children, crumbling
infrastructure, and concentrated all their collective energies
on destroying Amit Modi.

Everyone *cancelled* him. He was done with.

And then his girlfriend started calling him. And then his parents.

It took Twitter and Instagram twelve hours to destroy Amit Modi's entire life.

Ananth Khatri

Sarita and Saraansh had spent a nervous couple of weeks. They hadn't taken her mother's refusal well. Saraansh kept pestering me to try again which I did. He inundated my phone with texts, landed up at my house, chatted up my parents and even waited outside Mohini's house for me. He was like an annoying woodpecker who kept at it. *Bro, bro, bro, bro, bro, bro, bro, bro.* I could hear his 'bros' in my sleep.

It bore fruit when Aunty relented a little. I called Saraansh to the office and he asked, 'What did she say, bro?' even before he entered the conference room.

'She told me we could make the movie but on a condition,' I said.

'And that is?'

'I'm paraphrasing but this is the gist of what she told me. She told me I was a parasite, and that I wouldn't be anywhere if it weren't for the video Mohini had made for me.'

'You're not a parasite, bro. You're my loverboy, the chocolate hero,' said Saraansh.

'She said she would like the movie to be just about Mohini. Not me, not our love story, *just her*. And everything goes through Aunty first. It's either that or nothing at all,' I said.

'Are you sure, bro?' asked Saraansh.

'It's either that or nothing,' I said.

'Mohini is anyway the centrepiece of the entire thing,' said Sarita when she heard of it. 'Let's take this forward. We don't tell his story.'

'Thank you for the confidence,' I answered.

Sarita gave Saraansh the go-ahead to start the scripting of the movie. Soon after, Saraansh sent me a questionnaire which was extremely intrusive, but also detailed. The subject of the mail said, WE WILL KILL IT, BRO.

It took me a week to revisit the memories the questions unearthed and answer them. Aunty wanted to see the answers first. She reverted with red underlines pointing out grammatical mistakes and timeline anachronisms in the answers. I corrected them. She insisted to recheck them.

I couldn't get myself to send the answers to Saraansh. He was sincere but he was still a stranger and that didn't sit right with me. It was making me uncomfortable, and a bit angry, to share Mohini with him, and eventually everyone. Either Saraansh gets more hours in a day than everyone else or he's the best at multitasking because even though his timeline is full with Instagram stories, he's constantly sending me mails about rough ideas, scenes, story devices and references.

When I shared my concern with him, he said, 'I get it, I get it, but we got to start sitting on the story and make a move on, bro. I'm exploding with ideas so you got to help me out here, dude,' and then said nothing. He has been asking for the document every day since.

I'm meeting him tonight to thrash this out. He's coming with me to a home premier of a movie WeDonate has help produce. We got a mail to wear suits to the screening.

The suit I'm wearing is the only pair the family has seen through many weddings, right from my oldest Chachu's to my oldest Chachu's oldest son's. Countless *makhani* stains have been dry-cleaned off this suit, there's discoloration around the seams where it has been altered repeatedly. The laminated receipt is in a better shape than the suit is.

'You look great,' says Maa.

Papa takes a picture of me with their phone.

'This is why I can't trust both of you,' I say.

I take the phone, put it on self-timer and click a picture of all us together.

'We need to take a print of that,' says Papa.

'I will do it tomorrow,' I answer.

I don't look good at all. But I see this look as a subtle protest against the movie. Not only was the trailer dull and unentertaining, the director was a connected, rich girl. And that's my second grouse against Saraansh. His background is at odds with what we do at WeDonate; he's our donor profile not our beneficiary profile. Can't we find a director with no means? No connections? No real money or opportunity? Why him?

The more I see him on Instagram drinking expensive coffee and buying hardback copies of books that are available in paperback the more it grates me.

Saraansh calls me when he's downstairs. His suit is made of fabric that's glowing, probably plucked out of a unicorn's mane. He's wearing Onitsuka Tiger sneakers to go with it. They look new. That's how the rich look rich. He's at least worth Rs 50,000 right now not counting his watch and the thin bracelet he wears. He hugs me like we are old friends. His driver is driving a seven series BMW today.

'Did you like the trailer?' Saraansh asks.

'Did you like it?' I ask back.

'It sucked balls, fuckall trailer, bro,' he says.

That's exactly what I wanted to hear, maybe not in those exact words. He seems a bit angry that a movie like that got funded. At least here, we are on the same page.

'True.'

'Do you want to talk about the questionnaire, bro?' asks Saraansh.

'We will talk about it later,' I say.

'You have completed it, right?' he asks.

'I'm almost through with it. There are a few hitches,' I say.

'What—'

'I said I'm working on it,' I cut him.

The Delhi traffic is relentless and doesn't care for Saraansh's BMW 7 series. His driver curses the drivers of lesser cars, tells them he has a gun in the glove box. They shrug the threats off.

Sarita's house is in Alaknanda, she must come from the first cadre of upper-middle class people of Delhi. Dressed sharply in a saree that demands an occasion of its own she greets us cheerfully at the door. It's a small and tastefully done house, straight out of a Fabindia catalogue, minimal and exotic, reds and blues and deep browns mixing together, but not too much. There's still plenty of space to move around. The background score of a movie is playing on the music system.

'How's your project going?' Sarita asks us.

'I'm awaiting a mail from Ananth, once he sends that we can get cracking,' Saraansh says.

Sarita looks at me for an answer.

'We can sell Saraansh's car for the initial funding. That could be a good starting point. We can give him producers' credit for it,' I say.

Sarita laughs. Saraansh is not amused.

'You will make a great team,' she says and then marches away from us, greeting others in the same vein she greeted us.

'Is there something you want to say to me?' says Saraansh.

'I just think your car is expensive, that's all,' I say.

'And nothing else, bro? Because I can feel that—'

'Not that I can think of at the moment. Let the screening get over. We will talk about the questionnaire,' I tell him.

I walk away from him and towards where everyone has gathered for the screening. The screening is about to start on Sarita's TV. The girl who directed the movie is telling us why she just had to tell the story which throbbed inside her, how it was a story that needed to be told, and that she was just a medium of how this story is being transmitted. It's all pretentious nonsense.

'Fiction is important. It's how we repackage truth and tell it in a way that changes people,' Saraansh says to me when he sees that I am displeased.

The movie starts. *Dharti* is the biggest budget any short film has garnered on the website so everyone is excited about it. The movie is in Hindi and Tamil but everyone's whispering about it in English. My bias notwithstanding, the movie is terrible.

Most of them think the movie is brilliant because they don't understand it. I look at Saraansh to know what he thinks of it when it ends.

'Don't worry, it's going to be better than this,' he says.

The director is the daughter of a famous painter–writer–Jor-bagh–staple parents. What she thinks are praises from the audience are grovelling attempts at networking. The others are too scared to come across as stupid. They aren't products of convent schools, haven't studied abroad, don't live in Jorbagh, hold a rolled-tongue accent or a champagne flute correctly, and hence they can't say what they truly feel about it. The director is hugged and told that it was a difficult subject to make a movie on, and that she did a wonderful job of it. Does she know she is a sham? How can she not know? It's obvious that all art's a sham. A circle of people hating each other's work privately but lauding it publicly.

The medical team, unimpressed and busy, are the first ones to leave. I could hear them shift restlessly in there. Thrice in an hour, Rachita got up to take phone calls. Since the time I joined she has run three successful campaigns and collected over Rs 70 lakh. Rachita, who has made quite a name by saving lives and for clocking most number of hours in the office, informally heads the medical department. But it's a nominal position. Anyone who stays in medical wants to contribute. I try to find out about the girl who wants to swap entertainment with medical but Rachita refuses to talk.

'You're leaving?' I ask her when I see her booking a cab for herself.

'I watched the movie. This could be good for us,' she says.

'Are you serious?' I ask.

'Sonam Kapoor is set to retweet the link to this movie. Other movie stars will follow. It's an advertisement for us,' she says dryly. 'Sarita told me about you doing Mohini's story. Concentrate on that. You can help more people like that.'

'That's what everyone says.'

'My cab's here,' she says and turns away from me.

A little later, I tap on Saraansh's shoulder and ask him if he's ready to leave. He is. We meet Sarita and the director before leaving. The director asks us if we liked the movie. Saraansh tells her we reached late but will catch it once it's uploaded on YouTube. On the way back home, we stop at the tea stall near the Kashmere Gate ISBT.

'The questionnaire is done, Saraansh. I have got it checked and ratified from Mohini's mother,' I say.

'And there's something I have done to offend you that's keeping you from sending it to me,' he says and sips his tea.

'It's not one thing, Saraansh. First there was the ambush where you and Sarita had already decided what you had to do with our story and—'

'We're sorry about that, bro,' Saraansh interrupts me.

'Hear me out, Saraansh. I'm not foolish to hold that against you,' I say. 'But you do ride in a seven series, you have a thriving business, you have money and privilege. We are not here to help people like you and that woman whose movie we just watched get more visibility. People like you have way too much going for you to turn to us for help. It seems morally corrupt that you wouldn't slug it out like others do and use our platform.'

Saraansh listens intently and then says, 'Bro, I gave Sarita twenty scripts of possible advertisements for WeDonate. She convinced me, and she's right, that this is the best way, your story was the best way. I was selected because she liked my work, man. I didn't come grovelling for money, or trying to leverage your story to further my career.'

I didn't know that but it still doesn't negate my points.

'Even if I forget all of that, I don't know you enough to know you will do justice to our story. There's just one shot at this and I can't bear to disappoint Mohini or Aunty. There's too much at stake here, do you get it?' I say.

Saraansh says nothing.

'So?' I ask.

'What, bro? I'm not going to tell you a sob story for you to support me. I'm supposed to write and direct this thing and I know I will do a crazy job of it. If you don't think I'm up to it after you see my work, you can get me replaced. Nothing will change. I'm the most replaceable part of the jigsaw. You're free to choose,' he says.

I nod.

We sit there in silence for a while. He takes out the phone. From the corner of the eye I see him go to the YouTube app. He goes to the video of Mohini and thrusts his phone towards me.

'What am I looking at?' I ask.

It's a comment from his profile. He points at the timestamp.

'Check the date,' he says.

It was one of the first five comments on the video.

Saraansh Gupta: If this isn't love, I don't know what is. Why does this video have only 120 views? Are people blind? We need more of these stories.

I take out my phone.

'Are these the answers, bro?' he asks, his eyes light up.

I shake my head.

'Saraansh, here are forty-one questions,' I say. 'I want your answers for them, I need to know more about you. Let's see how well you tell your story before we start with Mohini.'

He takes the phone from me.

Anusha Sardana

Gautam! You're back in my notes. :)

Gautam, your parents were surprised to receive my call. They told me that no one from WeDonate had ever wanted to visit you. They had their reasons, and I had mine. I had taken a liking to what people hated about you. I had spent so much time reading your tweets, and thinking about them that it almost felt you were a friend, that we used to sit together and shit on the world. I now feel what I have heard other writers say in interviews—the characters I wrote about became my friends.

Your father told me to reach an hour later than I had planned to. I could hear your mother whisper in the background that the house was too dirty and there was nothing to feed me.

I told them I would come an hour later than planned.

The auto driver didn't want to go deep into the lane that led to your DDA flats knowing he ran the risk of brushing against the tightly packed cars. The cluster of modestly built apartments were disfigured by illegal extensions, mismatched paints and general neglect. Women in their nighties stood in their balconies looking for an excuse for a fracas with their neighbours. A strong smell of bhindi hung in the air. TV sets were on in every second house, women were transforming into lizards in the soaps that were on them, salt was being added *swadanusar* on cookery shows, and the doors were open.

Your house was on the ground floor. Your father opened the door. I folded my hands in namaste and he clasped his hands tightly over mine and nodded gently.

'Thank you, beta, for doing this,' he said.

I could smell the Lifebuoy on him, the kurta had a sharp crease in the middle from where it was ironed. Your mother came from behind him.

'Come, come. Come inside,' she said.

She now had the confidence in her house of a homemaker whose refrigerator has a 2 lt Pepsi bottle, and whose kitchen has steaming hot samosas and paneer pakodas with a packet of imli chutney.

She wiped the sweat off her brow, held my hand and led me inside. She made me sit on the sofa like a proper guest. There were chai and pakodas, just for me. They smelled great but I waited for them to insist on me having some.

I had some and then also had the samosa that had followed and realized how odd they must think that I hadn't asked about you. I looked at them.

'You want to see him?' your mother asked.

'That's what I'm here for, Aunty,' I said.

Your mother led me by my hand towards your room. Your room smelled hospital-like. If the room ever had your smell it had been obliterated by disinfectants. At the door itself, I heard the beeps of the machines that were monitoring you. The little beeps, their own Morse code, your body trying to talk through the pumps of the heart, the churning of fluids in your stomach.

'Gautam,' said your mother to introduce us.

You lay there sleeping, powerless, unmindful that you were going to be the first character I was to convincingly write about. Despite seeing your pictures, I was expecting a crooked face, pock-marked, uneven teeth, drooling, scarred. But you . . . you looked normal.

Your mother sat by your side, radiating sadness. She was holding your hand. The first thing I noticed about you was your hair. For someone who had had brain surgery they were long, healthy and shiny. In sharp contrast to your mother's hair—thin, strandy, most of which had fallen out.

We needed new pictures for your story on WeDonate, and you looked too handsome to look sick.

I took my laptop out. I needed to know more about you. I had spent the last week bingeing on your tweets, each more fascinating than the last. When people are assholes, and they know they are, they still try to defend their behaviour in a way. As if they know what they are saying is not acceptable, but it needs to be said according to them. You didn't give a fuck. You judged everyone without any qualms, and I loved how easily you could rile people up, make them angry enough to threaten to hack you.

Today, I was most interested in the bunch of tweets you typed before being wheeled into surgery. I wanted to know what was going on in your mind right before your possible death.

@gautam_gabbar: @ranmeeksingh *behen, your father is performing a brain surgery on me. If he had done one on you in time, he wouldn't have to buy a management quota for you. (1/n)*
|
Your father has a rolex. He's charging me for a full pair of gloves even though he uses one. Does he take one home to shag with? Does your mother know? Curious. (2/n)
|
How's your parent's sex life? Your father is rather fat and when he bends over to check me, he reeks of rotten eggs. Heard you're an only child. I think your mother had had enough. (3/n)

'Can you tell me a little bit about him? We need to tell our donors why they need to pay for his condition,' I said.

'Is it okay to let him die?' asked your father.

Your mother looks away from me, shaking her head in anger. She said, 'I have seen on your website. Many boys his age are saved every day. Why not my son?'

Your father said, 'You know why.'

'He never hurt anyone. Just few words,' argued your mother.

Your mother quietly left the room. There were no angry tears, no desperate pleas. It seemed like that phase of urgent, pointed, debilitating pain was over. I had seen your parent's look on Mumma—the one when you have accepted that the pain is a part of you—after Papa left us. You carry it to your death. Mumma tried her best to deal with it. She thought if she could find people to talk with about what she was going through, it would lessen the blow. Men—colleagues, neighbours, old friends—they all came. The pattern was unmissable. They would tell her they would come with their family and then turn up alone, smelling of Old Spice and Denim cologne, freshly shaved. They would all ask if I was home. Unlike Mumma, I knew why they were there. A picture, a smell, a gust of wind—anything could reduce her to tears. And she cried and sobbed and wailed in front of every one of these men. My mother is gorgeous, Gautam. She's a sight. And yet, when she cried, her screams seemed to stain the world with grief. The men shrivelled to half their size in front of her open, wild hair, her red veiny eyes. Her grief during the first few months was infectious, an epidemic. Everyone came out feeling they had lost something. Every man went back with their nefarious intentions unfulfilled. Some came back again to try their luck. Mumma, having deemed them useless in unburdening her pain, would ask me to tell the wolves she wasn't at home. I would refuse because I didn't want to talk to her. I had my own shit to deal with. And she was among all the people I blamed for our fate. I blamed the entire fucking world.

'What do you need?' your father asked once the uncomfortable air cleared.

'Your son had a troubling presence online. People remember that sort of thing. Every time we post about his campaign there's a lot of backlash. No one likes your son . . . even now.'

He stared right through me, and muttered the words, 'He was sick, his brain . . . it was rotting. He—'

'We need something to tell the donors. Something that contrasts with what people know about him,' I said.

Your father looked listlessly at me.

'I will be more specific. Let's start from the day he was taken for the surgery. He must have known there's a chance that he wouldn't wake up. So if everything went well, did he want to do something specific? What did he say before he was taken inside?' I asked.

There was a long pause. Your father steeled himself and then said, 'You have read the tweets . . . he was sick. It was his disease talking.'

He needed some time, so he got up and left me alone with you. I sat there looking at you. It seemed hard to believe that you hadn't opened your eyes in months. It looked like you would wake up this instant and start talking.

I wondered what made you who you had become and how you were like before that. We all have stories. You have yours and I have mine. I will tell you mine someday. As I sat there, I felt an urge that I didn't feel before, not this strongly, not even when I was watching Rajni cry. I wanted you to live. I wanted you to survive this so you could wake up, sit next to me and talk to me.

Ananth Khatri

If it were not for Saraansh's stupidly expensive car, we would have been chased down the road by the guards outside Polaris Technologies. It has been three hours that we have been waiting for Karan Jaslok.

'What does your father do again?' I ask to pass the time.

'He sells buttons, I told you earlier. Zara? UCB? Jack & Jones? The buttons you see. They are all manufactured by my father. My brother designs them.'

'That must be tough,' I say.

'He works . . . oh, you were making fun!' he says.

'Finding different ways to punch four holes in a plastic disc requires vision. I get it. You must be really proud,' I say. 'There he is.'

Karan Jaslok's limp isn't pronounced but it's there if you're looking for it.

'He's good looking, can't deny that,' says Saraansh softly.

Saraansh had insisted he needed to see and talk to Karan Jaslok, Mohini's first boyfriend on his own. He thought I had lied on the mail trying to make things more dramatic than they really were. He was also sure I had missed out on details. 'I want to do this right,' he kept telling me as if I didn't want the same thing. Although I have started to like him, this creative process is going to be fraught with trouble.

'Go through it again,' he says as we trail Karan Makhija's motorcycle though the streets of Connaught Place. 'Don't miss any of the details. Tell me everything you remember.'

'She was in the eleventh standard, must have been fourteen–fifteen. Karan was nineteen, older, second year of college, someone much wiser. He was much more handsome than he's now. Unlike other boys around her who were struggling, he had settled into his height. He had left puberty long behind. He knew of the strength in his arms, the energy, the sinewy muscles, the voice. His facial hair wasn't light but hard and grew vigorously. Karan was a man. He'd joined a call center in the second year of college. Every day he used to wear freshly ironed shirts, tuck them in neatly in his pleated trousers, and leave for work. A bus with similarly dressed people used to pick him up. Mohini's school bus and his shared the same stop. That's where Mohini first saw him. Despite the other men in the bus, it was his face that stood out for her.'

'For someone who doesn't like the entertainment vertical you paint quite a picture. Does thinking of him make you jealous?'

'It shreds my heart,' I tell him.

'Bro,' he says and looks at me with pity.

'On that bus stop, there used to be other girls from her school too. They would also notice Karan. The fear of losing Karan slowly gripped Mohini. She started to sleep uneasy. She was always worrying if one of the girls would roll down their socks or hike up their skirts to catch Karan's attention. To Karan's credit, he never once looked up from his books. She would never be that girl—her love story wouldn't start with looking at herself in the mirror thinking if more legs will draw her lover's attention.'

'Did you get all of this from Mohini? Her mother?' asks Saraansh.

'I have met Karan before today,' I tell him.

'Of course you have. Continue,' says Saraansh.

'Days passed, then weeks and then months, and yet he kept looking at his books. He never once looked up. He never missed work, she never missed school. Through fevers and chills, she would be there, at the bus stop to look at him before her day started. He had become her superstition. Like some look for two mynas, or a mail van for luck, she used to look for him.'

'Do you believe in the mail van too, bro?' asks Saraansh.

I nod.

'Go on,' he says.

'He looked up one day. Their eyes met. Once and then again, and then every day. On some days, she thought it was all in her head because why would someone like him look at someone like her. She would spend the entire day basking in that one gaze of his in the morning. She would build lifetimes starting from that one look, one gaze.'

'That's awfully romantic.'

'And then one day, he didn't come. His bus came, stopped, waited and left. An irrational fear gripped her. She felt scared; she thought something had happened to him. Why would he not come? She didn't board her school bus. She turned back not knowing where she would go. She first wandered around her colony, and then the neighbourhood, looking for him. Was he sick? Was he . . . dead? "Just keep him alive," she prayed. For a few moments she thought it was her wrongful desire for him that made him pay for his life. She had always felt guilty that she loved him, that she was keeping this from her parents. Things a teenager would imagine.'

'We have all been there,' says Saraansh.

'She promised to a god, just any god, that she wouldn't ever look at him, not wait for him, not think of him, if he was alive. She cut a deal with god. Little did she know that in the next few minutes, death would stare right at her.'

'You didn't write this in the mail,' says Saraansh irritably as if I had put a spanner in his plans. 'Continue.'

I continue, 'He was there. In a crisp white kurta, his lips slightly open, the name of Ram on his lips, and shouldering a fourth of a dead body. He chanted. *Ram Naam Satya Hai, Ram Naam Satya Hai.* Their eyes met. It might have been a second or a lifetime, it was hard to say, but when she wrenched herself free from the chokehold of time, true to her word, she turned, and she left. She promised to hang her head low if that's what it took to not look at him again. She didn't know if she boarded the bus the next day or the day after that. For days after that she kept hearing the chants in her head, "Ram Naam Satya Hai", over and over and over again. A few more days passed, and she learned Karan's chacha had died in an accident. Karan was driving the motorcycle. He had narrowly escaped death. It built her resolve.'

'That's hard,' says Saraansh.

'Mohini was convinced that it was Ram, the unknown god she prayed to, who had saved Karan. Mohini's parents weren't religious but, in that moment, she turned into a believer. She was so young after all.'

'You don't have to justify someone's faith,' says Saraansh.

'Mohini downloaded wallpapers of Ram who had saved Karan, learned a few chants to thank him. A few days later, she went to the temple near her house. That's where she saw him again. She tried walking away but he held her hand. He looked at her again. And it broke her resolve, the deal she cut. And that's where they came to be. In the three months that Karan and Mohini were together, Mohini surrendered everything. Karan destroyed her in return. All the grief, the guilt, the hate, the anger that he had for himself for surviving the accident, he unloaded on her. He abused her verbally and physically, broke her, closed his fist around her life and choked her. She wasn't allowed to have friends, she wasn't allowed time for herself, Karan was to be her everything. Mohini forgave everything, accepted everything as a part of the great love. Karan was a man in pain. He needed to let it out of his system.'

'How did it end?'

'Uncle could sense something was wrong. It didn't take him long to find out about Karan. He kept quiet for a week and then two, kept it from Mohini's mother who wouldn't have allowed this. His daughter needed to navigate these battles on her own. But his resolve broke when he knew that Mohini wasn't the only girl Karan was with. Mohini didn't believe her father at first. Her father who knew everyone around the neighbourhood tried to tell her that Karan and his chachu weren't close. That Karan's pain was an excuse.'

'What happened when she did?' asks Saraansh.

'She thought there was some mistake. She stopped going to school, talking to her friends, eating, drinking or bathing. Uncle saw her shed her innocence, her childhood like a robe, like a snake's skin. The veins in her heart constricted, her heart grew old.'

My heart sinks thinking of the details—now that I'm in the story.

'Mohini was in the school hockey team. She was brilliant with the stick. She picked one up. Her father followed her to Karan's house.'

'What did she do?' asks Saraansh.

'What's most humiliating in Delhi? *Ghar mein ghus kar maa-baap ke saamne pitai* (Getting beaten up in front of your parents). Uncle held off Karan's screaming parents. Mohini wielded her hockey stick like a mace. Three hairline fractures in his hands, two broken ribs. When she pushed him off the stairs, his broken femur jutted out of his thigh. That's the limp Karan carries today.'

'No police complaints?' asks Saraansh.

'Uncle was in the lock-up for a week. But don't pity him. He had made friends with the constables and then the inspector within the first day,' I say. 'Also, he was the father of a girl who had been violated and cheated on. The policemen quashed the FIR. The next week, they were all at Mohini's house and Uncle cooked biryani for them. He remained friends with the police guys long after. Mohini, in a number of ways is a carbon copy, cut from the same cloth, a little part of him.'

Karan parks his motorcycle. He enters the coffee shop. We enter after him, not particularly sure why. He takes a seat at the corner. There's a view so it's sure to be a date. When Karan spots me, he gets up.

'Now what?' he says, a bit scared.

It's been a few months since I last saw him. Saraansh and I sit in front of him. He shifts in his seat, trying to get up and leave.

'It will be better if you keep sitting down,' I say.

'Look—'

'Shut up till you're asked questions,' I say. 'This is Saraansh. Saraansh, this is Karan.'

Karan sits down with a hobble. The piercing pain of the bone cutting through skin visible in his eyes. He's scared. I tell him I'm not here to beat him up.

He says, 'I told you everything. Now what do you want from me?'

'Is he crying a bit?' Saraansh asks me.

'I'm not—'

'Calm down, Karan. We won't take long. Do you want something to drink? Coffee?'

'Water,' he mumbles.

Saraansh waves down the waiter and asks for water.

'Breathe, there's nothing to be scared of,' I say.

'What . . . what . . . do you want,' Karan stammers.

'Saraansh here is making a movie on Mohini. He thinks I might have embellished a few details in her story. He wants the truth. So everything you told me about her, you, about her father, he needs to hear it again. He needed to see the boy who made Mohini believe in god.'

Saraansh spots the fear in Karan's eyes and helpfully says, 'We are going to change names of course. That is if you help me, or—'

Karan hesitates.

'You don't have a choice,' I tell him.

Karan starts and tells Saraansh exactly what he told me a few months ago.

'She saw me at the bus stop . . .'

'Don't miss the details,' says Saraansh.

Karan continues. Saraansh orders a round of coffee for everyone. Karan's girlfriend comes and we make her sit with us.

'Can we not—'

I glare him down and he doesn't protest.

She hears the story too. Both Saraansh and I hope this will be her last date.

When he finishes and we leave the coffee shop, Saraansh asks me, 'He seemed scared. Did you beat him up too?'

'I'm not a part of the story,' I say.

Anusha Sardana

Rachita and Sarita would have lost their bearings with me dragging my feet on the Gautam case had Manoj Kumar's campaign not reached its completion. When it did, Manoj came to the office and made a huge deal crying and hugging me, telling me that they will always keep me in their prayers. They also came bearing gifts—clothes—which of course I didn't accept. I kept the card Rajni made for me. It warmed the cockles of my heart a bit, I won't deny that. I believe this was the kind of thing Rachita used to get off on—being a savior. I was sure there was a little board in her house with cards from sick children thanking her.

'Smile a little,' said Rachita.

If Rachita thought Rajni's campaign was a success and a reason to smile, she had to be naive. We collected Rs 15 lakh from 900 donors. Just 900 donors out of the hundreds of thousands of people who have money to spare. That's all it took to save Rajni's life, just 900 people tapping away at their laptops, feeling a bit cheeky and generous and superior on that day. It was less than what showrooms of Zara or UCB make in a day.

But how can you just think of Rajni and not of the thousands like her who die every day because 900 people didn't come together for them? Did their parents—with their daughters cremated—stumble upon the WeDonate website later and go, oh no, we should have known of this website before? They could have found 900 people to help them? Why has it come to that? Why do we have to seek out kindness?

The medical team now saw me as an asset, and invited me to their table quite a few times. I had to refuse because that's a stupid waste of time.

Sarita had given me a bunch of other cases to start working on simultaneously and it had kept me up at nights. I had been making minor adjustments to Gautam's campaign but every time we posted it from WeDonate's accounts, hate instead of donations started to stream in. The comment section used to fill up almost instantly. The post would be reported and the hate-comments would spill over to the other posts as well. We would have to take the posts down. Sometimes it felt like some of the accounts were fake accounts but we didn't have means to check.

I was dozing off at my table when Vishwas ji tapped on my shoulder and kept a big box on my table.

This is what I was waiting for!

I had been nagging Gautam's mother to send everything there was of Gautam—pictures, report cards, letters—to me. They had taken so much time I thought they had decided against sending it.

The box was taped and it took me ten minutes to get inside.

There was a small note inside.

This is everything about him—Aunty.

There were thirteen photo albums twice as thick as my arm, four academic files, two medical files and a bunch of files spilling with receipts. They were pretty thorough.

As I stacked them on the desk, others in the medical team turned towards me again, smiling.

'Good to see you have started enjoying being in the medical team,' said Rachita.

I didn't correct her, didn't tell her I plan to stay only till I find out everything about Gautam.

I opened the first album. The print pictures were in pristine quality, meticulously catalogued. I started to flip through the album.

Gautam was born an ugly child. Wrinkly skin, a scowl on his face, and not a sliver of hair on his head, a bit like a dried raisin. In the arms of his parents, he looked adopted. Yet, his parents seemed to be obsessed with him. There were a lot of pictures. I flipped through them.

A couple of months passed. He slowly filled up and started looking more human, more baby-like. His parents never looked into the camera, always towards him, their smiles bright, their grasp tighter. There were hundreds of pictures of him lying on the bed, at first supine, and then on his belly.

The albums changed. The pictures continued.

Ah, finally.

There was picture of him as a toddler. Standing up, a reindeer doll in his hand, his hair in a pony. And then a picture of him without any hair. *Mundan*. There were about thirty pictures of him just sleeping. Not doing anything cutesy, just sleeping. At this point, I felt resentful towards my parents for not having clicked as many pictures when I was growing up. I was a much cuter child.

I knew Gautam's parents weren't rich so paying for film, developing these pictures would have made a serious dent in their expenses.

I picked the next album. I flipped further.

A picture of him in his school uniform. He was crying, and so was his mother. It was cute I won't deny. And then there's another one. He's in his father's arms, wide smiles. I took the picture out and turned it. *After school*, was in the inscription.

It seemed like as an apology for sending him to school, his parents had bought him a bunch of toys because there were pictures of him posing with every toy. He was now making faces and gestures at the camera. The frequency of the pictures increased. Damn it. What were my parents doing when I was doing cute stuff?

He slowly grew cute. Another album came to an end.

I was warming up to him. First standard and then second and third and the fifth. This was where the photos became slightly sparse. Was it because he had a mind of his own? He became difficult to photograph? There are blurred pictures of him sticking out his tongue towards the camera.

Then came pictures of them on trips.

There were pictures of them in crowded trains and in buses. On the Mall Road and Jakhu Temple in Shimla, on the train to Jaipur, in front of the Taj Mahal, outside Fatehpur Sikri, in Rishikesh and Dehradun.

He slowly grew up in the pictures. Lost his baby fat, gained a lot of inches in height, sprouted facial hair.

Gautam regained his rat-like face by the time he turned, I'm guessing, twelve or thirteen? With it came the onslaught of pimples. He looked un-cute again. He now looked shy and yet angry in the picture. Gautam looked like he didn't like to be photographed. In the photographs, he stood a little away from his parents.

And then his pictures stopped.

Instead of him, his parents were in the pictures.

And then it dawned. These weren't Gautam's albums. These were family albums. And for thirteen years, his parents hadn't clicked a single photograph of just themselves.

Gautam seemed like he was making up for lost time.

The albums began to be flooded with the pictures of his parents. He shot them well and shot them rather indiscriminately. There were a *lot* of pictures of them. But unlike the pictures his parents clicked of him, there was a theme to every picture he clicked of them. He shot the pictures with a lot of love. These pictures were orchestrated. It took me a little time to figure this out. It wasn't a coincidence that his father was opening his briefcase in the background and his mother was pouring tea. It was staged and acted and conceptualized. The inscription was 'evening'. They would have prepared for the photograph.

Then there was a picture of his mother making tea, and of his father sitting on the counter with the inscription behind the picture as, 'a couple after a long day'. Another picture of his father sleeping in the bed, and his mother reading the newspaper was inscribed as 'Sunday morning'.

My favorite picture was of his mother eating a kulfi and his father cupping both his hands below that kulfi to catch its melted milk. It was inscribed as 'young'.

There were dozens of these meticulously planned pictures.

And then his father dropped out of the pictures. It was only solo pictures of her mother during different times of the day.

It took me a few pictures to realize that his mother was pregnant.

Gautam must have been thirteen. It came to me as a shock. Rachita had mentioned Gautam *had* a sister who died young. I had always assumed she was born before Gautam.

Through scores of pages of the album, there were pictures of his mother's pregnancy. Every picture taken with a lot of thought. When I was looking at these pictures, I had to remind myself that these were clicked on the film cameras where you had one shot to take a picture.

His mother looked beautiful, like a movie star in those photographs. There are pictures of her cooking with a big belly, there's a picture of her standing on the weighing scale in a doctor's office, there's a picture of his father looking at her mother's belly amongst others. If I flipped through them fast enough, it would have looked like a story board of an art film. There were no photos of Gautam in that period.

And then, there were pictures of another baby. This attempt by Gautam's parents was better. The baby was cute from Day One.

There was a single picture on two pages of the album. Gautam was holding the baby in his arm. The picture was inscribed, 'Anaira'.

Now Gautam returned in the pictures. There's the baby and there's him. There was a glut of pictures now.

I noticed a change. There were pictures in the mirror now with Gautam holding up the baby. The camera was no longer a film camera, it's a digital one. The baby grew up in the pictures. There were no pictures of the parents anymore. It was either the baby, Anaira, or Gautam. There were pictures of him feeding Anaira, there were pictures of Anaira sleeping on his shoulder, and there were pictures of Anaira crawling, and then standing up, and then there are pictures of Anaira and him drawing on the wall.

Gautam's pimples cleared up in the pictures, he turned handsome. I was on the fourth album and there were just pictures after pictures. Most of them were centred around the baby, Anaira. The digital camera allowed Gautam to capture everything he wanted.

Anaira turned into a toddler in the pictures. With every subsequent picture, Gautam and Anaira grew older. Anaira was painfully cute.

I flipped through an entire album of pictures of Anaira and Gautam; I skipped a few pictures. I picked up the next one.

There was a picture of Anaira, no longer a baby but a toddler in front of a huge cake. It was printed in black and white. The inscription said three. A few more pictures followed with

Gautam and Anaira with their faces plastered with cake. Soon, the same uniform from Gautam's earlier photos reappeared. Anaira's first day at school. Gautam's parents holding up Anaira, and then Gautam holding up Anaira. There were pictures of Anaira and Gautam in their uniforms, eating breakfast. Then there were pictures of Anaira in her own classroom. There were pictures of Gautam in her classroom too, looking like a giant in front of the little desks. Then there were pictures of Anaira with Gautam and his friends. The little girl amidst giants. There were pictures of Anaira and Gautam in front of an ice-cream vendor, in front of a bus, in front of their school ground, inside their library.

There were a slew of pictures of Anaira and Gautam in their own uniforms and then an abrupt stop.

There were pages upon pages of the album that were empty. Nothing.

I picked up the next album. There were no people in the pages. Anaira's uniform. Anaira's blanket. Anaira's toys. Anaira's things. Pictures of taped boxes marked Anaira, things that would never be used. Anaira's empty crib. Anaira's empty chair. Pictures of an empty class with little tables. Pictures of Anaira's tiny empty plates and spoons. This was when she must have died. At three years of age; Gautam must have been around fifteen or sixteen.

I had always assumed she died an infant, or in childbirth.

My heart sank thinking of all the pictures of Anaira and Gautam, and now the cold, empty picture of Anaira's things. It went on for a little while.

The first face to appear after a long while was of a girl. She was in a school dress and the inscription just said, 'Karishma'. There was no hint about who she might have been.

It seemed a little odd that Gautam's parents allowed solo pictures of a girl to run along for so many pages. There was just her for a huge percentage of the album I was at.

Was that how he grieved?

And then, the pictures of his parents returned. Older, a little hunched up, a bit tired. But the pictures became beautiful. They took on a professional quality. Even how the pictures were arranged in the albums changed. There were few pages just in black and white, some alternated, a mix of pictures of things, Karishma and his parents.

And now more people came into the pictures. People in the same uniform as his. His school friends, I gathered.

I picked another album.

It seemed this was when he started college. There were a bunch of guys in the pictures. He's there in a bunch of pictures too. He seemed to have peaked here, looking gorgeous with his long hair. Gautam seemed to have realized this because the number of pictures of him took an uptick.

In most of the pictures, Karishma was with him too.

Though a world of difference between the pictures he clicked of others and what others clicked of him remained.

Of all the guys in the pictures, there's one guy whose portraits kept cropping up. I checked for inscriptions and found a name behind one of them. 'Arvind'. Both portraits of Arvind and Karishma were, if I might hazard saying, art-like, ones clicked out of love and of knowing someone. These were pictures taken for posterity. As if to say after a few years, *Look there's you!* Every expression of theirs was deftly captured, every angle, every blemish, every type of smile; there details were so rich I could imagine them talking out of their pictures, I could imagine their voices, their gait, their fears, their hopes and their dreams. They felt like people I intimately knew.

These must have meant something to him. There were other faces too, almost as frequent as Arvind and Karishma, also clicked with intention but not love.

With time, pictures of some people petered out but Karishma and Arvind's remained. There were a stream of pictures of them, each more beautiful than the last. There were some pictures I paused for over a minute just looking at them over and over and over again. I didn't know a picture could elicit that emotion in me. The faces remained the same, yet they drew me in.

I picked the next album.

There were pictures of his new experiences that the freedom of college brings. Food. Restaurants. Pictures of movie tickets. Chaat eaten late at night. Friend's motorcycles. Empty streets. Maggi at the roadside joint. Endless pictures.

A lot of pictures of Arvind had a single-word inscription. 'Friend'.

A lot of pictures of Karishma had a single-word inscription too. 'Girl'.

And then he started to feature in pictures that were taken well too. A photographer friend? Self-timer? He appeared confident at the way he looked in those pictures. He looked straight at the lens and peered into it as if he was listening to me, inviting me to talk, to hear his secret. The quality of the photos of him peaked and became sparser. I loved these pictures. There was a piercing handsomeness to him.

But then something different happened.

The stream of pictures clicked by him became denser. He was capturing everything. Did he get a phone with a larger memory space? Some of them were great. But most were passable. The quality of the pictures Gautam took dropped. And it kept dropping. It was obvious.

It was a strange experience for me because before these albums I couldn't have told the difference between a good picture and a bad picture. A picture is a picture. Talking endlessly about photographs is just pretentiousness.

These pictures were *average*. It seemed like I had stepped out of an art gallery and found myself looking through a teenager's phone.

There were less people and more things in his pictures. Roads. Cars. Streetlights. Pens. Anything but people. Of the ones with people, they weren't memorable. They didn't have the feel or the look of the earlier pictures. It seemed like Gautam had clicked them half-heartedly. The glaring difference between his previous good pictures and the ones I was seeing now jumped out at me.

People started dropping out. I saw less of his parents. The last two to go were Arvind and Karishma. Even their pictures lacked the sharpness, the depth, the semblance of a story that his earlier pictures had.

After Karishma also dropped out of the pictures, there were no pictures of people anymore. Just things. Just his books, his laptop, his room. A barrage of pictures of things.

And then the pictures disappeared. There were empty pages. Pages after pages after pages of emptiness.

I picked up the last album.

There were pictures of a clinic. Of files and reports. Pictures of his parents sitting in front of doctors. Then the inside of their house. There were pictures of X-rays.

The photos then came to a stop.

By the time I was finished, it had been three hours and Rachita was leaving office. She said, 'Take some rest. You can't be sitting like that for that long. Your back will give up.'

I took her sound medical advice and headed back home. That night I had vivid dreams of being Gautam's friend, his classmate in school, his friend in college, and his ward-mate in a hospital.

I couldn't think of anyone but him. The tenderness of his photographs was at odds with his tweets. He seemed like two different people. How do you relate the pictures taken with so much love, intention and mastery to someone who only saw the worst in people? I felt like Gautam had been betraying me all this while. He wasn't in my team after all. Disappointingly enough, and unlike me, he still had a working heart.

The thought kept me up all night.

The next day, I rushed to the office. I cross-referenced the photographs with Gautam's tweets, and I realized what had happened.

I saw why the quality, the love behind the photographs had suddenly vanished. I saw when the tweets started getting more caustic.

Everything coincided with the last good picture of Karishma. The inscription on that photograph was 'Finished'.

Was this their break-up picture? Was it when their relationship started to sour? When they started fighting?

There were pictures of Karishma after that too but none of them had the intention and the mastery of the earlier photographs.

Gautam was turning out to be a cliché. Here's what I surmised. She broke his little heart, and he lost the will to photograph and record things as beautifully as he did, started to hate the world, and what better place to dump that hate than on Twitter?

Now, I needed to meet Karishma to confirm my hypothesis.

Ananth Khatri

There's seldom a time when I'm allowed in Mohini's room without Aunty's looming presence.

But today is one of those days. I'm in her room and Aunty has had to leave the house for some office work. Today's a big day, Saraansh will narrate to us the opening montage of the movie, and yet with her in the room, all I can think of right now is to hold her hand. It feels like I should take the plunge. My hands are trembling, I can feel the reverb of my beating heart. It's like a subwoofer going full blast in the boot of the car. She won't mind, I know. She will even like it, give me one of those looks that she does. That confounding, loving look. It does nothing for my child-like dread and excitement. But maybe not taking the plunge has its own advantages. Till the time I hold her hand, I can experience this over and over again repeatedly. Once I do hold her hand, this anticipation, this thumping of my heart is never going to come back; that's going to be it, isn't it?

I'm in the middle of my indecision when Saraansh walks in.

A week ago, he had accompanied me to Mohini's house as a friend and had ingratiated himself to Aunty. How he did that is beyond me. Why wasn't she wary of the expensive car, the rich-people clothes, the rich-people scent, is confounding. As someone whose husband had been properly fucked over by rich customers time and again, she should have harboured a mild hatred towards Saraansh. Not her. She even spilled all the details of the Ramneek Aunty incident, an episode I had to gather from the other neighbours.

Ramneek Aunty lived in the street behind Mohini's house. The only times Ramneek Aunty and Mohini's mother had met were when Ramneek Aunty tried to recruit Mohini's mother for her kitty group. Between her books, her job and Mohini, she led a full life; she always respectfully denied. The meetings took a spike when Ramneek Aunty wanted Uncle to remodel their two bathrooms. The demand was ordinary. Uncle had worked on a lot of houses in the locality.

It was Mohini who first noticed the boundaries Ramneek Aunty would cross. A casual touch here, a flirtatious comment there.

'You can bathe here and go,' she would tell Uncle after the day's work.

Mohini was eleven but she had seen enough Hindi movies to know what Aunty was trying to do. She relayed everything to her mother.

Ramneek Aunty's blouses became deeper and the sleeves shorter till in July, there were no sleeves to talk about. Two months of construction were drawing to a close when Ramneek Aunty made her move. She locked herself in the bathroom with Uncle. Mohini was outside. She heard her father shout like she never had before. Then moments later, her father had pulled the door clean off. He held Mohini's hand and stormed out of the house. Aunty hadn't asked Uncle for the details.

But her revenge was far from over.

She let a couple of months pass. It was October and winters had crept in. She took Mohini along to Ramneek Aunty's house to collect the money owed to her husband. But Aunty wasn't there just for money. She dragged Ramneek Aunty by her hair to the bathroom her husband had constructed, bound her under the shower, turned it on and walked out. Aunty was found three hours later, drenched, and dangerously close to catching pneumonia.

Over the years, there have been many Ramneek Aunties in Mohini and Aunty's life. One stray, loose comment about Uncle had always sent them into a wild tizzy. If these were the medieval times, mother and daughter would have ripped out countless tongues from people's mouths and fed their children biryani made from it.

Aunty—when she narrated the same to Saraansh—told him she had no regrets.

I sat there cursing her. Why wouldn't she tell *me* all this?

Saraansh addresses Mohini before me. It's what he does, talks to everyone as if he has known them for a lifetime. Saraansh is great at small talk and tries to initiate one when I cut him.

'Can we do what we are here for?' I ask him.

The earlier he wraps up, the more time Mohini and I will have with each other. Aunty had asked me to keep this from Mohini, but I think she has the right to know what we are making. When Mohini wakes up tomorrow, I want to be on the right side of history.

'Sure, sure,' says Saraansh. He looks at Mohini and says, 'I have gathered everything Ananth had to tell me about you, your childhood, etc. Since the movie won't cover your entire life, we will put in a montage for the first fifteen years of your life. Dude, you know, like those scenes where a little boy is running on the track and suddenly he grows up? Exactly like that but with more story and context. Things will play out to a musical score in the background with a few dialogues here and there. It will help us establish the world.'

'Stop treating us like children,' I tell Saraansh.

Saraansh takes out his writing pad. There are random words scribbled on the pages. There's no *Sc-1/Various locations* anywhere on the page. He catches me staring.

'Everything is rough right now,' he says.

'Shall we start?' I ask Mohini.

Mohini looks on; waiting.

'So we begin,' says Saraansh. 'These are your first fifteen years. Condensed.' Saraansh smiles and begins.

'A busy hospital. A woman screaming, legs splayed apart. The doctor holds up a baby. It's a girl. The woman smiles nervously. Cut to the nurse coming out of the labour room, baby wrapped in a hospital cloth. The father comes and holds her. After a pause, he smiles. He looks at the mother. The mother looks a little scared. The father runs a loving hand on her mother's face. They both have tears in their eyes.

'Cut to the parents and the baby enter the house. Dada and Dadi look at them, and then away. They are not happy. The father's brother smiles politely. No one's happy. The parents take the baby inside.

'Cut to the little girl crying. The mother gets up. The father taps the mother, asking her to go to sleep. He then picks up the child, lulls her to sleep.

'Cut to the girl crying at the gate of a nursery. Other children are playing at the background. A smile begins to appear on the girl's face. We pan and see the father and the mother are here to pick her up.

'Cut to the father shouting at Dada and Dadi who are pointing their fingers at the door. The mother is holding the little girl's hand, cowering at a distance. The fight goes on.

'Cut to the father teaching the girl. It's a different house now. The mother is looking at her from a distance. The girl turns and looks at the mother.

'Cut to the girl, hardly eight, is teaching the mother how to read English. They are both laughing. In the background, the father's watching on. He takes the book and starts teaching the mother.

'Cut to the girl is sleeping on the father's back. In the corner of the room, under a little lamp, the mother's reading a thick mathematics book. The girl and the father look and then close their eyes.

'Cut to the father's on the bed, plaster on his leg. The mother's looking at the father. She turns and looks at the bills on the table.

'Cut to the family in the new house. It's half-constructed. The father's cooking, hobbling about on the broken leg. On the table besides them are Amway packages. Cut to a random house's gate. The girl in a school uniform and her mother are standing outside. The girl jumps up and rings the bell.

'Cut to the girl's school friends eating *chhole kulchhe*. She has the money but pushes it back inside her skirt. A friend shares it with her. Sharp cut. She's doing the friend's homework while the friend is playing a game on the phone.

'Cut to the girl and the mother carrying Amway packages on the street. Smiling. Sharp cut. A door is closed on their faces. The girl rings the bell again. It opens. The girl motions as if asking for water. The door is closed again. We charge on the girl's face. Sharp cut. The girl is outside doing her homework. The mother gets down from a rickshaw. The girl runs to take her mother's bag. She gives her bottle of water to the rickshawalla.

'Cut to the father is laying bricks. The daughter is watching. The mother's shouting at the daughter to come down. The daughter doesn't listen. We follow the mother as she's cooking and reading a book. On the side, there's an admit card.

'Cut to the girl is in her new room. New cupboard. New desk, new everything. She can't sleep. She gets up. Walks down the stairs and tip-toes into the parents' room. They are sleeping. She puts her bedding on the ground and sleeps there.

'Cut to the father's in the hospital. The mother's with him, holding his hand. The doctor is pointing to the lungs. They all look tense and worried. Sharp cut. The girl is older, a teenager. She's taking a dance class for very little kids. The class is about to end. A mother hands her money. Sharp cut to her offering the money to her father. The father hugs her mother.

'Cut to the father is bedridden. The mother and daughter are leaving. The mother's leaving for work. The daughter for school. The father looks sick, unkempt. He smiles at them. As they leave, we see the father get up from the bed. He's really sick.

'Cut to the hospital. The girl is running. Tense. She opens the door. Pan to the doctor's eyes. Tension builds. We pan and see the father and the mother. They are smiling. The father gets up. The girl runs and hugs the father. The father has recovered. The doctor shakes the mother's hand.

'Cut to a busy morning. The father's leaving for work. The mother's leaving for work, the daughter's leaving for school. They all smile at each other.

'Cut to a wedding dance floor. The girl's watching on. There are only two people dancing like teenagers. Her parents. There's a big smile on the girl's face. She joins her parents and starts to dance.

'Cut to her father working at a construction site. There's a woman who's looking on. Just then, the mother and the daughter barge in, they both pick up a rod and start to beat up the woman. The father intervenes and takes them away.

'We slow down the music. Everyone is happy. And that's where our story starts. From the time you were fifteen to the time you met Ananth for the first time.'

Mohini and I have nothing to add. It's perfect the way it is. Both of us know that.

Neelima Ji

Of late, Neelima ji, Gautam's mother, was finding her days to be shorter than usual. Until a few days ago, after she was done with caring for Gautam in the morning, and Rajesh ji left for work, she used to have nothing to do. The silence and the sound of Gautam's beeping machines used to echo around the house. It reminded her of the early days of her marriage. Rajesh ji would go to work and she would wait beside the phone for it to ring.

Now, with the girl from WeDonate, Anusha, the days seemed to fill up. The girl would come to the house every alternate evening for a couple of hours. Sometimes she would talk about her son feverishly for hours at an end—she loved those days, recounting the old times with Anusha—and at other times she would just sit in the corner of the living room and type on her laptop.

Caring for Gautam had forced her to leave her job, and though she taught tuitions every now and then, it was a part of her life that was gone.

'It's a lot quieter here than in the office. Everybody chatters a lot there,' the girl would tell Neelima ji.

Sometimes the girl would flip through Gautam's albums with Neelima ji. Neelima ji would tell her exactly what went behind each of the pictures.

One day, Neelima ji had showed Anusha the cameras they had bought Gautam over the years. The most expensive of them was the one they had bought Gautam months before his sister was born. She told Anusha how her husband kept a little money aside every month to buy Gautam his next camera.

'He liked clicking pictures,' she told Anusha. 'On Sundays, Gautam would not let us do anything. He used to write extensive notes about the pictures he wanted to click. He would prepare for the entire week. His father loved it. He even applied make-up to me for some of his pictures. He was really good at it.'

Neelima ji showed Anusha the negatives of the pictures Gautam clicked.

'Gautam wouldn't let us develop all his pictures, said they were bad,' she told Anusha. 'We liked everything he clicked. We would spend hours looking at our own pictures. He turned us into narcissists. He made us look beautiful. I think I liked your uncle more because Gautam made him look so nice.'

Anusha had smiled like a child. She held each one of them up against the tube light and marked the ones Gautam had not developed.

'His father and he used to spend a lot of money on photographs. You couldn't argue with the two of them.'

Anusha asked Neelima ji if she could have the negatives. Neelima ji had fetched the negatives from the loft, dusted them and had given them to Anusha. She knew she wouldn't have shared them with anyone else but her.

The next day, the girl bought two albums filled with pictures she had got developed from Gautam's negatives. Neelima ji had offered to pay but the girl had refused to take a single rupee. Instead, the girl just asked Neelima ji to talk about the pictures, what she felt about them, what Gautam had said during the photographing of them.

'Gautam was hard on himself, these pictures are really good!' the girl told Neelima ji.

Neelima ji could barely keep from crying. It had been a while since she had heard anyone say good things about her son.

'Why didn't he pursue it as a career?' she asked Neelima ji.

Neelima ji told her about how her son had fallen in love with a girl who had wanted him to follow her to an engineering college and he did.

'Rajesh ji's colleagues used to ask him to not encourage Gautam's hobby. There would be no jobs for him, they told him. But we knew Gautam would find something. He was brilliant, wasn't he?' Neelima ji told Anusha.

'He was brilliant,' said the girl.

Neelima ji didn't tell Anusha how she didn't like Karishma. Everyone found her pretty, but Neelima ji found Anusha much prettier and well-behaved. Unlike Karishma, or anyone else, Anusha took interest in Gautam's work and she would find her sitting on the floor, Gautam's pictures scattered all around her, and she would be scribbling in her little notepad.

Neelima ji also found Anusha staring at her son sometimes. It was flattering. She had caught her in the act one day and asked, 'He's handsome, isn't he?'

Anusha had answered without missing a beat, 'He is quite handsome.'

Neelima ji had been surprised seeing how upfront the girl was but didn't mind. She was used to Gautam being called good-looking at family engagements and weddings and such. Sometimes she thought it was because of their *nazar* that Gautam had found himself where he was.

Neelima ji had always felt possessive when girls giggled near her son, trying to snare him away from her. But with Anusha, she didn't mind.

'She's lovely, isn't she?' she had told Rajesh ji a few days ago.

Rajesh ji, a realist, had answered, 'She's just doing her job.'

That morning Neelima ji and Rajesh ji were going about their schedule, unmindful that Anusha had reached early and was watching them from the bedroom door. They took off Gautam's clothes, and started with Gautam's toilet care. Neelima ji emptied Gautam's toilet bag and Rajesh ji checked the catheterization. They hoisted Gautam's naked, limp body off the bed together. Earlier they used to struggle with his body but now he had lost so much weight. Then they gave Gautam a long sponge bath, talking about the day to their unresponsive son as if he was listening. Neelima ji dried Gautam, gave his lifeless limbs a little movement, while Rajesh ji changed the bedsheets and cleaned up. They then put a diaper on Gautam, dressed him up, moisturized his face, parted his hair, blow-dried it for a couple of minutes, and put him back into bed.

When Neelima ji turned to leave, she found Anusha standing there, feet bolted to the ground, pity and horror in her eyes.

'Are you okay?' Neelima ji asked.

Anusha turned and left without answering.

Neelima ji got worried when Anusha didn't return for an hour. Her bag was still in the living room. When she returned, Neelima ji made her a parantha to take to office with her.

'This is why I didn't want to be in medical, I didn't want to see these things. I just don't . . .' She met Neelima ji's eyes and said angrily, 'Doesn't it break your heart?'

Neelima ji understood where she was coming from. A young lifeless man in bed, his elderly parents burdened with taking care of him at an age where it should have been the other way round. People had suggested a day nurse but why wouldn't they do it themselves.

'Gautam's our child, our baby. He had grown up but he has come back to me as a child. Your uncle and I used to do the same things when he was an infant, and then a toddler. We used to clean him, bathe him, put him to bed when he was a child, didn't we? It's like that time has come back for us. We don't mind,' said Neelima ji.

She saw tears in the girl's eyes for the slightest moment and in the very next she was her calm, strong self again.

'I wish I could do more for you and Uncle,' said Anusha.

'You're doing enough. We saw the changes you made in Gautam's story,' said Neelima ji.

Rajesh ji showed her the story changes every time Anusha made them. Not everything in there was the truth, but neither she nor her husband minded.

Their son, Gautam, told stories through his pictures all the time. Now, when Rajesh ji and she sat in the evenings and saw the pictures Gautam had clicked of them when they were younger, they believed the photos captured what their life was like back then. Even though they knew Gautam had staged and directed every scene before he photographed it. Neelima ji knew stories were important.

'It's not enough. They still read Gautam's name and immediately connect him to those tweets and . . .' Anusha sighed.

'Change his name,' said Neelima ji.

'Aunty?'

'Change his name if his name is the problem,' said Neelima ji who never liked her son's name. Gautam was a common name and she had been forced to keep it by her husband's relatives. None of the people who had fallen over each other to name the child had parted with a single rupee.

'We can look at changing the name,' the girl muttered to herself. 'Sure, why not. But . . .they know how he looks,' said Anusha.

'I never liked his long hair. Only his father did,' said Neelima ji.

Neelima ji took Anusha by her hand and led her to Gautam's room. She opened the drawer and handed Anusha the trimmer.

'Let's see how we can make Gautam look different?' she said.

Neelima ji noticed Anusha flinch. She took the trimmer from her and buzzed the right side of Gautam's head clean.

'That looks so much better, a bit like Tiger Shroff?' said Anusha, lightening up. 'Let me try.'

For the next half an hour, Neelima ji saw Anusha meticulously trim Gautam's hair.

'Do you think we should give him a Mohawk?' the girl asked her.

Neelima ji didn't know what a Mohawk was but she nodded. Neelima ji then gave Gautam a shave.

'He looks different now, doesn't he?' asked Neelima ji.

Anusha nodded.

'What do we name him?' asked Anusha.

Neelima ji knew exactly what to name him. It's the name she wanted to keep instead of Gautam.

'*Ananth*, after the serpent Vishnu rests on,' Neelima ji said.

She watched Anusha say the name under her breath, Ananth Khatri.

Neelima ji continued, 'And you're his Mohini, Vishnu's female avatar, and from where Ananth derives life from, aren't you?'

Anusha shook her head. 'I have done nothing yet,' she said. 'But I will find a story, Aunty.'

Neelima ji was sure she would.

Ananth Khatri

Saraansh
Did you think about it?

Saraansh
Now?

Saraansh
Ab?

Saraansh
Waiting?

Saraansh
You didn't pick my call.

Saraansh
Are you thinking?

Saraansh
It's important.

Saraansh has been sending me these texts every second hour since the past few days. He has been hammering in the fact that we have the beginning of the story, and we have the end—when she meets me.

117

'We need the middle before we go any further. It's where the story changes. The interval, the cliffhanger, the plot point.' He has repeated this a few dozen times.

As much as it's important for the movie, it's more essential for my relationship with Mohini and Aunty. As much as Mohini loves me, she wouldn't think twice before walking away if I screw this up.

To tell the plot point that revolves wholly around Uncle is paved with trouble.

Saraansh knows that too. He has been to Mohini's house more than a few times now. He had been confused the first time as well. Nothing can prepare you for it. There are men's shoes at the entrance. They have been there for the last six years. Just the way her father left it the last time. Her father's clothes are hanging in the closet like he was going to come back. Even his dirty clothes lay above the washing machine.

Saraansh and I are on our way to Noida to see the house.

'Bro, you have been there before, yes? I have heard people get lost in Noida for years,' jokes Saraansh.

Nothing he says will lighten the mood. We leave behind the oddly placed sectors of Noida and enter Greater Noida. I guide the driver off the highway and into a locality with mid-sized houses.

'What are we looking for here?' asks Saraansh.

And before I can say it, he sees it.

'Fuck!' he mutters.

Fuck is right. It looks like Mohini's house had been uprooted and placed here. The house we were in front of is an exact reproduction of Mohini's. The same structure, the same iron grills, the same gate, the same paint job.

'A new English teacher had joined Mohini's school,' I begin the story. 'She had called Mohini's father to see her. A few months later, the teacher called Mohini to her staff room. She asked Mohini why she pretended in school that she doesn't have a brother. 'Because I don't have a brother!' she had told her teacher. Then she went back home and told her parents what the teacher had said. There must have been some mistake, Uncle had said. Months passed without incident.

'A few months later, the teacher mentioned the brother again. You're Anusha *Sardana*, right?' her teacher had said. Not every Sardana is my brother, Mohini had snapped at the teacher. Mohini went to her father again. Her father told her not to listen to the teacher, that she must be crazy. The teacher asked Mohini to call her father to class but her father refused. Mohini believed her father, but she also began to wonder if there was a boy in the teacher's earlier class who looked like her. Curious, she went to the teacher's old school's website and browsed through the passport-sized pictures of the students.

'And there he was, a boy, who anyone could mistake to be her brother. Sameer *Sardana*. At first, she hadn't noticed the surname. But when she did, she couldn't push it out of her head.

'A few weeks later, she took the road we did following him after school and reached here. She stood where we are standing now, and looked at this house, *her* house, but miles apart. The same doorway, the same shape of the windows, the same wall paint.

'As expected, the boy, a couple of years younger than her, the boy her teacher thought to be her brother, Sameer Sardana, entered the house. He walked to the first floor of the house, the floor she imagined his father would have built for him, like he had built for her. Then she saw a woman walk inside the house, tall, beautiful, slender. Her heart pounded in her chest.

'She knew what was going to happen.

'And then as the sun dipped below the horizon, the man of the house came—her father. She saw her father play cricket with the boy who shared her likeness, her surname, her father. She saw her father drink tea with the woman on the terrace.

'When it was dark, her father left the house and revved his scooter. He left and came home—Mohini's home. He told her mother that work had taken longer than expected. He lied with a smile on his face and took Mohini in his arms. He said he didn't want tea. Her mother had wondered for years if she made bad tea because her father, otherwise a tea-drinker, wouldn't want one after work. Her father loved her and her mother, like they meant everything to him. He laughed and joked around with them.

'He did the same the next day and the day after that, and the week after that.

'It took Mohini a month to confront him. He was leaving the locality of the other woman, when she walked in front of his scooter. He braked. Her father looked at Mohini, knew that she knew, and then said, "Your mother knows." He asked Mohini to get on the scooter and took her home. Her home. All the way, she could think of just one thing—if her father, someone who gave their house all that was possible and more, could have another family, cheat and lie and dupe, what about the others? Was there any good in the world?

'That night Mohini heard her parents fight and her mother cry. The next day, Mohini came here again to tell the woman about herself and her mother. She found where Sameer Sardana played cricket in the evening. She slammed his head with a bat till he bled. She then went to their house, jumped on the woman's neck with a knife, and asked the woman to leave her father. The woman—who knew of Mohini—acquiesced. Mohini waited outside the house again till her father came and took her home. For the first time, her father addressed her mother instead of talking directly to her. "Keep your daughter in check." That, broke her heart. Mohini's mother said, "She's your daughter too."

'That endless night, Mohini had only two questions for her mother. How long had she known? And why was she still with her father? Mohini's mother told her she had met the teacher after she had mentioned the brother. She had found about the woman just a few days ago. Her mother told her they were together for Mohini's sake. The next morning, Mohini and her mother asked her father to leave the house.'

'And he left? Just like that?' asks Saraansh.

I nod.

'Mohini dropped out of school that year. They were left alone. Mohini's mother asked her father to not try to contact them or anyone they knew,' I tell Saraansh.

When the neighbours started to ask where Mohini's father had gone, Mohini's mother told everyone he had died in a construction accident. Since Uncle's family was estranged and lived far away, everyone believed it to be true.

People eventually knew.

But for Mohini and her mother, this was the new truth. Even while being cognizant of reality, they chose to believe the story they had constructed.

'Do you think—'

Saraansh's voice drowns out.

'They aren't delusional.'

Believing their own version of truth gave them some control of what they felt.

The man their world revolved around, their sun, their source of strength and happiness, turned out to be someone else.

It broke them in ways no one can imagine. Everything that they held dear had turned to ashes in an instant. As a last act of decency, her father let them have the house they lived in. Though ever since her Surinder Chachu has got to know of her father deserting them, he's been trying to lay claim to the land saying it's Mohini's grandfather's land the house stands on.

'Families are the worst,' says Saraansh.

Mohini wished her father had died instead of breaking her heart. She was inconsolable. When the clouds of grief cleared, she was a different person.

With her father's departure, the joy within her died. If her father, her hero, the love of her life, could turn out to be like this, what was there to love in this world? She grew up overnight. Her heart shrunk and shrivelled, the light in her eyes died, hate and doubt consumed her. She only saw darkness in people.

Saraansh, who was usually quick to jump on plot points, looks morose. This plot point has drained the happiness out of it.

'This is the pivot from where the story swings,' I tell him. 'This is where Mohini starts to hate the world, sees the worst in people.'

'And this is the Mohini who met you.'

'This is the Mohini who met me,' I say. 'She was Anusha then, a name given to her by her father. She shed it like a skin when my mother suggested she change her name to Mohini. It was then that I was rechristened as Ananth from Gautam.'

Saraansh says, 'She found it in her heart to love you.'

'I was in more ways than one like her. When I met her, I couldn't feel love too, I couldn't feel anything.'

Saraansh closes his notepad.

'Do you miss your old name?' asked Saraansh.

'Not in the least bit,' I tell him.

'Mohini and Ananth sound much better than Anusha and Gautam,' says Saraansh.

I agree.

Amit Modi

The first time Amit Modi met @gautam_gabbar was two months after the tweets that destroyed his life. For an entire month, he was trying to put together the million pieces his life was shattered into. God knows how hard he fought and yet nothing changed. He did everything he could—apologized publicly, admitted he was ignorant, and vowed to change, but no one listened, no one was interested. They had tweeted about their anger towards him, got their tweets retweeted and then forgot all about him.

He realized that all this wasn't because people didn't feel like forgiving him, it was because they couldn't care less. They weren't angry at him— they had moved on to the next, fresh outrage, too bothered to look back. They had enjoyed seeing him falter and stumble and now he was useless to them. They enjoyed his downfall. Fucking, opportunistic madarchods. They sat with a popcorn and watched it unfold and now that it was done, they had moved on with their lives.

He wasn't the same person four years ago, he wanted to scream at everyone.

For a month after the tweets, he hadn't thought about Gautam. He wasn't the one who had disappointed him but the others who pretended to be more erudite, more enlightened than him and yet couldn't understand that people change. Once they had branded him as a sexist, possible-molester, they were set in their ways. No matter how loud he shouted it didn't matter.

123

Once he knew the people he lost would never come back, he turned his attention to the man who was responsible, that madarchod, Gautam.

When he first planned to meet Gautam, he had half a mind to bash his fucking head in. The rest wanted to ask— why? Why would he do this to him?

He could do neither. He had noticed a drop in tweets There were tweets where he talked about going to get operated for a brain tumour. Then the first WeDonate campaign came and Amit Modi felt his anger rise up. Thankfully, no one felt Gautam deserved the money to get better. The posts attracted a lot of hate—some of it from Amit himself. WeDonate had to take down the posts. Gautam's tweets stopped. Had the madarchod died, he wondered. He found Gautam in the hospital, languishing in a coma. Was this another fucking joke? Would there be any closure for him? Months passed and Gautam had not woken up. Amit Modi waited. And then thought, it would be much better if the bhenchod died in his sleep.

Amit Modi was now desperately trying to rebuild his life.

He went back to Twitter. His last tweet was the apology for the video Gautam had shared. For a week, he tested waters by retweeting some safe jokes from comedians outside India. He timed those tweets to be bang in the middle of assembly elections so that people were too busy discussing elections.

When that went well, he needed to strategize a new opening.

The left, woke Twitter, would never accept him. He couldn't be the feminism-talking, fascism-resisting, hyper-secular, hyper-moral, performative, privilege owning-and-showing comic anymore. There were many who were doing well and monetizing it.

He chose to go the opposite way.

The centrist who's really right-wing. That's what he chose.

He started with siding with the right, retweeting the safer tweets. There were some who noticed his return to Twitter and trolled him but he blocked them, put them out of sight. He planned further. He would emulate himself on the out-of-work actors and directors who shouted from rooftops that the majority of the country is under threat. Amit had realized that there could be many things wrong with the right—but they were loyal and forgiving. He followed all the major players and liked their tweets. He would drop them messages when the right time came.

He spent the next couple of weeks working on his comeback comedy set. It was poking fun at the Opposition leader, the woke community who took offence at everything, the outrage industry, the women who thought not shaving is feminism, the people who believed they were saviours of the Muslim community, etc. He imagined himself as being retweeted by all significant right-wing handles. That would be slap on the face of hyper-moral comedians who had made activism their business. He would destroy them, call out their double-standards.

It was easier said than done. Before the tweets came, he was just a year away from selling out a stadium. But now he couldn't even get an open-mic slot. When he asked why he couldn't perform, he got the answer he had heard from many organizers before.

'If someone gets to know that we allowed you to perform and tweets about it on Twitter, you know what will happen, right? We don't want to be dragged into it,' said the organizer.

'And you don't have a problem with me performing?' he asked the girl.

'Naah. You were young, it's fine,' the girl said.

'No one will tweet about me, I'm irrelevant,' Amit Modi insisted.

'It's not about you, it's about them. They will feel relevant tweeting about you. It's easy retweets. We can't let you go on,' the girl explained.

Amit Modi sat through the open-mic. One after another bad comic came with their silly jokes and bombing their sets. No one in the audience laughed.

Amit Modi leaned back in his chair, and let the darkness of the venue wash over him. He thought about the only thing that loomed over him—Gautam.

That night, he had just finished a practice session of his set and sat down on his laptop when he saw the subtle changes in Gautam's campaign. There were restructuring of a few sentences. *Why the fuck are they still working on this?*

The next morning, he went to the WeDonate office. He sat outside, in the waiting area, pretending that he was waiting for a friend to leave the office. Every now and then, he peeked inside. Every other face was familiar except one. Vishwas ji told him she was the new girl—Anusha Sardana, medical.

'Seems like it's another long day for my friend,' said Amit to Vishwas ji and took his leave.

When he went back home, he saw the girl had shared Gautam's campaign on her timeline. There was still no movement on the donations though.

Sarita Sharan

Sarita Sharan's proud of what she has created in WeDonate. She's prouder of her recruits than the Rs 340 crore in donations they accrued last year. No one sticks around in office just to show her that they're working.

She's the last one in office today. There's the opening montage sequence lying in her Inbox since two days and she hasn't gotten around to reading it. She's promised herself this morning that she will read it today before she leaves office.

She owes it to Ananth and Saraansh who have just run with her idea of making this movie. She's hoping this would translate into some veritable visibility for WeDonate. It seems obvious it would. She also hopes the boys will do a good job at it. Anusha, or Mohini, as everyone calls her now, deserves it.

She still remembers how she walked into this office, a frown on her face, a caustic remark always up her sleeve. Except Rachita, everyone else in the medical team, took umbrage to how she just sat on her desk and made up stories about the patients she had never met, lied guiltlessly through her teeth and improved collections.

She remembers how Rachita and she used to read Anusha's stories and marvel at their ingenuity.

'She says she hates people, sees the worst in them blah blah blah, but she appeals to their good side by changing the stories. What does that say about her?' Sarita had said to Rachita.

'She's just heartbroken,' Rachita had answered. 'She's taking it out on the world.'

At that time, Sarita had thought there had been a boy. Later she knew it was her father. A father she claimed to be dead in her interview. When Sarita had later raised it with Anusha, she had brushed it away saying, 'I will let you know when he dies.'

Sarita keeps the rest of the work aside and downloads the document. She reads it all in one breath and loves it. She leans back into her chair and texts the two boys that she likes what they have written till now.

She thinks of her, and is immediately taken back to Anusha's best work—the Gautam/Ananth case. Everyone had called her crazy back then.

And just like that, she types Mohini's name on YouTube to watch the video because of which Ananth is walking around today, the video that opened the floodgates of donations to his campaign.

A smile creeps up on Sarita's face as she watches a tearful Mohini/Anusha confess her undying love for a dying, gorgeous boy named Ananth.

Where will the boys ever find an actor as good as her?

Ananth Khatri

Saraansh and I are sitting in front of Mohini's English teacher. She's the one who had first mentioned the brother.

Archana Kalra is now the vice principal of the school. She has her own room, her own peon. She orders for tea. It's not been long because last year she and I had met in the reception of the school and not here. I congratulate her and she nods slightly. She has the look only English teachers have—a friend when you're younger, a possible crush when you're older, and a reflection of what you might be when you reach adulthood.

'Anusha,' she says shaking her head, 'She changed. She was no longer the bright girl we knew.'

'Mohini,' I correct her.

'Oh yes, she changed her name,' says the teacher.

Saraansh takes out his pad and asks for permission to take notes. He starts to scribble and Archana ma'am recalls in fits and starts what she remembers about Mohini. It takes about an hour for her. Saraansh fills up an entire page with little words here and there. I lean in to see what he thinks as important and can't make out anything.

'Sometimes I wish I had never said anything,' she says.

Saraansh responds with a platitude: 'Everything that happens, happens for the best.'

She wishes us luck when we are leaving her staff room.

'Can we walk around the school for a while? I want to see where we can shoot?' asks Saraansh.

She nods.

129

For the next hour, we walk around in the corridors Mohini would have once walked. A deep melancholic sadness grips us.

'Can you imagine?' says Saraansh and points to a corner. We are on the floor where the tenth standard has its classes. 'She in that corner, friendless. Just a few days ago, she would have told everyone that her father died. Her friends would have sympathized. She would have lapped it up. She was a child. But a few days in, people would have known about her father's affair, his alternate life, the brother in the other part of the town. Hurt and exposed, she would have shouted at them. That's where she would have stood, casted out, alone, friendless, anger and loneliness taking over her body like cancer.'

Saraansh's words bring up the world in a way I hadn't been able to imagine.

'That's the washroom she would have cried in for hours. That's where she would have eventually decided that she wouldn't cry anymore,' says Saraansh pointing to the girl's washroom.

Saraansh walks around the corridor. His speech changes from past-perfect to the present, he shifts from a conversation to screenplay. He's now imagining the scenes out of the movie.

'We see Anusha coming out of the washroom, wiping her tears. Her group of three girls and two guys are standing in that corner. She looks at them and then turns away. She doesn't need them. She has a smile on her face. There's a hint of madness in her eyes. We can see something has changed. Like someone has drained out the pretenses from her worldview and she can see the world for what it is behind the garb.'

Saraansh is walking around in circles, imagining scenes and camera placements in his head. He continues.

'We see Anusha walking through this corridor and to the class. We follow her as she enters the class. Everyone looks up at her. Unlike other times, she stares right back at them. It's surreal but she catches everyone's gaze at the same time and makes them look away. She will wreck them all.'

Saraansh walks towards where the tenth-standard classes are. In an empty class, he points to the last desk. I can see what Saraansh is trying to show me. He continues.

'Sitting on the last desk, three rows separating her desk from the last inhabited desk, the difference between her and the rest of the class accentuated, she makes her Twitter, Reddit, Facebook account. And sitting right there, she spills out the lies her own friends and classmates have been hiding behind.

'We cut to her eyes. Angry, hurt. She looks up. Her maths teacher, Raman, walks into the class. We track Raman sir's eyes. She watches them dip towards the legs of the girl on the first desk. We charge on Mohini's face. We do a time-transition. The class is empty. She gets up and approaches the teacher's table. She picks up a chalk and writes on the board: Raman Sir watches Akriti's legs all day, every day.'

We walk away from the class. Saraansh walks towards the end of the corridor where the mathematics staff room is. I follow him.

'We cut to her standing outside the staff room a few days later, watching as Akriti's parents, Raman Sir and the principal are talking in animated tones. A smile comes onto her face.'

Saraansh and I are crossing the washroom again. Where everything started.

'We cut to her in the classroom again. It's empty. She has a chalk in her hand. There's a hurt smile on her face. She's writing on the board. Graphics appear on screen. Things she's writing on the board.

Karanjeet from class XI was kissing Sameer from class X in the music class.

Tarun Sir spends too much time at the swimming pool when XII A students are there.

Ankur Khetrapal and Chetan Sandhu were touching each other's penises in the basement.

Manasi Pathak cheated her entire assignment from Manisha Chugh who copied it from Meekal Bajaj.

Teacher's pet, Khushboo Jindal, called Namrata Ma'am a slut. Says she's sleeping with Ramesh Sir.

Saraansh and I walk through the corridors. We leave the building. We are now in the skating rink that's bang in the middle of the two buildings that house Mohini's school.

'We cut to the corridors. People are talking about it. Horrified. Mohini walks through the corridors, head up high. Everyone's shocked at people's transgressions. She's not.'

'Sharp cut to the principal's room. The fabric of the school under threat, the principal shakes his head. We cut to the skating rink. The principal is up there. He says they will put CCTV cameras.

'We see the students groan. We pan and cut to Mohini's face. She smiles. She raises her hand. The principal points at her. She says, "The lack of CCTVs aren't the problem, the truth is." We charge on her.'

Saraansh walks away from the skating rink. We are leaving the skating rink. I don't ask where and why. Outside the school, there's a gola-walla and there are a few students there. At a distance there's a broken RCC pillar.

'We cut to Mohini here, sitting alone, we track the camera around her. As we do a trolley shot, her clothes are changed. She's in college now. She looks up from her phone. We see her stare straight into the camera. Dispassionately, she walks

into the college. A boy approaches to talk to her. "Fuck off",
she says and enters the college gate.'

Saraansh looks at me.

'What do you feel?' he asks.

He doesn't want criticism. He wants me to pat his back.
Which is what I should have done because he brought the
scenes alive for me.

'Won't it paint her as too harsh?' I ask.

Saraansh shakes his head. I sense a shift. It's his story too
and he's going to fight for the way he's going to tell it.

'We need to be true to the story, bro. And why would
you think of her as harsh? She's only using the truth. This is
the moment people will see why she was drawn to you, why
she fell for an asshole like you. She saw her reflection in you,
and made that beautiful video,' he says.

I don't correct Saraansh.

She might have seen herself in me, but she didn't fall in
love with me. That's a lie everyone believes in. That video—
the one with the millions of views—was playacting, not love.
That video—was a lie.

Rachita was the first choice for the actor and not Anusha.
Rachita was meant to play the role of Mohini, not Anusha.

That video was shot to save me.

Rachita Somani

Rachita Somani has been reading portions of the movie Sarita has been sending her over the past couple of weeks. If made well, they can reach out to hundreds of new potential donors. After Saraansh and Ananth started to work on the movie, Sarita had sought out Rachita to ask her about what she felt of the idea.

'I hope we aren't doing the entire story, Sarita? Just the parts about Anusha before she met Ananth/Gautam, right?' Rachita had said to Sarita.

'Yes, but I think once that is done we should do the second part. The one with Anusha's love story with Gautam. That's going to be a worthwhile sequel,' Sarita said. 'We can't do that,' said Rachita.

'Why not? We should do it. It makes complete sense,' said Sarita strongly.

'We can't,' repeated Rachita.

'Give me one reason why not,' insisted Sarita. 'I have signed on Saraansh for the year. I won't have him sitting idle. Why should we let go of such a good story?'

Rachita shook her head.

'Tell me why then? Convince me otherwise. One good reason why we shouldn't?' asked Sarita.

Rachita wondered if she should tell Sarita. Maybe it was time Sarita knew the truth about what she had since long suspected.

'We don't know if Anusha loved Gautam. So morally, we will be in the red, though I'm sure Anusha, or Mohini as we are calling her now, wouldn't mind,' Rachita had told Sarita.

'Yes, we assume that she didn't love him because the video just came out of the blue, we assume that it's fake, and because we all knew how she was—'

'*Is*, how she is,' corrected Rachita.

'But we can assume for the sake of the movie that she was in love with him? We can assume that Anusha's feelings in the video were true. She might have changed her name to Mohini in the video, but there's no way to tell if her feelings were fake too?' said Sarita.

Rachita knew fully well—now and then—that the video hadn't fooled Sarita. All Sarita was trying to do was to eke the truth out of Rachita.

'We can't assume that her feelings were true,' said Rachita.

'I think they were. The video was pretty convincing,' said Sarita sternly.

Rachita gave up; she knew Sarita knew, there was no longer any need to keep up this charade. Sarita needed to know the truth.

She then mailed Sarita the video that only Anusha had seen.

In the video, it was Rachita who was reading out the script of being in love with Ananth; she was playing the role of Mohini. The intonations, the places she cried, the words, everything else was the same—only the face was different.

Up till that moment, Sarita only had assumptions.

'I knew it was the two of you,' said Sarita.

Rachita couldn't tell if Sarita was angry or not.

'It worked, Sarita,' said Rachita.

'How did she convince you to act in this?' asked Sarita.

'Anusha could be quite convincing if she needed to be. 900 people, we just need 900 people to donate, she kept telling me. Shoot the video and we will take it off later. She said I looked more haggard, more pitiful and shot me first. She told me I was a great actor. Also, she said, I would be harder to fire for you,' explained Rachita, shaking her head and smiling.

Sarita nodded. 'That's true.' And then she added. 'Do you think Ananth knows that the video was fake? That it was acted out to save him?'

'He's a sharp boy. Didn't he dissuade you from making their love story? Didn't he ask you to not make the second part of the story?' asked Rachita.

'He didn't have a problem with us showing their entire love story. It's just that he said that Anusha's mother didn't allow—' Sarita's voice trailed because she just realized.

'Maybe that's what he wants you to know, because, you know, he himself doesn't know the nature of their love story, if it exists or not,' Rachita had said.

Rachita watched the video Anusha and she had shot of her talking to the camera. Even by her own admission, she believes she acted very convincingly. If she were a viewer, she would believe that the girl on screen was Ananth's one true love. Anusha had written the script smartly.

Rachita remembered what she had said when she had read the script.

'Sounds like a Bollywood movie, a decent Bollywood movie,' she had said.

'And to think of it, we need to make just Rs 15 lakh and not a Rs 100 crore,' Anusha had answered.

Rachita leaned back into her chair. She missed her; she was one of a kind. She remembered having asked Anusha why she didn't use Rachita's video and used her own instead.

Anusha had side-stepped that question.

Arvind Mohan and Karishma Jaiswal

Arvind Mohan sat three desks away from Karishma Jaiswal and could see her if he adjusted his seat a notch higher. There were times when he wished he sat a bit further away so he could concentrate on his job better.

Arvind Mohan landed a job on day zero of placement, with an unprecedented salary structure as an analyst at Silverman Finance. And yet, every time he looked up and found Karishma sitting amidst a sea of men, apparently far better than him, he felt undeserving of her. She was smart, sassy, quite attractive, and while he knew he was smart he couldn't claim the rest about himself. On their now-numerous dates, he would find himself wanting to say something funnier or smarter, do something grand and romantic. Their sex, too, was blindingly hot for him, and he often wondered if it were as exciting for her. He could never fully believe her frequent reassurances. He would have to distract himself thinking of spreadsheets in the middle of sex so that he could last and she could have a good time or what he firmly believed, an average time. Sometimes he would open their selfies on his phone and wonder what people must talk about when they saw them together. The small mercy was that neither of them was on any social media, having sworn off it after what their friend Gautam did to them.

Karishma Jaiswal, his girlfriend, the love of his life, and now his fiancé, was not the only distraction he gave into every day. The second was the godforsaken WeDonate website. No matter how hard he tried, he would find himself on the website at least once every day, and there was nothing he hated more. Invariably, he would type in the name 'Gautam' in the search box to find how much the campaign had generated.

It was never enough. Sooner or later, Gautam—his best friend from college—would die in his sleep.

'He deserves this,' he would say to himself, looking at the bastard's handsome face.

Then he would search for his own handle on Twitter—now deactivated—to remind himself that his hatred for Gautam wasn't misplaced, to assure himself that he wasn't an evil person for wishing death on someone.

@gautam_gabbar: This is shout-out to my friend @12MohanArvind, my best friend who couldn't stop looking up my girlfriend's skirt.

@gautam_gabbar: @12ArvindMohan has a small dick. I have seen it. It's like someone kept it in the sun to dry and then forgot. I'm curious what it does to the confidence of a man?

@gautam_gabbar: @12ArvindMohan prefers big boobs. Once told me that he feels sorry for all the girls with small boobs. He also thinks the smaller the boobs the more intelligent the woman. Boobs and brains share tissue matter, he said.

@gautam_gabbar: @12ArvindMohan doesn't pick up my calls anymore. I'm almost sure he's sucking the professor's cocks, making sure he gets attendance on a mass bunk. Suck it well is what I will say.

@gautam_gabbar: Can someone like both Japanese bukkake and articles about toxic masculinity? Asking for a friend. The friend's name is @12ArvindMohan

The tweets only got worse from here.

He would give up reading the tweets within the first few minutes. He would close the window and look around to see if anyone was watching. No one ever was. 'It's in my head,' he would remind himself. If a group of boys in office sat around and laughed, he couldn't help but think that they were talking about him.

But Arvind knew people at his company had read those tweets even before he joined the office. He knew because he had been asked to meet the HR head before he joined and explain the tweets.

'Haven't you read the other tweets? The man lost his mind, he was a moron! He tweeted nonsense. He had reasons to say things like that about me. His girlfriend left him for me,' Arvind had explained in his defence.

He could have lost this job.

Arvind got back to his computer. He marked out the date. He wouldn't check Gautam's WeDonate profile ever again. He had done that in the past and had failed but this time he would stick with it.

Maybe this time . . .

A few desks away, Karishma Jaiswal never missed Arvind's surreptitious glances at her during the day. She liked when he did that. There were always people looking at the two of them. Being a high-performing couple in the same department had made things uncomfortable for those around them. But this was everything Karishma and Arvind ever wanted—to be in this company, together, in love. She loved their evenings. Sitting in the corner of their favourite coffee shop, talking about their day, their career strategies, companies they would eventually want to switch to, leadership positions they wanted to aim for. Sometimes Arvind would drift away from these strategizing talks to lighter subjects and joke around; she didn't mind that either but they weren't entirely necessary. When she had first met Arvind she hadn't made much of him, he was just another boy.

But how things change . . . Arvind was now her entire world.

She couldn't wait to be married to him. They lie when they say opposites attract. You should always look for someone just like you. She never thought she would be that girl who would pay a photographer an arm and a leg to click pictures of them in love but now she often found herself Googling pre-wedding photographers. She knew Arvind would never agree to posing and getting photographed. It brought back memories of Gautam and how he used to make the two of them model for his pictures. Arvind had his reasons.

He—and they—had come so close to losing all of this, the job, the life they had together, everything.

Gautam's tweets about Arvind had put him in the dock with the HR even after he had the offer letter.

'I told them it was their damned loss if they let me go. I gave them no explanations,' Arvind had told a nervous Karishma after the meeting with HR.

Karishma knew Arvind was not that type. He would have convinced them that Gautam had lost his mind in his dedicated-but-firm employee voice.

Karishma was dating Gautam for a couple of years when she first met Arvind. They had come from the same school and Arvind was the first friend both Karishma and Gautam had made in college. Arvind liked to tell people that she left Gautam for him, to position himself as the alpha male. Karishma let him have this little win; he deserved it after what Gautam had dragged him through. Even though she was thankful she left Gautam, this was far from the truth.

Karishma looked up and found Arvind staring at her. They smiled at each other and got back to work. Like right now, there were times she felt exposed and guilty when she found Arvind staring lovingly at her, because away from his eyes she would be looking at Gautam's, her ex-boyfriend's, WeDonate campaign.

For the past few weeks, she'd made sure she was on the website in incognito mode. A few weeks ago Arvind had stumbled upon the history of Karishma's web browser and found out about her daily, obsessive visits to the WeDonate website.

He hadn't said anything to her but he mailed Karishma a bunch of screenshots—her ex-boyfriend's tweets about her:

@gautam_gabbar: JK wears a special padded bra to all her vivas and then talks about the discrimination against women.

@gautam_gabbar: JK told me her brother hit his wife. But then said, her bhabhi is very irritating at times and really pushes her brother over the edge. So it's fair dinkum it seems.

@gautam_gabbar: To anyone who needs to know. JK's pubes are like the Ents from the Lord of the Rings. In the darkness of the night, they will creep over you and choke you.

@gautam_gabbar: No complaints but JK doesn't swallow on Tuesdays. She's vegetarian and she doesn't want to kill the little tadpoles. True story, not kidding.

@gautam_gabbar: So I won't take names but JK feels really bad for one of her friend's boyfriend because her friend's thighs chafe and she stinks.

*@gautam_gabbar: Found @12ArvindMohan and his
girlfriend on a date. They were staring for a straight ten minutes
into their phones. It looked fun.*

Karishma deleted that mail. Even in the Trash, the mail with
the tweets gave Karishma anxiety. She had never been on
Twitter and didn't think she would ever be. Unlike Arvind,
the people in the office hadn't connected JK to her name,
Jaiswal Karishma. But every now and then she would wake up
sweating and panting in the middle of the night thinking what
if they knew.

What people suffered virtually from Gautam—through
words on Twitter—she faced in real life. He would say the
meanest things to her without a second thought. It was hard
to forgive him, but she always did. Despite the anxiety, the
panic attacks, the hate, she forgave Gautam for everything. It
had taken time and effort but she had.

Everyone around Karishma thought it was because of
Gautam's online behaviour that they'd broken up. Only she
knew their relationship was doomed from the very beginning.
Gautam's online behaviour was only the nail in the coffin of
their already dead and defunct relationship.

She had been thinking of Gautam when her phone lit up.
She did not answer the call. It was from a girl named Anusha
Sardana, Gautam's campaign manager at WeDonate, the girl
in charge of saving him. During their first phone conversation
Karishma had asked Anusha not to call her again. She had been
calling Arvind as well. Arvind and Karishma had decided that
they wouldn't answer her calls.

Karishma had promised herself in the morning that she
wouldn't check Gautam's campaign page but Anusha's
incessant calling pushed her over the edge. She broke her vow
in the afternoon when she typed in Gautam's name.

Nothing came up.

Her heart sank, her stomach churned.

What had happened? Did they get the money? But how would they? What could have happened in one day? Or did he . . . had he . . . died? Her heart pounded in her chest.

She almost reached out to her phone and called the number she had been getting calls from for the last few days. She texted the girl.

'Is he alive?'

There was no reply to that text.

Anusha Sardana

Arvind Mohan, once Gautam's best friend, and Karishma Jaiswal, Gautam's ex-girlfriend, hadn't wanted to meet me or talk to me. Dozens of calls to them were rejected. The one call that he did take, he screamed and asked me to fuck right off, to not call him or Karishma Jaiswal, his fiancé, ever again. I told him I didn't have the luxury to do that.

'Let us know when he dies!' Arvind had screamed into the phone.

He cut the call instead of understanding my urgent need to save Gautam.

His outbursts contrasted with the story Gautam's photographs said about him. He looked like the mild-mannered teacher's favourite sort of guy who spent half his day adjusting the spectacles on his nose and the rest helping his classmates out with trigonometry and calculus. He looked the kind who would reject the idea of a mass bunk on principle and not just to gain points from a professor.

My texts to them went unanswered, and so did the WhatsApp messages.

I went back to Gautam's house and pored over the pictures once more. In a way, I was confirming what I felt about them. But I was also there because I loved the photographs. There had been writers I liked, poets whose words made me feel something, actors who became characters for me, but I had never met any of them. Gautam, who pushed me to find art in his treasure trove of photographs, was in front of me, and

144

though he couldn't talk I could talk to him, tell him I loved his work. I found myself lost in the photographs again. Sometimes I would turn to him and utter half a question before realizing he wasn't going to answer and then say it anyway.

It's clear that Karishma had jumped ship and had started dating Arvind while they were in college, but it was Gautam's parents who filled me up with the details.

'He was in love with that Karishma girl. *Life barbaad kar di usne Gautam ki. Khatam kar diya mere bete ko* (she ruined my son's life),' said Gautam's mother with scorn.

Gautam's father added, 'He should have pursued photography but he ran behind that girl and did engineering. Look what happened. She left him for that Mohan boy. All that photography equipment . . . ' he shook his head. 'Waste.' He then looked up with a twinkle in his eye and said, 'He had magic in his hands, magic.'

'She wasn't a good girl,' said Gautam's mother.

'He tweeted some bad things about the two of them,' I argued.

Neither of them said anything. This is where every conversation came to a stop.

There was one piece of the puzzle that I had to figure out in Gautam's story.

Every story has a pivot. In my own story, my revelation, my moment on top of Mount Hira, was when I found out about my father, and knew instantly that people were not who they pretended to be. There was at least one ism they were deeply afflicted with—racism, casteism, ageism, assholeism.

What was Gautam's pivot? When had *he* changed?

I had two hypotheses and one of them has been proven wrong.

The first was the diagnosis of his disease which sort of gave him the license to lash out at the world, take his revenge.

This was the obvious one but it was wrong. His behaviour predated his diagnosis by a couple of years.

The second one—a bit filmy but totally believable—was the betrayal of Karishma. Nursing a broken heart, Gautam went on to unleash his worst on the world. He wouldn't be the first one to go down that path. We glorify heartbroken boys everywhere in fiction and boys ape that shit; only that no one really likes them in real life.

It's what most people thought too.

There was a little problem with this hypothesis again.

His supposed bad behavior—under my assumption a direct effect of relationship trouble—overlapped with a lot of photographs he had taken—quite lovingly—of Arvind and Karishma. There were some great pictures of them, but there still were some nasty tweets—not about them but still nasty.

If their problems had started by then, if he knew that Karishma was leaving him, and leaving him for Arvind, and that made him angry, why would he still photograph them? Why would he still tolerate them?

The end of those photographs should have signalled the start of the tweets but it didn't happen that way.

What was I missing? Did they play patch-up-break-up-patch-up for a little while before they broke up for good?

I needed to fit this piece of the puzzle.

When neither Arvind nor Karishma agreed to my meeting requests, I dangled a carrot in front of Arvind and he reached out for it.

Arvind and I were meeting at Silverman Finance. His LinkedIn profile said he was a financial analyst. He had reached before time, and was waiting for me at the reception, legs crossed, calm. The gold-bridge rimless spectacles, the sharp

crease on his trousers, the crisp check shirt, the greenish tinge
that comes with shaving too much—all pointed out to the fact
that he'd spent a lot of time giving presentations. He seemed
proper—a far cry from what Gautam's acerbic tweets painted
him as—and just as the photographs showed him.

'That bastard is the last thing I want to talk about,' Arvind
said sitting in front of me.

He had a presentation voice, sharp, precise and effective.
His passport-sized photo was on the college's website under
the achievers. Both his and Karishma's, both clicked by
Gautam.

His face was at odds with his body. He had the face of a tall
man. But he wasn't. He couldn't have been taller than 5'6".
He walked and sat upright, with a sense of purpose. That's
what Gautam had captured in his photographs too.

'I will get those tweets deleted,' I told Arvind.

'The Instagram posts? The tweets? Everything?'

'Everything will be gone, Arvind,' I told him. 'I talked
to his parents and they have the passwords to everything. But
they don't have a reason to share them with me yet.'

It looked like he wanted to take up the offer but he didn't
believe in the authenticity of it.

'He's dying so we don't have much time,' I said.

'And who's responsible for that?' he asked. He didn't
wait for my answer and said, 'Karma, this is karma. He would
find this funny, he always found stuff like this funny and look
where it got him.'

'Look, Arvind. I know he was an asshole and he said a
few things about you, but he's a person and it's our moral
responsibility to save him.'

'Is it?' he asked, frowning.

'I met his parents yesterday and they were . . . in a bad
state. I don't know what they would do if he dies,' I said in

a dulcet tone, lightly putting the blame of a possible double-suicide on Arvind's shoulders.

Arvind was unmoved. Like he could smell my dishonesty.

I made my pitch stronger. I continued, 'You stand to gain out of it too. Everything goes. A fresh start for you, and Karishma. Think about this.'

Arvind Mohan leaned back into his chair.

'He reduced me to a laughing stock. I almost lost my job because of him.'

'You can be better than him. This could be your moment to shine,' I said.

Arvind weighed his options.

I continued, 'He would be thankful for the help you extend. We will delete his profiles anyway.'

'I won't donate a single rupee,' he said.

'I don't want money from you,' I said. 'I want to know something about him.'

'What?'

'The first year is when the two of you became friends and I would say spent a lot of time together, didn't you? From the pictures, I would say you two were very close. I'm sure he thought quite fondly of you, these pictures show that. I have never seen any boy treat his guy friend with such tenderness,' I said and pushed the pictures of the two of them in front of him.

He stayed quiet. He looked at the pictures briefly and then kept them back on the table. There was a moment of softness in his face which disintegrated as quickly as it came.

'And you thought kindly of him, too. But then something changed. He started to tweet nasty stuff from the second year of college. I had assumed—like everyone else—that was because Karishma broke up with him and went with you. He started to take out his anger on the world. But there are many pictures that he had taken of you and Karishma while he was tweeting horrible things.'

'Yes,' said Arvind.

'But he wasn't tweeting about the two of you,' I said.

'So?' snapped Arvind.

'So clearly, his anger wasn't from the break-up. Where was his anger coming from? When did he snap? What am I missing? What else happened? If not Karishma, then who? What broke him?' I asked.

Arvind didn't answer for sometime.

'Why can't you just believe he was a jerk? Why should there be a reason?' he argued.

'Umm.'

'Answer the question?' he grumbled.

His face flushed with anger when I kept quiet. In hindsight, his question was correct. People are nasty often for no reason at all. It's who they are and I should have been the last person to question it. *Why was I looking for a reason then?*

'You know what? I'm done,' he grumbled and got up. 'I don't need to do this. I had put everything behind me. All the things he said about me? Let them fucking stay. Let the tweets stay. I didn't mean all those things. I was young and we all used to say those things. So fuck him and fuck you for trying to save him.'

He stormed off leaving me hanging at the reception.

I ran after him but he disappeared behind the turnstiles. A part of me wanted to call her and threaten him. It wouldn't take me much to drop an anonymous tweet that JK was Karishma Jaiswal. No one had connected the two—and people had long moved on from Gautam's tweets—but I could tag a few office folks of Arvind and Karishma and point them in that direction. That could have been quite uncomfortable for both Arvind and Karishma who were turning out to be unhelpful pigs.

I was standing there thinking about whether such a threat would be an overkill when I saw her. I could recognize that face in a crowd.

Karishma Jaiswal.

*

Karishma Jaiswal wore a dull-grey suit LinkedIn seems to hand out to everyone who makes a profile on it.

Karishma marched towards me with purpose, her heels pounding on the marble floor. Her face looked like someone had drawn the lines with a ruler and had forgotten to leave stray marks to give her softness around the edges. Her jawline could slice through Arctic ice with ease. Her light eyes were big and it seemed they were staring right inside your soul. In most of the photographs, Gautam had made her look softer.

When she came closer, I saw a hint of tears in her eyes.

'Karishma,' I said.

She held me by my hand and led me outside the office. She looked over her shoulder to see if anyone was watching us. The tears had retracted. The harder, unfeeling version was back. It was uncanny.

'Is he alive?' she asked.

'Yes, he is,' I answered.

'Then why isn't his campaign live?' she demanded to know.

I told her about the change we had made. I showed her the new campaign. His name was Ananth now, the story had changed. I showed her the new pictures we had posted. I felt the tension in her dissipate.

'It's doing a little better,' said Karishma, like a teacher.

'I needed to talk to you about something,' I said. 'I asked Arvind too but you saw how he abruptly left.'

'It's hard for him to talk about this, I can't blame him,' she said.

I reframed my question to check if the break-up led to the tweets, or vice versa. 'I will tell you what I thought. You broke up with him and chose Arvind instead. It broke him and then he started tweeting nasty things. The only hitch is, he was still photographing the two of you while he was tweeting those things. So the first question I wanted to ask you was, could it be that he was hanging out with the two of you while knowing that you two had feelings for each other and that's why tweeted the stuff he did?'

Karishma looked amused; the softer Karishma was back. She said, 'I felt nothing for Arvind for a really, really long time after I broke up with Gautam. He wasn't even a consideration and Gautam knew that.'

'So he didn't tweet those things because he was angry at Arvind for trying to steal his girlfriend?' I asked.

She shook her head. 'He wasn't the kind who would get furious about a break-up.'

'So was it because the two of you were not getting along? Was that making him angry? Did that push him over the edge?' I asked.

'You couldn't be more wrong,' said Karishma, almost a bit angry.

And just as she said it, I realized. Of course, I was wrong and Arvind was right! Why was I looking for a life-changing event for Gautam for the turn that he took? Why was I going against the assumption that people can be generally unkind? Maybe there *was* no pivot! He was made like this, hardwired to be judgemental and unthinking of other people. *Why was I trying to make him into a good person in my head?*

Karishma said, 'I really loved him at one point. I really, really loved him. Sometimes when I look back and think how devoted I was to him, I feel surprised. We are capable of so much more love when we are younger.'

I nodded.

'Are you going to write this?' she asked.

'Not if you don't want me to.'

'I don't want you to,' she said.

'What made you fall out of love with him?' I asked.

She lit a cigarette. She leaned against the wall and took a few long drags. She offered me one and I refused. She composed herself before she began to talk.

'It wasn't one thing. It's never one thing because of which it all ends. We were really, really young, and you know how that is. We were in school when we got together. It was supposed to be puppy love but he never assumed that. For him, and for me at that moment, we were lovers for life from the word go. I revelled in it. While the other girls were with boys I was with a man, someone whom I could see would be with me for a long time. No one had what I did. It was quite something. He could really make you feel like a queen, you know? He could make you feel that you were the centre of the universe; that nothing else mattered but you. He would hold your hand, and look at you like no one else would. He would talk to you like no one would, ask you things, like he really wanted to know you. The photographs you see are a tip of the iceberg; he would really know you before he made you pose. He was . . . quite incredible.' Karishma's eyes welled up. She waited for the moment to pass, her breath to settle and then continued, 'But we were very young . . .'

'You don't have to justify yourself, Karishma.'

She nodded.

'It had been two years since we had been together. College was a new world and I realized I was nothing without him. I needed him for everything. I felt too dependent . . . I don't know how to say this, I felt like I couldn't enjoy anything without him. I wanted him around for everything I did. That scared me, it consumed me. What if he left me? What if something happened to him? I thought he would be angry when I said that I wanted to enjoy other things aside from him. He wasn't and so we decided to put distance between us. We both made new friends. He had Arvind among others, and I made friends with a few people in my class. I started to feel more at ease, started to learn to be in my own company and with others. But he still kept me at the centre of his world and after a while I couldn't. While he clung on to the idea of *us*, I learned little by little to let go. He never used to complain. Maybe he should have, maybe that would have been better. I could sense the sadness, the disappointment in his eyes. I used to keep asking him if something was wrong and he used to lie that everything was fine. His dishonesty made me so angry. He didn't have to be nice, did he? His steadfastness made me not like myself, like I was cheating on him. His perfectness, devotion, love started to put me off. It only made me push him away. While he remained the boy in love, I changed. That relationship was my everything but as I grew I realized I would be unfair to myself if I made a relationship my everything. That's not right, is it? Things changed between us a lot before his behaviour did. That was the last straw. But I had decided by the end of first year that I wanted out.'

She looked away.

'No one can blame you for that.'

'Every time we broke up, he used to walk away without questioning it. He didn't fight it. I wanted him to. It would have been easier that way if he just hated me. But he would treat me like a friend still, like he would treat Arvind or his other friends,' she said.

She sighed. The silence was heavy around us. She stared at her fingers and wept silently for a bit.

'Then he changed. It had nothing to do with the break-up. We were over long before, but when he changed . . . when he started to tweet the way he did, it was impossible to be even friends,' she said.

'You weren't the reason why he became what he became,' I said out aloud.

'He wasn't that person,' she nodded. 'A break-up could never change him, nothing could change him,' she said. 'He had seen much worse.'

'But he did change?' I asked.

'You don't know, do you? Or do you not want to believe? Like I didn't for the longest time and Arvind still doesn't,' she said.

'What do I not want to believe? You need to be clearer,' I said.

'It was the cancer that changed him,' she said.

'That's not possible. He was tweeting all that way before the diagnosis. He couldn't have been angry because of that,' I countered.

She shook her head. 'You are looking at it all wrong. He wasn't reacting to the tumour, or the diagnosis. It was the tumour in his head that was making him say the things he was. It was the disease talking. Didn't his parents tell you that?'

I faintly remembered his father say the exact sentence. *It's the disease talking.* It seemed like an excuse at the time to weakly defend their son's behaviour.

Karishma continued, 'We were as confused as you are at the time. We didn't know why he had become . . . so strange. For two years, we wondered too. We hated him for the things he said. We tried to make him stop but he wouldn't. Then once he started tweeting about Arvind, and then about me, we knew we couldn't be friends. Our hearts broke to see him like that. We couldn't accept it. It wasn't until the last year of engineering that he was diagnosed with meningioma and we were told the reason why he changed.'

'Still not getting your point though,' I said.

Why wasn't she coming to the point!

She said, 'The tumour in his head pressed against the frontal lobe.'

'So? What does that have to do with anything?'

'It blocked out his emotions. For two years, he couldn't feel anything. Happiness, sadness, of his own or of others. It made him unfeeling, blind of other people's reactions. He lost his filter. It all made sense to us later. All the things he said in those tweets came from a place where he couldn't empathize with the person he was talking about,' said Karishma.

'What does that even mean?' I said.

'If he thought someone was bad looking, he would tell them they were ugly. It wouldn't be wrong to him. A lot of tumour patients go through the same. They don't know any more what should be said aloud, and what shouldn't be, what should be done, what shouldn't. You lose your sense of right and wrong.'

'That seems . . .'

'It's the first thing doctors tell the family after the diagnosis. It's something that doctors counsel the family for, prepare them for the behavourial changes that come with it.'

'*It was the disease speaking,*' I whispered.

'To watch him like that . . . it was heartbreaking. We didn't know about the disease, or about the compromised frontal lobe! He went from feeling too much to not feeling at all. He abandoned us. He would meet us in the most dispassionate way, like we were strangers, and then tweet horrible things about us. I know it made him feel nothing but for us, for me, it was heartbreaking. Arvind and I would shout at him, and he would sit there unblinkingly. I tried to give us another chance but . . . he was too unfeeling.'

She shook her head. 'We suffered. His parents, I, Arvind, the others.'

'He was having the time of his life, not feeling anything,' I said.

Karishma smiled sadly and said, 'Except for a hammering headache. The doctors were surprised he carried on with it for so long without seeking treatment.'

Just then, her phone rang.

'Arvind?' I asked.

She nodded.

'He knows about this too?' I asked.

'He does,' said Karishma. 'But that's the thing about those tweets. They weren't lies, they were in more ways than one, truths. But the truths we don't say because we think kindly of others, because we know we can hurt others, because we know everyone is struggling and trying to change. We all think about the things he tweeted but we don't say them aloud. Which is the right thing to do, which is the kind, humane thing to do. Which he also wouldn't have, had he been himself. But it wasn't him. But Arvind can't accept that.'

At this point, I was scrolling through Gautam's tweets. I pointed at them and said, 'If this isn't him, then he's dying for no reason.'

'I'm doing what I can,' said Karishma. 'I have donated a few times but . . .'

Karishma left when Arvind called a few more times.

I sat there and Googled the effects of brain tumours on people's behaviours. Hundreds of pages of research jumped at me. Forums of people talking about the same thing—the sharp, acrid change of personality, the lack of empathy, the cruelness that came with a tumour of that sort, the effect it had on caregivers and family. There were people who had gotten divorces from their husbands and wives only to later find out that their partners had been suffering from a brain tumour. Men and women had lost their children in custody battles, their jobs and careers, things they held close to them only to later find out it was for no fault of theirs. Numerous people had wrecked their relationships because of the apathy, the lack of feeling resulting from brain tumours.

This was Ananth's pivot.

This is what had changed him. All this while I had been thinking he was like me but that theory turned out to be wrong.

Fuck.

That evening, I had dinner with Gautam's parents.

'It's easier said than done,' said Gautam's father. 'To hear someone say hurtful things and forgive them for saying them because there's a problem in their brain. It's not easy. The words are coming out of their mouth. How can you not believe them? But we knew he was a good person . . . if what happened with his sister didn't change him into a bad person, how could anything else?'

When I asked him about Gautam's sister, he started to weep. I waited and waited for him to stop. He didn't. *How long can you watch a grown man weep?*

'Sorry Uncle, I asked—'

He walked out, leaving Gautam and me alone in the room. I turned to look at him. He looked like he was smiling, mocking me at my failed attempt to find what made him the way he was, questioning me—if he didn't change, why did I?

I stayed there for a few hours; the reclining chair by his bedside was comforting. I edited and re-edited the other stories that came by. Every now and then, I would look at the photographs Gautam clicked and add notes for the campaign manager to mimic those angles. When I was done and tired, I heated some water in the kettle in the room and made myself a dip tea. I called Mumma and told her I wouldn't be coming home. She told me Gautam's mother had already called and told her I was there.

'Don't watch movies on your laptop on high volume,' said Mumma.

'Why would you—'

'Because you do that,' said Mumma and added before she cut the call, 'I will call Neelima ji and check tomorrow. Come in the morning, I'm sleeping.'

'Please don't call his mother—'

She had already disconnected the call.

She was unconcerned about me staying out the entire night in a boy's room. She was wise; the only men who couldn't hurt you are the harmless ones, sleeping. But could she be more wrong about the harmless part? This guy, lying there calmly, was causing quite a havoc in my head about my life choices. He had already proved me wrong once by turning out to be nice. Why would he be nice? It takes courage to hate the world. Why was he turning out to be a coward?

Once I wrapped up the rest of the stories, I rearranged the photographs, the receipts, the mark sheets in a chronological order. It was only later that I realized that his room was beginning to look like a shrine. I was contemplating messing up my good work when his father walked in again and beamed like a child looking at a clean room.

Ananth Khatri

Saraansh insisted today morning that he will come along to help me buy a gift for Mohini's birthday. It's the exact opposite of what I wanted. It's weird to go buy something with someone so rich. When Karishma and I were dating, and I would haggle, and she would say that it embarrassed her.

She wouldn't say that after I would bring down the price of a knock-out Adidas bag by 50 per cent.

Rich people like to shop differently; she interacted only with the product. Others, like me, interact both with the product and the one selling it. That's how you get a good deal. And yet, Saraansh insisted on accompanying me and now we are in the car hurtling towards Nehru Place.

'What are you getting her, bro?' he asks in the car, all excited.

'You will see,' I say.

During the rest of the drive, he comes up with honest but useless suggestions for what I can get Mohini. When he realizes he has failed, he tells me he doesn't get cis-het gender-binary relationships; when he talks it's like a Buzzfeed in person is sitting next to me. I know none of those words he uses and remind myself to Google them later.

We reach Nehru Place before the shop opens so we wait outside Khan and Khan Hospital Equipment. I know Nehru Place inside out. Back in college, I had helped Arvind get the gaming laptop he had his eyes on. I had spent a month upturning every shop for a second-hand machine. I vividly remember how happy Arvind was. It was the first memory of Arvind that came flooding back to me when I woke up after the surgery—his sincere, toothy smile. I don't think he would cradle his child the way he cradled that laptop.

'It would be an awesome gift,' says Saraansh looking at the signboard. 'Thoughtful, bro.'

He sits on the steps and does his rich-boy thing. He googles 'best hospital beds' in Delhi, and then shows me the ones with the most features. None of the beds are less than 8 lakh.

'I'm sure we can find some of them here,' he says.

'These are too expensive.'

'But they are Swiss made, and over time it will hardly cost anything—'

'I'm hoping that over time whatever bed we buy is a huge waste of money. I'm hoping she wakes up tomorrow and the bed becomes useless,' I counter.

'Er . . . what's your budget?' he asks.

His face falls when I tell him my budget for the bed is 1 lakh; his phone's more expensive; his laptop is more expensive; his watch and shoes and clothes combined are more expensive.

'I would have pitched in with the rest had my parents not cut me off,' he says.

He would have pitched in 7 lakh? How rich are the rich exactly? If they have 7 lakh to spare, why aren't they sparing it? Why are they fluffing their pillows with all that money? He sits there pondering about the have-nots, and I about the haves.

'You have been bouncing ideas off Mohini's mother? The documents? The storyline?' Saraansh asks after a while.

'Aunty sends me page-long feedbacks every other day. I'm not sending them to you because she also retracts them every other day and sends a fresh batch. She has read a lot of books so she has a strong sense of how to tell a story,' I say.

'I would like to narrate a few scenes to her as well, if you're busy someday that is,' he says.

I haven't let Saraansh meet her without me. This isn't the first time he has made this request. 'I don't think I will be that busy,' I say.

'Even otherwise, it will be nice to get some first-hand feedback,' he says.

'I don't think that's necessary. I will tell you what she says. Or else, we can both sort of go together,' I argue. 'This is the only thing on my mind right now, so I will always have time for this.'

Does he suspect something? If he does think I have lied to him, how long before he finds out?

He doesn't press further. Maybe it's all in my head.

A little later, the shopkeeper's helper comes and opens the shutter. He asks us to look around till the time the owner comes in.

I know which bed to pick. It's a Dupont Elitis. It's a new model and the reviews online are mostly favorable.

Saraansh gets on the bed and fiddles with the controls. 'It's comfortable,' he says.

He tries some other beds and concludes, 'Good choice, bro.'

He's trying to make me feel good.

'Have you checked online? Does it have good reviews?' asks Saraansh.

'*Gadha thodi hu?* (Do you take me for a fool?) It's the highest-rated hospital bed in this price range,' I say.

When I was reading the reviews online, I couldn't help but wonder what it must take for parents, partners, children to buy a hospital bed for their comatose, paralysed or handicapped relative and then post a review about the product. Like, they'd bought a shampoo.

Even in the worst of times, normalcy creeps in.

I start to wonder if I will post good things about the bed once Mohini uses it for a while.

The one she uses now has creaky hinges and has rotted in places. Mohini's mother and I joke that maybe the uncomfortable bed might be the reason why she finally opens her eyes. We wouldn't want her to get too comfortable in her bed.

I'm strictly not allowed to sit on the bed.

'It will break, it can't take as much weight,' Aunty says.

I know for a fact it wouldn't break; it has taken my weight quite well before. Her bed was once mine. The bed did take my weight for a long time.

It was on this bed that Mohini and I first met. It was this bed that Maa–Papa chose when the doctors told them I would be shifted home into their care, it's on this bed that I lay on while they cried for months at end, it was this bed I lay on while Mohini sat beside me figuring out who I was.

It was on this bed Mohini shot the video of me. It was there, eyes closed, mind shut, brain damaged, that Mohini lied that she loved me, and that she desperately needed me to be saved. But there were things that she didn't lie about. She didn't lie when she said I wasn't as bad a person as people made me out of be from my tweets; she didn't lie when she urged people to believe her when she said my behaviour was the disease speaking and not me; she wasn't lying when she said I had loved people with all my heart. There are moments in that video when she turns towards me and looks at me with love in her heart. There are moments that her tears seem real.

How could I not believe her? Millions of people did.

I wish Mohini's mother had never told me about her lie, about the fakeness of the video. Rachita Somani had kept her mouth shut, why couldn't Aunty? She could have let me believe what the world did—*Mohini loved Ananth*.

I was the happiest person to wake up from the coma, not so much because I woke up from it, but because I woke up to find someone like her to be in love with me. It was like god was making up for his goof-up of putting a tumour in my head and a wedge between me and everyone I loved.

But Aunty loved the truth.

'She did it only because you were dying,' Aunty had said to me once I recovered and hounded people to make me meet Mohini.

For a moment I think I am imagining Aunty at the shop.

The wind chime at the door stopped tolling, and Mohini's mother is there. Behind her are Arvind and Karishma. They spot me immediately. They walk towards me with big smiles. Karishma hugs me first and then Arvind shakes my hand. Maybe it's in my head but they have started to look like a married couple; their smiles and their gait seem to have merged into one. Which is strange because there couldn't be two people who used to look more different than each other. That's why I used to love photographing them. There was a certain contrast between them but now . . . I saw their pre-wedding pictures and they were badly done; I could have done a much better job of it.

'Saraansh told us you're here and getting something for our Anusha,' says Karishma.

'Mohini,' I correct them.

'Yes, Mohini,' says Arvind.

They knew her as Anusha, and they knew her before I knew her. They were friends with her before she existed for me, and that's deeply discomforting for me. I feel I have lost out. I bear a smidge of resentment towards them, as if they wrested away the time that was meant for me. They even have selfies together. They are all badly taken with terrible lighting and focus, a waste of a good face. I bristle when they talk about her like they were friends, which they had become, when they go like 'Remember she said that' and 'remember she said this'.

'We thought we will pitch in for the bed,' says Aunty.

'It is supposed to be my gift,' I snap.

'We can't let you spend that much. You gave your bed too. We will buy this one together,' says Aunty. She looks disapprovingly at the bed I have chosen. 'Is this the one you have chosen?'

I protest but Mohini's mother and Karishma have moved on. Their research is deeper and they know more about the models of the beds. It irritates me to no end. While they are talking, the owner walks in and they harass him with questions about the newer models. We can afford them with more people pitching in. It's three hours before we select the bed and despite my reservations, we split the cost five ways.

Like always, here too I have had to share Mohini with the others.

'Haldiram's?' says Saraansh after we are done.

Everyone nods and a little later we all huddle around a small table at Haldiram's and order a plate of chaat each. I request if I can leave but Aunty asks me to stay.

'I like the new nurse,' says Aunty.

'I will be nice to the nurse,' I insist.

Aunty shakes her head. Aunty never leaves me alone with a nurse. My nitpicking has made a bunch of nurses quit in the past and Aunty doesn't want to take a chance. As if I don't want the best for Mohini.

'Ananth has been telling me that you're giving him feedback,' says Saraansh.

'A little but I'm not sure. It's not a medium I understand well,' says Aunty.

'Do you think it's a bit incomplete? The story? Do you think it misses something, Aunty?' asks Saraansh.

My heart pounds. He's going to ask her. He knows.

'As in?' asks Aunty.

'I think it's fine the way it is,' I insist.

'I mean it would have been better if we tell the story through and through, no? Tell everything there's to know about her,' says Saraansh.

'We are already doing that,' I interrupt.

'*Aunty, mai kya keh raha tha ki naa* we should add Ananth's part too. That way it's going to make more sense. Her story will reach out to more people. That's what I think. I know you rejected that proposal but I still stand by it,' says Saraansh.

Aunty takes a few seconds to process that information, and then looks at me. She realizes what must have transpired.

'I like the way it is right now, Saraansh. Ananth doesn't need to be a part of the story,' she says and puts it to rest.

I had never told Aunty that Sarita and Saraansh had planned to run my story, too. Because there wasn't one to be told. There was no love story, just a fake video.

'Are you sure?' asks Saraansh.

Aunty glares Saraansh down like only she can.

We finish our chaats. We go back to see the hospital bed we have chosen for Mohini. It's fancy and we all like it even better now. Arvind and Karishma leave, chiding me again for not meeting them enough.

Saraansh and I drop Aunty home. She doesn't let me inside the house lest I nag the new nurse.

We have barely turned the corner when Saraansh says, 'Aunty was lying. You never told her what we were planning to do, bro.'

'I don't know what you're talking about,' I cut him.

'She didn't reject doing your story with Mohini's, *you* did! Don't lie to me, bro. It's on your face.'

'You have an active imagination, don't you?' I tell him.

He pesters on.

'I'm not doing your story, that's a given, but I want to know why,' he says. 'We know that doing your story will take this to another level. So give me a reason so I can put this to rest in my mind.'

'Stop overthinking,' I snap.

'*Mummy kasam khao*, bro, swear it was her idea,' he says.

'What? Are you in third standard?'

'You're lying,' he snaps back.

'Hey—'

'You might think you're not in third standard, but your superstition is just as strong, bro. You paused when I asked you to swear on your mother. So tell me, because it's going to keep playing on my mind when I work and neither of us want that to suffer,' Saraansh tells me.

He drives to the side of the road and parks the car.

'We are going to stop work if you don't tell me,' says Saraansh.

He looks sincere in his threat, and I figure I can't bullshit him anymore.

'The story will fall flat if we tell the entire truth,' I say.

'As in?' asks Saraansh.

'The video that you have seen, the one which was the beginning of it all is fake. Mohini wasn't in love with me. She shot the video to get me the money I needed,' I tell him as concisely as possible. 'Aunty told me once I recovered how she shot it only for the campaign.'

'Fuck.'

'If you tell the entire truth, we will have to show she lied in the video. Once we do that, she loses credibility, and more importantly, so does WeDonate. It will defeat your purpose of making this movie,' I say.

'Bro.'

'. . .'

'She wasn't in love, then? That video, your love—'

'This can't be made common knowledge. It ushered in a new phase for WeDonate. Video testimonials by partners and parents bring in a lot more money. Showing the entire story is not an option we have,' I say.

Saraansh nods.

He says after a while, 'We stick with the plan then.'

'We do.'

We don't talk for a bit. He drives slower than he usually does. I turn to look at him a few times and he's looking out of the window vacantly. I remember his comment on the video. He was one of the first few people who had believed in this love story, my love story, the love story that didn't exist.

'How does that make you feel? Because this is breaking my fucking heart, bro,' he says after a while.

'What?' I ask.

'Knowing that she doesn't love you. When did you get to know that the video was fake? How does that make you feel?' asks Saraansh almost in tears.

I keep my hand on his. I don't want to cry and if he does, I will too.

'I was in love with her long before Aunty told me anything, so I mean . . . I saw her in the video once I woke up and I knew she was the one. Of course, it was an easy choice to make at the time seeing how she saved my life and all. Like you at that point in time, I didn't know the video was fake. '

'Anyone in your position would feel the same,' says Saraansh helpfully.

'But then Aunty told me the truth about the video and it . . . didn't matter. The more I found out about her, trying to know everything there was to know of her, the more undeniably in love I fell. It was irreversible. I needed to know about the person who saved me. That the video was fake, didn't matter then and doesn't matter now,' I say.

It matters.

If and when Mohini wakes up, what will be I to her? An interesting story she wanted to pursue? A possible friend? A prospective boyfriend?

'So you're okay, bro?' asks Saraansh putting his arm around me.

'I am. I'm fine.'

Anusha Sardana

The last couple of weeks have been terribly busy.

I understood how it was possible when people said they started working and then one day found themselves to be forty, boring and with the mild onset of arthritis.

Sarita and Rachita had made a nice little conduit that ended with me. The worst, most horribly done campaigns where the truth needed to be relooked at were sent to me. We were now peddlers of fake news, the good kind, probably the only good kind.

Rachita soon pointed out to me that I had stopped complaining about being in the medical vertical. Little did she know that I had realized staying in medical allowed me to be more creative. It opened me up to a gamut of emotions that I wouldn't have access to anywhere else. Someday I would be the champion writer of misery porn; god knows I have seen enough for a few lifetimes. People dying, people suffering from abject poverty, people living with loss—they are going to be the stepping stones to my eventual literary success.

The nights at Gautam's bedside had proved to be helpful. I had a dozen story ideas where a character like Gautam could be placed in and could drive the story. Also, Gautam's parents cooked well, way better than Mumma, and they loved having me over.

'It feels like Gautam's got better now that he has a friend over every day,' Gautam's mother had said with a sad smile on her face. 'Sometimes I think I will walk into the room and find the two of you laughing.'

Whether it was genuine or she had tried to manipulate me into coming there every day I wouldn't know. But it was successful.

Last week, Mumma had come to pick me up. I knew it was a pretext to meet the people I was spending so much time with. She liked Gautam's parents and what I thought would be a fifteen-minute interaction dragged on for three hours.

Rachita was the only one who had questioned me on spending too much time at Gautam's place. The rest of the office—like juvenile three-year-old kids—teased me about it. When we first talked about it, Rachita was militant in her views.

'You shouldn't fraternize too much. You don't know what's going to happen tomorrow. You know what happened to Karan, the boy—'

'The boy who jumped off the building because he couldn't save the children? Yes? You have warned me quite a bit already,' I said to her.

'This isn't a joke,' she had snapped.

'Is this because of what you went through—'

She had her headphones on before I could finish the sentence. Every subsequent conversation just bolstered my belief about the rumour of her having lost a patient she had fallen in love with.

Rachita eased off one day. She was leaning in her chair when I asked her what she was thinking. She said, 'Maybe it's okay that you're being pally with him. He's not like the others. He already has a foot in his grave.'

It was the unkindest, most real thing I had heard Rachita say. For a moment, I thought she was being sarcastic, a sort of a reverse psychology thing. Whatever it was, she never mentioned it after that. Maybe she wanted me to stop quizzing her on her rumour.

'Why don't you accept you like doing good?' Rachita would say once every day.

I never dignified her nonsense with an answer.

Though I won't deny I loved working on Vishwas ji's case too. He brought his daughter to office—who all of us thought was wonderful and brilliant. She had just cracked her engineering entrance and she was beaming when she distributed laddoos for it. We didn't see the point of it until later. Rachita realized—after googling the fee structure—Vishwas ji had needed money and was too ashamed to ask for it. The education team put up a toothless campaign by the end of the day.

By the end of the week, it had failed. We knew it would never reach the money it intended to generate.

And every day I would have to look at Vishwas ji's sorry face while entering office.

Rachita and I found a better way out. We gave the fundraiser another seven days and on the seventh day, during lunch, we printed out the campaign, and passed around a donation box in office.

The 'thoughtful' and wholly incompetent employees raised enough money to cover her education for four years. Vishwas ji was in tears and thanked everyone profusely. He hugged everyone when he left the office. None of us deserved it though. It only laid bare our true selves. We hadn't thought of giving the money to him in the first place. What did we do instead? We ran a charity campaign instead of doing charity ourselves. Our online charities are shopping not charity.

I was ranting in front of Rachita about this when she started to smile.

'What?' I asked.

'See? You're a nice person. Unlike what you say, maybe you're not a raging witch,' said Rachita.

'Oh, I know I'm a nice person because everyone else is a fucking asshole,' I snapped.

'You never used to get angry at people exhibiting selfish behaviour. That was your expectation from them. Which tells me you believe they can be better? No?'

'Fuck off, Freud,' I argued.

Rachita didn't back off. 'Is it because you found out your boyfriend was a nice person after all? All those mean tweets were just his disease speaking? Is that it?'

It was my turn to put my headphones on. She pulled them off.

'Or maybe finding all these things about him, the photography, how he was with friends, his parents and what not is making you see the good in people?' she asked, smiling her stupid smile.

'Rachita, did I tell you that your undereye serums are not working and your dark circles are worse now? You also have crow's feet,' I grumbled.

'Did I tell you that you have them too, now? You would be interested to know that Nikhat told me that you have started to look like me a little,' Rachita joked.

It was true I wasn't getting a lot of sleep. Writing, editing and sifting through Gautam's memories took up a lot of hours. And yet, there was a missing piece of the puzzle.

No matter how much I tried I couldn't pull out the story of Gautam's sister from his father.

His father apologized to me for crying that day when I had asked about his sister. Though he never told me the story, I hadn't found the heart to prod him or Karishma or Arvind about it. It seemed wrong.

But I needed to know, and every time I hinted at it, his parents seemed to start to crumble.

There was a limit to my good-hearted patience.

So today, I was meeting Karishma.

She and I had been talking a lot about Gautam, and she would keep asking me to delete her texts lest Arvind sees them. It felt like we were in an illicit relationship. Which would have been great, because she seemed like a warm person. Her sharp edges seemed like warm butter now. As much as I started to like her, sometimes she also put me off. Gautam and she were perfect. Why would she give that up for a journey of self-discovery? Didn't she know what she was risking was exactly what people desired? Most of all, it reminded me of Mumma and my father until it all went to shit. On some days, I would comb through Gautam's pictures just to see if there was another girl in his life, if he too was a cheating, lying bastard.

I had just left the office when I found Arvind waiting for me. He didn't seem angry.

'That's creepy,' I told him.

'You think I wouldn't know that she was talking to you?' he asked.

'That's even creepier,' I said.

'She told me, and she asked me to talk to you,' he said.

'And you agreed?' I asked him.

He took a deep breath, shifted in his place and said, 'I did. She wouldn't have it any other way.'

'Did she clench her jaw to intimidate you?' I asked.

'You noticed that too? And the eyes? The way she stares into you,' said Arvind.

'It's very effective,' I said.

He nodded. 'Help me select a ring for Karishma? And I will tell you what you need to know about him,' he said.

'Just because I'm a girl I would know which ring to buy?' I said.

Arvind walked to his car and I followed him. How people his age could afford cars, I had no idea. He was a lot softer this time. I reckoned Karishma had worn him down; I didn't think that was possible but then I reminded myself how I too happened to like Karishma, even have a bit of a crush on her. Mumma, too, was as surprised by this sudden turn of events of me wanting to text people back. First Rachita, then Gautam, and now Karishma. This was unprecedented.

'They will all disappoint me sooner or later. Baba took years to show his true self and he was the best at deception and driving you close to a murder–suicide. These guys are still young. They will find a way sooner than later to screw it all up and disappoint me,' I said to Mumma when she mentioned my *friends* to me. Whether I was being defensive I didn't know.

I had underestimated how tough it could be to choose a ring for an indecisive person. He dragged me to half a dozen jewellery shops in South Extension and Greater Kailash, fussed over multiple rings, and yet couldn't decide on one. He was taking the ring business very seriously and it was pathetic and boring. I wanted to remind him that marriages were conceived to bind a woman down to a legal, unpaid contract because a sexual, liberated woman is a nightmare for men.

'Do you know if she even likes rings?' I asked.

'She hasn't given any indication that she doesn't,' said Arvind holding up a ring that cost Rs 2.5 lakh plus some other charges I had no interest in knowing. 'I should get one just in case.'

I let him play around with other rings while fighting the curiosity to ask how much they were getting paid. I showed varying levels of interest in the rings he was picking up. I wanted to get over with this as quickly as possible.

The salesmen squinted at Arvind's Tissot—an expensive one—and brought out a solitaire on white gold with none of the look-at-the-pattern-it's-set-with-rubies-too nonsense. This one was a huge rock on a band. That's it. In that tiny moment of seeing the stone scatter light, I experienced the stupid allure of owning a diamond. Blood have been spilled because of the diamond trade, there are child soldiers in Sudan, people have lost their limbs because of the rock, not to mention the artificial jacking up of prices—in spite of the knowledge about everything that goes into a diamond reaching a showroom, for a brief moment, it seemed worth it. And then it went to ash.

'If you have decided that you're going to encourage the blood lust behind this industry, buy the one you're holding,' I said to him.

Arvind wanted his parents to have a look at it before he spent Rs 4 lakh on a ring so we left the shop empty-handed. Again. I was full from the numerous cups of tea we had had in the jewellery shops but Arvind insisted that we have tikkis at this place he knew.

There was a long wait at the roadside stall Arvind took me to. The tikkis weren't as crisp as I had expected them to be.

'We used to come here often, the three of us,' he said.

'Is this where we start talking about Gautam? Because I thought dragging me around jewellery shops was your revenge for me trying to save Gautam,' I asked.

Arvind poured more chutney on the tikki. We joined the other patrons sitting on the pavement.

'Are you sure it's not just nostalgia that makes his tikkis better?' I asked.

'It's the chutney,' he said.

'Tell me about Gautam.'

He nodded. He put a big piece is his mouth, chewed dramatically, and only then started to talk.

'We hated him so much. God knows he gave us reasons to do so. You have read the tweets. As horrible as it sounds, Karishma and I bonded over hating him. He was embarrassing himself, embarrassing us. None of us deserved what he did to us,' said Arvind.

'Don't start with the end,' I said. 'How did the two of you become friends?'

'We were in first year. We had just joined college. It hadn't even been a week. I texted Karishma, actually my classmates did. You know how engineering friends are,' he said.

'I have heard engineering boys can be insufferable.'

'They knew I had a crush on her, so they got her number and texted her. Much to everyone's surprise, she replied. She asked me to meet her. No one could believe it. The text was sent to embarrass me. This was going the opposite way,' said Arvind.

'You must have thought of yourself as a stud, no?' I asked, nudging him.

'Everyone knew she had a guy. Gautam, from civil engineering, good-looking guy. My classmates kept pumping me, kept telling me she's looking for someone new and what not. It was college, after all,' he said shaking his head.

'So what happened when you met her?' I asked.

'She wasn't there, Gautam was.'

'You serious?' I asked.

'Have you noticed that Gautam has the look of a fighter? Like, I don't—I don't look like someone who would fight at all,' he said and then stared at me for a bit. 'You do. You look like you're okay with a fist fight. You look like you could be carrying a knife.'

I took it as a compliment and let him continue.

'I thought he would have a go at me. I contemplated telling him to not go for my face. Instead, he sat me down, offered me a cigarette. I had never smoked before but I felt the pressure. Without mincing words he told me he was with Karishma and that he knew that I hadn't sent the messages on my own.'

'That was it?' I asked.

'Nope. He made me meet Karishma,' said Arvind.

'You're joking!' I said.

'I thought he would ask me to apologize but he introduced me as a friend. We went to McDonald's that evening. We ate burgers Karishma paid for. He clicked pictures of us. It was awkward, him pointing the big camera at us.'

I remembered a picture of Karishma and Arvind in that McDonald's. I always thought Arvind looked a bit scared in the picture.

Arvind said, 'I never quite believed till the very end that he was taking it this kindly. I kept thinking, this is the moment, this is the moment, when he punches me in the face. It never came and we started to hang out together. He told me later he found me to be a decent chap.'

'I used to joke that Gautam likes me more than he liked her,' continued Arvind. 'He gave us plenty of reasons to think so. He would do anything for me.'

'And why do you fathom he liked you so much?' I asked Arvind.

'I guess I was at the right place at the right time. He had to reinvest all his love and time somewhere,' said Arvind. 'Karishma and he were drifting apart and I was there and I liked him.'

Arvind took out his phone and swiped to Google photos. He typed 'laptop pictures' and it threw up pictures with laptops in it from his gallery.

'What am I looking at?' I asked.

'I was quite good at Counter-Strike. That laptop you see there? Gautam scoured every second-hand laptop shop in Nehru Place for that. Karishma and he pooled in money for it. I earned it back through college bets in a year. They knew that I would, but still. A lot of people talked about it for a long time.'

'I have seen pictures of you playing on that laptop,' I said.

'He loved photographing me like that. He said I looked like I had just fallen in love,' said Arvind. 'After he changed for the worse it was easy to forget all the good things he did for us, for me. I mean . . . it was . . . he wasn't there to defend himself . . .' He lost his train of thought for a bit. 'I don't know how all this will help you,' he said.

It probably wouldn't.

'You have been making fictional changes to his story anyway,' said Arvind.

'I have,' I answered.

'So why do you want to know more? You could write anything you fancied,' he said.

'I want to know more about him. He interests me,' I said. 'As a character.'

He nodded; although he did not voice it, he must have thought my behaviour was strange. He didn't speak for a bit and then said, 'I still can't forgive him for the things he said.'

'I have been thinking about that,' I said. 'I find it very acceptable. Everything, no matter, how nasty.'

He shook his head dismissively.

'You're going to say it was the disease and not him. The same nonsense Karishma keeps talking about,' he said.

'Hear me out, Arvind,' I said.

He was still shaking his head.

'Keep an open mind. Look at that guy, red shirt, near the signal. Look at him. Now what is the first or the second or the third thing that comes to your mind. Some opinion about him. Something that you shouldn't think, something that you're trained not to think,' I said.

He looked at me and then at the seemingly lower-middle-class person. He said, 'He's ugly.'

'No, dig deeper. You're covering up a few things, you're still trying to be nice. Okay, let me help you along. You do the next one, I will do this but don't judge me. So yes, he's ugly. That shirt is horrible. But let's dig deeper, be meaner, be Blair Waldorf but worse. Now I'm thinking if he's married. And if he's married, is his wife attracted to him? Now I'm thinking maybe she's ugly too.'

I dug deeper and let myself go. What if we could say out the first things that came to our head? If it felt right to say anything. If our frontal lobes didn't stop us from being assholes.

'Now I'm thinking whether his wife will stray if she comes across a good-looking man. Or do ugly and/or poor people not get attracted to the rich knowing that that world is unachievable for them? Or do they live their lives in discontent having lacklustre, ugly sex with each other? If two ugly people look at themselves having sex in the mirror, do they realize how ugly they look? Do they have the awareness of how better-looking people are much more watchable? Now I'm thinking who would watch their sex scandal. No one, not even as a punishment. Pretty sure, ugly people spend their lives thinking about other people while having sex with their ugly partners. How can they not?'

I stopped. Arvind looked at me, horrified.

'I know that's hard,' I said.

'Brutal,' said Arvind.

'This is what Gautam's mind was like. He had no checks and balances. His tumour made him lose his sense of right and wrong. Or he would have stopped where you said that man was ugly. He would have reasoned and questioned that statement. He would have asked himself—*why am I saying this? Is he worse-looking because he works in hard labour? Because I have set notions of what is good-looking? Is that shirt that's making him look worse the only one he can afford? I'm sure he feels love in the deepest of ways and can't think of even touching anyone other than his wife, and his wife feels the same way. Maybe they are content in the lives they lead?* That's what we all do. We ask ourselves to empathize with the other, put ourselves in their shoes, rummage around in their stories and know them,' I said.

He didn't seem to totally buy into it so I put him through another one.

'That one. That uncle,' I said pointing to a man coming out of the shop. He got into his Mercedes and drove off.

'I don't know,' said Arvind.

'Don't tell me you don't hate him a little bit?' I asked.

'A little yes,' he said.

'So tell me what you think? Without any checks and balances? Let yourself go.'

'He's fat. I would never get that fat. That paunch, nope. That's unacceptable. I'm now thinking what will happen if I get that fat? That stomach hanging over a belt? There's no way I could be happy. How does one be *that* fat . . . and you know . . . not think about it all the time. How does that not consume you? I would be sad. That's just horrible. And it looks horrible. He's just horrible to look at,' he said.

I could see he was pushing himself. He already felt sorry for the man so I encouraged him.

'That's true, exactly what I thought,' I said. 'Go on.'

'Now I'm thinking of all the overweight . . .'

'Honestly, is the word in your head overweight or fat?' I asked.

'Fat, all the fat men and women on Instagram who talk about loving their bodies. How can they love their bodies? They can lie, they can try but there's no way they love their bodies, no way they don't want thinner bodies. How can they not? Those rolls of fat, that freckled, dimpled ugly skin . . . no. They are all lying about it. They feel disgusted with their bodies and they don't want to work hard enough to change that. So they sit there taking offence at anyone calling them fat. But they . . . are fat.'

He stopped. He looked at me.

'We are all Gautam. We are all his tweets without our sense of empathy.'

'We are all unkind, loveless animals?' he asked.

'Technically umm . . . we were made to be just wild animals, roam about hunting and eating, so yeah,' I said. 'But we invented humanity and defined what it means to be human, and we constantly update the definition. Killing babies, impaling them on spears was okay six centuries ago but is unimaginable now. Was Gautam—even with his disease and his tweets—worse than those brutal soldiers? Debatable, no? We learn and we strive to be better. That's what makes us humans now. The disease robbed him of that learning. If he were conscious and well today, he would hate himself as much as you hated him. Or as much as you're hating yourself for saying those things you just did. You didn't mean any of that,' I said.

He nodded.

'But had I said those things to those men on the street or a fat person on Instagram, would they have got over it? It's about them, not Gautam. It's about me, I can't get over it,' said Arvind.

It was a fair point.

He looked at his watch.

'Karishma will be here in a bit,' he said. 'What did you need to talk to her about?'

'His sister,' I said.

'Yes, she's the best person to talk about it.'

He shook my hand and took my leave. I entered a coffee shop and checked on Gautam's campaign. A donation of Rs 4 lakh had just been made to Gautam's campaign.

There would be no ring.

Saraansh Gupta

It's now that Saraansh realizes that he had been overconfident with the subject matter. He had thought he would waltz in, dazzle people with his portrayal of their story and walk out with one of the best short movies ever made. That's what he had always done. Back in college, he was leagues ahead of the others in class. *How could this be any different?*

He had been wrong on two counts. He hadn't taken into the account the richness of the story, and his meagre understanding of the people in it. Second, he hadn't anticipated that he would come to think of these people as *people*. They weren't characters but real human beings.

But also, he hadn't expected Ananth to be the incredible raconteur he turned out to be.

Ananth, when he woke up and recovered after the DBS surgery that WeDonate paid for, and found out about the girl who saved his life, scourged for every scrap of detail he could find about her. He met everyone she knew, talked to them for hours, till they exhausted their stories about her and then some. Mohini had made it a smidge easier for Ananth by shedding friends like autumn leaves after her father left her. Ananth relayed everything to him in explicit detail. Saraansh knows now that Ananth—given his history and his newfound obsession to help save as many people as he can—keeps away from anything that's creative, thinking of it as a waste of time, but his talent for picturing things is unmissable when he paints a scenario, a history of something. Saraansh has been to Ananth's house a bunch of times, he has seen what Ananth can do with a camera, and it seeps into how Ananth narrates a certain incident. He describes the entire milieu in painstaking detail.

Ananth took him to see everyone who played a role in her life, and he had heard the stories again but none could tell it like Ananth did. But there was one glaring but obvious omission—Mohini's father.

He was off-limits.

It wasn't the only thing that had completely occupied Saraansh's mind.

The entire project seemed disingenuous to him now. It had already taken a big hit right at the start when he was forbidden from telling Ananth's story and only asked to stick to Mohini's. The story was incomplete but at least it was honest. It ended with the right, true assumption of the girl finding love and recovering from the damage her father had caused her.

The story of the movie was simple as well:

A girl who believed in love and all things fair, is heartbroken when she discovers that her father has an additional family. The girl turns into a judgmental, insufferable asshole who sees the worst in people. But contradictory to her then behaviour, she joins WeDonate and is offered to work on helping people and is put on Ananth's case.

It ended here. The credits scene would show the YouTube video that saved Ananth's life. People would assume that the girl changed after meeting Ananth, that she fell in love.

THE END.

But, as it turned out, the video was a lie. Mohini wasn't in love with Ananth; the assumption they were ending the story with was *untrue*. Mohini hadn't changed. She had remained the same—both before and after Ananth. Every story has to have a character graph, this one had none.

It shouldn't have mattered to Saraansh, whose job was to tell stories and this was just another one—but it deeply rankled him.

'I need to not think about it,' said Saraansh to his boyfriend.

He tried his best to brush the discomfort away—there was nothing to be done—and concentrated on the first part of his problem.

Though Ananth had told him strictly that there would be no meeting her father, he knew he had to find him. He told himself it was the ethical thing to do. After all, he was a character in the movie. It was their responsibility to tell him what they were doing.

Saraansh is waiting in the car. He had called up Mohini's father to tell him he has a construction project for him. Plus he had called from the office landline to give himself credibility.

Mohini's father walks towards the car with big, purposeful strides. He's wearing a starched blue kurta and a jeans underneath. He looks like an aged student union president. Unlike the behaviour Saraansh and the people in his family business are used to from small vendors, Mohini's father is not meek and there's no attempt to grovel. He introduces himself. His voice is self-assured, and Saraansh can see why someone can believe everything he says so readily. The man has aged well. Indian men seldom do.

Saraansh drives to a nearby food stall and parks the car. He orders chai for both when Mohini's father asks about the construction project. Without mincing words, Saraansh tells him why he's really there. Mohini's father is quiet for a bit and then nods.

'A lot of people are going to watch this?' he asks.

Saraansh had expected anger. He had imagined her father walking away. But he sat there, listening, absorbing.

'That's why we are making it. Everyone's going to know,' says Saraansh.

Despite everything, Saraansh feels warmly towards the man. What's with the human tendency to glorify pain. *Why?* He corrects course, reminds himself of what *this* man had done. How hollow, how cowardly he had been.

'I don't have to tell you what I know by now. It's corroborated by multiple accounts. What I want to know is if there's something you want to add? Something you might think they would have missed out? Your justification?' asks Saraansh.

'There's no justification,' he says and sips his tea. 'How's Anusha?'

'She's hanging in there,' says Saraansh.

How to hate this man? Are humans so debased that just a little honesty makes them likeable? Hate, hate, hate, Saraansh reminds himself.

'Did you ever think of going back to them? Did you ever think you should have stayed on?' asks Saraansh.

The man shook his head. 'How can you not, beta? But staying required courage, the ability to apologize every day, to overreach, to fix, to be better every moment. I couldn't— *mujhse nahi ho pata.* Going away, being with my son, my wife, was easier. They were thankful I was there. They are still thankful. Isn't that pitiful?' he says.

'It is cowardly,' says Saraansh. Does he not see the horribleness in calling the other woman his wife? But, of course, the fault lies in him. He should have been no one's husband.

Mohini's father nods.

'You never went back? To see her?'

'I have,' he says. 'I have seen her around the house too.'

'Did you ever talk? If yes, when?' asks Saraansh who wants to know if it comes under the timeline of the story.

'Yes, we did. Once, I went to the house. It was when she was working at WeDonate,' he says. He then adds, 'I needed to sell that house.'

'You what?'

At this point, Saraansh can't tell if this man is just a good actor. You have to be, right? To have two families, to lie every day?

'*Bohut udhaar tha.* I needed money for a project, was under debt, so . . .' His voice trailed off. 'Anusha's mother threatened to go to the police if I ever tried to contact them. You have met her, so you know she's capable of that.'

'What did Anusha say?'

'She drove me out of the house,' says Mohini's father.

'Seems like the right thing to do,' says Saraansh.

Saraansh thinks he has got what he needed from this man. A superstar prototype with an inflated sense of self but lacking a spine; an awareness of his own cowardice, his vulnerability which he exploits to get people, mostly women on his side.

'But some days later, Anusha visited us. She came to our house,' says Mohini's father. 'She clicked a few pictures of us. When we asked what was it for, she asked us to keep our mouths shut. A few days later, she put up a story on her website, WeDonate.'

'What story? What picture?'

'It was my . . . wife's picture. She was holding my son's hand and crying.'

Mohini's father shows him the screenshots of the campaign. How did no one know about this? Sarita? Rachita?

He says, 'The story was that she had an abusive drug addict husband who had wasted away all the money and now they had nothing left to pay the boy's fees. She had made us rehearse the story lest anyone tried to confirm. We got the money in two weeks.'

'That's illegal. She could have fucking gone to jail for this, bro. When exactly was this?' asks an angry Saraansh.

'Did she get in touch later?'

Mohini's father shakes his head.

Saraansh nods. He asks, 'I think I have got what I needed. I have to go somewhere. I'm sure you will find your way home.'

Saraansh gets into his car. He puts the car in gear and is driving away when he spots Mohini's father and slows down beside him. He rolls down the window and says, 'Uncle?'

'Haan, beta?'

'Fuck you, madarchod.'

Saraansh leaves him in a plume of dust and smoke. He hasn't reached the next red light when the anger against Mohini's father settles. He feels relief wash over him. He thinks at first it's because the uncertainty of how he's going to portray the father is gone but it's something else. It keeps nagging at him.

And then he gets it.

Mohini would not get anything out of it. It wasn't even an interesting story she came up with it. There was nothing for her to even gain creatively. If anything, because of the deeply personal nature of the story, it would have been very painful for her. If Saraansh knew the old Anusha correctly, before Gautam and her fake love story, she would have loved to see her father suffer. She would have sat back and enjoyed watching her father destroy himself.

This was out of character.

There could be only one reason for it.

He remembered the screenshot, the time of the post. It would have been during the time she was working on

Gautam's campaign. She would have been knee-deep in Gautam's history.

This meant only one thing.

This meant, finding Gautam, finding his story, being around him, had changed her. In the video, she says she loves him, which might not be true, but the rest of the things she says about Gautam, about his niceness, about his stodgy kindness even when life threw the worst at him, were true.

And it changed her. This made sense.

Gautam changed her. That was the truth. And that's why he was relieved. There was a story here, might not be love, but it was something.

She changed.

He buzzes with excitement. He wonders if he can tell Ananth this. There's no right answer to that, he realizes. Should he create more hope based on a hypothesis? Inject more uncertainty in his life? Or let him live with the truth he has already accepted?

His train of thought is broken by Sarita's phone calls. She had been calling incessantly to get hold of him.

'Saraansh.'

'I was—'

'We need to shoot the trailer as soon as possible. Come to the office tomorrow and sit with me for the commercials. Lock the cast immediately,' she says and cuts the call.

Saraansh opens the folder containing the auditions of the actors he had worked with.

He stays up all night creating an audition call for girls playing Anusha/Mohini.

They have to shoot the trailer soon.

Anusha Sardana

Hmmmm. Gautam, you're filling up my notes with alarming density now.

I must concede that you have disappointed me of late. I thought we were the same, you and I. But as it turns out, we are quite different. The doctors' confirmation that your behaviour wasn't in keeping with your true nature, and it was all because of the tumour, might work in your favour if put across in a way that people warm up to it and donate to your cause, but it broke my heart.

What good were you to me if you didn't hate the world with the vengeance that I did. How stupid of you to resist the temptation to loathe the world when you had plenty of reasons to do so.

You were quite the opposite of what I had hoped you to be.

You were there today, lying in front of me and you looked the good, kind type of handsome. Your handsomeness is fluid and takes on different personalities. When I first saw you, with your long, flowing hair, the long fingers and the puffed up chest, you were the Disney villian kind of handsome. And now that I know you a little better, your hair looks lovingly unkempt from all the ruffling it gets from people who love you, creativity flows from your long fingers, your chest is a nice resting place. It annoys me even more.

I talked to your father about your sister. Again and again and again. And though he stopped crying after a bit—I can take some credit for desensitizing him—he didn't tell me a thing.

He refused to talk about it. Which only made me want to know more about her.

I gave up my good grace of trying not to gossip, and hearing it from someone in the family, and turned to Karishma whom I am good friends with now.

Unknown to Arvind, we have started hanging out. I see why both you and Karishma like Arvind. He's a simple guy who loves his girlfriend, a stable job, money and big breasts. He has been easy to fool.

Karishma was the one who told me what had happened to your sister, and how you had changed post her death.

Needless to say, your reaction and the entire story infuriated me. *How naive and stupid can one be?* Maybe it was a good thing you had your brain messed with so you could finally see things as they are.

Karishma told me you were in tenth standard when it happened. Your sister had just started to go to school. Every afternoon you would wait for her bus at the bus stop and then take her home. I have seen the photographs. There are pictures of you both in uniforms, holding a bottle each, in your hands. There are pictures of her in two plaits. I know you braided those plaits because there's a self-portrait where you're doing just that. There are photographs of you and her eating breakfast together in your school mornings. There are photographs of you with your tie hanging loosely, your sister on your lap and you feeding her. There are photographs of her pointing at an open book and you mouthing something. There are photographs of you and her at your bus stop. Of you in her class, looking like a giant amongst the little tables and chairs. Of you and your friends with her. Of you surrounded by her friends from Mont 1 D. In most photographs she had been making faces. And then, there are photographs of her sitting on the bench at the bus stop.

The first summer of her school, your vacations had started before hers.

The day she died was the last day of that academic year.

The bus was more or less empty. Many students had cut classes, opting to start their vacation earlier. You were at the bus stop. The bus driver had spotted you. He didn't bother to take a U-turn that day. There was just your sister who needed to be dropped off on the other side of the road. The driver had waved at you and you had waved back. He had assumed you would cross the road, he had assumed your sister would wait for you to cross the road. So had you.

Your sister had seen you. She had jumped with joy. It was the start of the summer vacations.

You had called out, screamed to her not to cross the road on her own.

She hadn't listened. She had run towards her brother. She had a big smile on her face. She was screaming your name in happiness!

She didn't see the car that hit her. You saw it. And you saw it over and over and over again.

By the time you got there, held her bleeding head in your arms, her little hands hanging limply by her side, you knew it was terrible. This was unfixable. The car drove off without stopping. Other cars slowed down. The people on motorcycles slowed down but didn't stop. The pedestrians stopped and watched you cry hoarse for help but didn't move from their places. They just stood there watching you and your sister drenched in blood. The blood you tried scooping from the road and putting back into her. What else were you supposed to do?

Could she have been saved had someone reacted earlier? Could she have been saved had three auto drivers not refused to stain their autos with blood? Could she have lived had the drivers of other cars stopped without thinking if they would have to buy new seat covers? Could she have lived had anyone come forward to help in the first fifteen minutes that you carried her in your arms and run about begging for help?

There are no answers for that. You know that better than most.

Your sister was declared dead on arrival.

This was enough ground. Why on earth would you have not turned against the world? Why wouldn't you be angry at the people who stood around watching your sister die? Why wouldn't you wish the worse for them who went back to their families while you went back to a bloodied tattered bag, a broken water bottle and a uniform that no one could wear again?

This would have been a great turning point. The triggering incident to make you that asshole you were on Twitter. But it didn't. This pre-dated your behaviour by a bunch of years.

What you did instead was foolish.

After the debilitating part of your mourning was over, you asked Karishma—the girl you were secretly in love with for six years before that—out. You, naively, thought life's short and one should fill it with as much love as possible. Blah.

But that wasn't the stupidest thing you had done.

That was the forgiveness you extended to the people who had watched on.

'He said people would have been shocked to see what had happened. He said maybe this world needs more love, not less of it. Maybe if everyone felt it in their lives, things would have been different. This was a young boy. I knew how much he loved his sister. I mean those weren't empty words.

He changed. Everyone in the class saw that. He had so much love to give and share, he seemed like a lunatic sometimes. We were at an age where we were developing personalities—he chose to be the giver of unbridled love and kindness as his identity and it baffled us all. He embraced everyone with a kind of mad love which was unprecedented. You just had to ask him and he would do anything for you. For even the most gone-cases in our class . . . and you know, we saw a few others start behaving like him. It was infectious what he did. Who wouldn't want a friend like him? Someone who would drop everything and help you out with whatever you needed? It was crazy. Of course, for me, and a few other girls, he became quite the heartthrob. That tragedy-struck brooding look, that uncompromising kindness. He told me it would be an insult to his sister's life if he let her passing destroy him. So he became a better person, better than all of us. It was madness, just madness.'

It was madness.

I couldn't have put it better than Karishma.

Why would you betray me like this, Gautam? I thought we were together in this. Seems like you were always in the other team.

Now I feel small in my hatred towards the world. On your part, this was a dick move. With all due respect, fuck you.

Ananth Khatri

The trailer auditions have been blowing up on social media. WeDonate and Saraansh have made a public spectacle out of the entire thing; they are not entirely to blame. How things progressed is a surprise to all of us. Also a testimony that this story will find takers.

Saraansh made a call-for-auditions video for the main character—Mohini—and WeDonate shared it across platforms. The people interested had to upload a video of their own and send us the YouTube link. The script that the auditioning people had to follow was the video Mohini had made.

We had expected a decent response but since then we have been deluged by the number of entries; mails had been bouncing back from the WeDonate mail IDs so we had to share our Gmail IDs. There are people—guys—sending in their entries who want to play me. We haven't told them I'm not a part of the story.

It's all a bit surreal. It's no longer just a script, it's no longer in our head, it's happening, and it's making me feel nervous.

I stopped watching the clips after a while because I felt what could be described as a sharp, piercing, debilitating pain in my heart seeing all these actor Mohinis when my own was strapped to a bed.

For the last two weeks, I had been told to rush things a little. Sarita wants me to step on the project. She wants us to put the trailer out before we work further on the script. There's a budget already earmarked for the trailer and she wants us to claim it before other projects start to clamour for it. Once the trailer is shot, we can put it up asking for funds. Which—after seeing the response to the audition call—seems to be the least of all our worries.

Saraansh tells me he has been approached by a few streaming partners as well. Sarita and Saraansh have both vehemently shot them down. They need the autonomy to do what they want. A streaming partner will shackle them creatively.

Last night Saraansh called me to book a conference room for the entire day. It's been a week since we last met. He has been working on the script of the trailer. When I see him, his stubble is threatening to become a beard. I didn't know he was capable of facial hair. He is beginning to look more and more like the romanticized image of a director. He has been wearing shirts that aren't ironed, jeans with stains. I believe in his talent more now.

'I haven't slept in five days,' Saraansh says to explain the scraggly beard and the bags under the eyes. 'Where are the others?'

'Show me the faces you choose,' Sarita says as she passes the conference room. 'Nothing gets through without my approval. Okay?'

And, of course, she walks away before I can answer. A little later, the door to the conference room opens.

'Hi,' says Karishma.

Behind her, Arvind walks in. They are both thinner and older than they were the last time I met them. But that's every time I meet them now. I wonder if the two of them know that they are being sucked dry by their corporate jobs or they are on Keto diets before they get married.

When I reach for a hug, Karishma hesitates for a second and then hugs me warmly. It happens every time we meet now. When I had woken up from my coma, and remembered what I had put Karishma and Arvind through, I knew I had seen the last of them. I mourned my relationship with them, went through all the five stages of grief only to realize later that Mohini had mended the bridges I had burned. It couldn't have been easy for Mohini, or for them, to make this happen. I nearly destroyed the two of them.

Arvind and I shake hands. It hits me how much I miss them; I make a mental note to meet them more often. They are holding hands now.

That's how I remember them in college. After my brain played truant and I started badmouthing them, Arvind would always reach out to hold her hand as if I was going to run away with her; it was amusing at the time.

That's how I saw them after my surgery.

It wasn't amusing then. Just as my counsellor has warned me, when I saw them, it felt as if someone had ripped my heart out. The tweets about them came rushing back to me and I was drowning in guilt.

I started to cry and tell them I didn't mean any of those things. Seeing them felt like waking up from a drunken sleep and regretting the things that you did the night before which seemed fine, even entertaining, at the time. I had struggled to find words to apologize. It was me who had written out those nasty tweets; I clearly remember having said those things. *How could I have taken them back?*

'It wasn't you,' Arvind had said.

It was also what the counsellor and my doctor had said. They kept drumming it in—it wasn't you, it wasn't you, it wasn't you. And yet, every time, I meet them I can sense their anger (and mine) at the things I had said. Now some times when we meet, we do the exercise Mohini had done with Arvind to tell ourselves that without our empathy

checks, we are all harsh, nasty people and it helps a bit. And
yet . . .

'I called them so we could reach some kind of consensus
on who should play Anusha,' says Saraansh.

'Mohini,' I correct him.

'You look horrible,' says Karishma to Saraansh.

'Thanks.' Saraansh continues, 'I have seen so many auditions
over the weekend that everyone is looking the same to me. I
have shortlisted 123 auditions. They are all coming in today.'

'How many were there?' asked Karishma.

'870, give or take,' answered Saraansh with a sense of pride.
'But if I leave it up to Ananth, no one is going to match up.'

Karishma rubs her hands, looks at us and says, 'Let's get on
with this then.'

Just then, there is a knock at the door. It's Rachita,
followed closely behind by Nimesh and Nikhat.

'We want in. We are the first people she made friends
with at WeDonate,' say Nimesh and Nikhat.

'Friends is an overstatement,' says Rachita.

'It might be a little intimidating for the actresses to see so
many of us sitting for the auditions,' says Saraansh.

No one budges from their position.

'I'm not going anywhere,' says Rachita.

'Neither are we,' say Arvind and Karishma, fiercely
possessive of their seats.

It's obvious the only one who shouldn't be here is me—
the rest have all met her.

Rachita looks at the script. It's the same as the video.

'We are using this?' she asks.

Saraansh nods.

'We can't use this. Your shortlisted candidates already
know this dialogue by now. We need to add two more
variations to the dialogues,' she tells Saraansh.

'But—'

Rachita cuts Saraansh. 'You're not just auditioning for the trailer, you're auditioning for the entire movie, there will be more scenes in the movie than just this one, I'm hoping? We need to see how these girls would be if they were to act in all ten episodes and not just in an one-minute cut. We need to see their range.'

'She's right,' says Karishma.

Rachita quickly scribbles a few dialogues.

'Not bad,' says Saraansh when he reads them.

The paper is passed around and they all agree it sounds like something Mohini would have said.

'These are her exact words,' says Rachita to confirm what we are all thinking.

In the next hour, the line outside our office keeps getting longer. A lot of girls have come dressed like Mohini/Anusha and it's a little confusing to see that.

One after another, the girls walk in. They leave the room as swiftly as they come in. Saraansh was wrong. It wasn't me but Rachita, Karishma and the others who are ruthless. Some girls hobble out crying, calling the audition unfair and the judges ruthless. Most do really well on the video content, but when it comes to delivering the sarcastic, caustic lines, they falter. None of them have the bite that Rachita and Karishma want.

'You haven't heard her be that,' says Rachita in the most offhanded way to me not realizing she might have broken my heart in a bajillion pieces.

Rachita is uncharacteristically harsh on most of them. Even when we do like someone, she looks at us and snaps, 'Do you really think that's how she used to talk?' She would then turn to the girl and ask her to leave.

Sometimes, she would tell the actresses exactly how to intonate the lines and yet most of them would miss the mark.

After the first couple of hours, Saraansh steps back as he's no longer running the show. Rachita whose organizational skills are par excellence takes over. She walks around the serpentine line of hopeful faces and culls half the hopeful just from the way they look and carry themselves.

'Not fit, not fit, not fit,' she says to the waiting girls.

As for the rest, she tutors them exactly what to say before getting them to audition.

The process is quicker but fruitless. No one gets through.

It's six in the evening and we are still where we started in the morning.

Someone doesn't look right, someone's accent is all off, someone is not smart enough to get the character, someone doesn't have the spunk. The optimism we started the day with has already withered. Disappointment, and then panic, set in. Where were we going to find her? By the time we wrap up the auditions, the team has sent many a grown women crying back to their homes. We are all slumped forward in our desks except Saraansh and Rachita. Saraansh is leaning back on his chair, looking into his phone. Rachita is still tweaking the dialogues for the future auditions.

'I won't be able to come tomorrow but you can keep sending me auditions on WhatsApp,' Karishma addresses Rachita.

'Forward them to me as well,' says Arvind.

'We will do that,' says Rachita. 'How many more people can you get to audition by tomorrow? Or should we give it a couple of more days? Give out more variations of the script?'

'I don't think we will need to do that,' says Saraansh. 'I think we have found the girl.'

Rachita glares Saraansh down. 'None of these were good. I'm not letting any of these girls play Anusha,' argues Rachita.

'Mohini,' I correct Rachita.

'Can you hook up my phone to the projector?' says Saraansh and gives his phone to Arvind who does so. The projector is now the wallpaper of his phone screen. He looks at us and says, 'Are we ready?'

He clicks through to his mailbox where there's a mail from Sarita Sharan. There's a link to a private YouTube video.

'The girl sent her audition to Sarita? The gall!' snaps Rachita. 'I'm telling you some of the wannabe actors—'

'I'm playing it,' says Saraansh and presses the button.

It's a tight close-up. Rachita's face fills up the screen.

What.

Rachita is now talking to the camera. She has tears in her eyes. She says she's Mohini. She points to the bed in the background introduces the boy on the bed as Ananth. She's telling the viewer—us—how she met me, how she's in love with me, she's defending my tweets, she's urging us how we should all donate to WeDonate to save my life, how it would mean the world to her. The video is an exact copy of the one we have all seen multiple times—one of Mohini. It's uncanny. It's like only the face has changed. It's an incredible performance. The video, her broken voice, her trembling fingers, the twitching face, the welled-up eyes bring us all to tears even though we have heard the same dialogues hundreds of times since the morning.

It strikes all of us. *Rachita*. She's perfect. She's the same height, the same complexion, she has shorter hair but that can be grown out, or we can use extensions. A little make-up will make her look younger. The video plays on. We have heard the same script—different people, same emotion—hundreds of times today, and yet Rachita's version hits hard.

'You recorded an audition too?' Karishma whispers.

Rachita shakes her head.

As she talks, the camera pulls back. It's a familiar frame. It's the *same* frame. We see the full bed. And now I'm in that frame, I'm on the bed. Motionless. In a deep coma. My heart breaks a little.

This isn't an audition video.

This video was shot before, much before, alongside Mohini's video, as an option to Mohini's video. Both Anusha and Rachita shot as Mohini.

I can feel everyone turn and look at me. I knew, Saraansh knew Mohini's video was scripted, but Arvind and Karishma? They didn't.

The video ends.

'I think you should do it,' I say to Rachita.

Rachita feels sorry for me.

'I knew,' I say to put her at ease. 'I knew this video exists.'

'You did?' she asks.

'Of course, I did!' I say, a little too brightly, like you do when you're lying.

She looks at me for a bit, as an apology and to check if I was bluffing.

'Can I think about it? This was just . . . a video. I am not sure if I will be able to pull off an entire movie,' she asks.

'Sure,' says Saraansh.

Even though Saraansh makes it sound like Rachita has any agency on the matter, we all know who's going to play Mohini. No one else comes close. She's *Mohini,* too.

A little later, Karishma and Arvind leave. They both hugged me before they left. Karishma's lingered a bit longer. They found it hard to say anything to me and I don't blame them. Unlike me, they didn't know Mohini never really fell in love with me. For them it was just revealed to me; for them I was heartbroken.

This was the proverbial nail in the coffin of my unrequited love story. I feel my stomach churn.

'I don't know how Sarita got this video,' says Rachita as if it would make things better. 'Anusha got me to shoot this video because she thought I will be good at it. She chose to upload hers. I'm sorry . . . I didn't.'

'It's okay, I'm fine. I told you I knew this existed. I needed to be saved and both of you did what you had to. I would have done the same if I were in your position,' I say.

'But—'

'You don't have to say anything, Rachita. I'm fine, really, trust me,' I say and pat her arm.

She hugs me in return, and then leaves the room. Saraansh looks at me and struggles for words to say.

'So they both shot a video,' I say out aloud what I have been saying inside for the last ten minutes. 'They were both Mohini.'

'Bro—'

I interrupt Saraansh. 'I know what you're thinking, Saraansh. If Rachita's video had been uploaded as Mohini, I would have fallen in love with her?' I shake my head. 'I wouldn't have. I fell in love with the story of hers, of what she was, of the things I have told you about Mohi . . . Anusha. That's what I fell in love with.'

'That's true, bro,' says Saraansh.

'I knew but I didn't wholly believe that she felt absolutely nothing for me, you know, that all that love was just for the camera, just for show. But this video—'

'I understand,' says Saraansh.

'Saraansh, when I see Mohini's video, I know it's a script. I know she's mouthing words she designed to save me. Aunty told me that and I believe it. But . . . but I always thought she must have felt something at least saying those words.'

'That still doesn't change, bro. This video changes nothing,' says Saraansh.

'Of course it does. It changes everything. This video means Mohini was replaceable, no?' I try my hardest not to cry. 'Rachita said the same words as Anusha. She even said them better than Moh . . . Anusha did. So it didn't matter who said the words, who was in the video. Hell, even Karishma could have said the words, or anyone else from the medical team. She felt *nothing*,' I say.

I turned to Saraansh for solace but he was looking at me, grinning.

'Are you sure about that?' asks Saraansh, that grin still firmly in place.

It was a strange thing to do for someone I considered a friend.

'You're not helping. Your tone is teasing and it's hurtful. I fucking knew but . . .'

Saraansh smiles and says, 'I met Anusha's father.'

'You did what?' I ask, even forgetting to correct her name.

He's still smiling and it's not helping his cause.

'Let me get to the good part, bro,' says Saraansh.

He tells me about the campaign Mohini ran to save her father from bankruptcy and looks at me like it should make me happy but it doesn't. What does it change?

'So yeah, she did that, so what?' I say.

'Are you not seeing what you did, bro? Bro! You made a difference! So while she might not have felt what you would have ideally wanted her to, but you changed her.'

I changed her?

He continued, 'You think she would have helped them out had she been the old Anusha? Absofuckinglutely not! She helped them because she knew of you, because she knew of your story, of your mad kindness. Anusha didn't help her father, Mohini helped her father. You damn well changed her. From Anusha to Mohini.'

'Wait.'

'Yeah, yeah, absorb it. Be the stupid, optimistic Ananth you can be and think about it,' he says.

'Did I?'

'It's the only explanation,' he says.

Now that he puts it like that maybe it's the only explanation. I lean back on my chair, close my eyes, and dream her up. I imagine the situation and yes, it fits. I want to believe it.

I changed her.

'You're right,' I tell Saraansh. 'But why didn't you tell me earlier?'

'I mean I wasn't confident about my inference. But you just confirmed it,' he says.

While we mull over it, we order burgers and a KFC bucket to tide over the gloom. The food makes the silver lining clearer.

I changed Mohini.

Saraansh watches Rachita's video repeatedly. Each time, he comes out more impressed.

'Can you stop playing that now?' I ask.

'Look at this?' he says and points to the screen. He pushes play and then stops. Then pushes play and stops at another place. 'Do you see the edit jumps? It's very smooth but the light changes. Also, look there.'

'Where?'

'The window. You can see a shadow. That's Anusha directing Rachita, bro,' says Saraansh.

'So? That's all kind of obvious?' I say even as I squint to make out Mohini's shadow.

'It's, bro. But . . . but . . . if you check Anusha's video, it's a one take. There are no edits, nothing. Now I don't believe she would have got it done in one shot. Also, I don't think they shot it on the same day. I think she directed herself unlike Rachita who was directed by her. What I want to see are the shots she rejected and the outtakes,' says Saraansh.

'What will that give us?' I ask even though I have spent hours going through the videos of Mohini that Aunty had showed me.

'It will be you and her, alone in a room. We can see how she was around you, bro? See . . . my point is that she made the entire world believe that she was in love with you. She was great at lying, we can all concur, no? Could it be possible there was another lie? After all that she has gone through with her parents, the betrayal and all that stuff, don't you think she's capable of fooling herself that she wasn't in love with you? Maybe she was? One look, one tender moment, that's all it takes,' says Saraansh with a smile. 'Maybe it's not the world she was lying to, maybe she was lying to herself?'

Fuck Saraansh. Fuck Saraansh for giving me hope. Fuck him.

Anusha Sardana

The more I wrote, the more I read what I wrote, the more I wanted to write. Gautam was a wholesome character; there was so much to bite into, so much to explore, so much to dive into. This was the problem with my attempts in the previous books. I didn't have a character I liked enough to write about; they became boring after a while. But with Gautam, just the notes about him, ran into 14,000 words. Which brought me to my problem. How was I supposed to condense a rich story like his into 500 words for WeDonate?

I gave up after a week. It wasn't for the lack of trying. Fifteen drafts were approved by Gautam's parents, Sarita and Rachita, and fifteen drafts had been rejected by the *junta*. Money slowly trickled in, but we were still Rs 12 lakh short on it.

Other times, I would have minded reworking the story multiple times. This time, I enjoyed it. Previously, writing always meant finding creative ways to procrastinate; but that was not the case with Gautam's story.

But that day, after tracking and being disappointed with the traction of the story, I clicked on YouTube, browsed through the vloggers I used to like. They are my happy place, my escape. I don't believe their lives—of course they are fake and they are probably cutting their wrists in their spare time—but for those eight minutes starting with them shouting 'Hey guys' I believe them. I believe their happiness, I believe their excitement, I believe their smiles, I believe those eight minutes is what every minute of their lives are like, I believe they don't have disappointment, I believe their courage.

I was still mindlessly clicking through the videos when I stumbled upon what is clearly a click-bait video titled HELP. One of the YouTubers I once liked was selling his merchandise. A five-minute sales pitch on how the t-shirt he's selling is going to pay for the trip he wants to take that in turn would help him make better content for the people who watch him.

What!

Who in the right mind would pay for someone else's trip? Turned out, a lot of people. Droves of intellectually stunted fans bought the t-shirt and into the stupid plea. And there I was, struggling to sell a legitimately great story to people!

I was reading through the comments, getting angrier and angrier at people who'd typed 'BOUGHT' when it struck me that my anger was misdirected.

You can't blame the audience. Most people don't know right from wrong, smart from stupid. They only think they know what's right for them. They buy cars and then resent the traffic, they litter and then resent the garbage pile outside their homes, they make casteist slurs and then resent that there is reservation, they raise girls to be submissive and then resent dowry, they elect right-wing governments and expect peace. Most political analysts trying to figure out election results should fall back on what every one of us has said one time or the other—*log chutiye hote hai*, people are fuckers. It's the universal truth.

This vlogger knew it.

And I realized rather than trying to make people know better, fool them into doing better. If people weren't willing to read a long story—can't blame them, no one reads—SHOW them the story.

WeDonate is a successful organization. They do a great job at getting money for the poorest, most desperate. Maybe that's why they haven't felt the need to jump on the video bandwagon.

I called up Rachita and asked her to meet me. Rachita who had dragged herself out of her home on a Sunday was unimpressed.

'You really think this is your "Eureka!" moment?' asked Rachita with a shrug. 'The cost is prohibitive. We would need to hire cameras, lighting, and find someone to edit it. It doesn't make sense. Writing stories mostly does the job,' she explained.

'*Mostly?* Are you saying this knowing that the alternative is that a few campaigns end up underfunded and people die because of that?' I asked.

'When did you start caring about that, Anusha?' she asked in turn.

I wanted to ask myself the same question but I had an argument to win so I said, 'Okay, let's say your campaign gets funded, now what? What happens to the story you wrote?'

It was a rhetorical question. They closed the fundraiser and it was archived on the website. No one visited successfully closed cases except people who were running fundraisers and wanted to check if there were others like them who were successful.

I continued, 'Those successful fundraisers are our advertising material and we let it rot in some corner of our website. Instead, people should have access to those successful, happy stories. People love their dopamine hits. Haven't you seen videos of YouTubers handing out money to homeless people, beggars raking in millions of views? Ellen DeGeneres giving out cheques to people who need it? Those have like a billion hits! This is even better! We are saving lives here. They will want to be a part of this happiness. Go, see the number of views on the sad-happy stories of *India's Got Talent* and *Dance India Dance*.'

'You want to turn WeDonate into *Dance India Dance*?'

'Say someone sees a video today of a parent crying for their child, asking for money, and then finds out that the fundraiser was closed two months ago, that the money had been generated, and the child was saved. What will he think? Of course he will think well of WeDonate and its model. He will also want to be a part of it, no? He will look for other videos. People love these positive stories!'

*

I continue, 'So here's where we start. We make videos—let's just start with the ones that aren't going well but we believe that they should—and post them online with a click-bait title, YOU CAN SAVE THIS POOR 3-YEAR OLD FROM DEADLY, BONE ROTTING CANCER. When the fundraiser is closed, you can change the title or add in the caption, PEOPLE SAVED THIS 3-YEAR OLD FROM BONE ROTTING CANCER.'

'Why are you shouting?'

'Isn't everyone on the Internet shouting?'

Rachita nodded like she bought it and yet argued, 'No one's going to earmark money for campaigns that aren't working.'

'We don't need to. Did you know Karunesh's team just got flooded with money?' I asked.

Last month, after the multiple failures of the entertainment team to find projects they could fund they had pivoted to a different model. They were now looking for people and not projects. They would fund their scripts and their trailers themselves. The trailer would then go up and the junta would be asked to fund them. They were flush with money at the moment.

'We borrow Karunesh's fancy equipment to shoot it. I will edit it. It's not that tough, and neither is it expensive. We don't need it to be overproduced anyway. It has to look natural.'

It required several repetitions for her to buy into the idea. Internet taught me that. You repeat something—or make a bunch of people do it— and people start to believe in your idea. You can change governments on the back of it.

'Are we making the video for your boyfriend, Gautam?' she asked.

'Actually, your boyfriend,' I corrected her and gave her the script I had written.

She thought it was a joke till she read it. Hiding her shock, she said, 'Why can't the parents do it?'

This is why I like her; others would have said the parents should do it. Unlike others she knew there was a possibility that the parents weren't the best choice.

'When I see a truant, misbehaving child, I blame their parents, I don't sympathize with them. I would say he was raised badly. This campaign is getting backlash from the young, and we need someone young to side with him. Who better than a devastated girlfriend?' I asked.

'Why me?'

'Who else? You're the only one who hasn't questioned the moral and ethical boundaries we will cross when we make this video. I can't think of anyone else who would say this is the right thing to do,' I said.

'But—'

I interrupted her. 'Also, you're a good actor. I have seen footages from your theatre days. And you kind of didn't ask why I couldn't do it. After all, this is my idea. Only an actor can be that vain to put her talent over anyone else's. You already know that you're better than I am.'

'I'm not sure—'

She was lying. She was sure of it. Rachita had seen way too many people die to deny this. Numerous times, she would have felt shackled by the reach of WeDonate. The money was out there to be collected, but unreachable. And then, there was the rumour.

'You know you want to do it, Rachita,' I said. 'I have heard the rumours.'

'What rumours?' she asked.

'Of you losing someone you got close to, someone who couldn't get the money?' I said, a little unsure.

She smiled sadly.

'It's true, then?' I asked.

She looked at me and said, 'You think there was one?' She added with a pitiful smile. 'I fall in love pretty easy.'

That was literally the last thing I would have ever expected Rachita to say.

She continued, 'Anyway, I'm guessing you have already told his parents?' she asked.

'I have.'

I didn't tell her that Gautam's mother hadn't been completely thrilled.

'Why is she going to be Mohini? You're his Mohini,' Gautam's mother had said rather forcefully. 'You are Mohini. *Tum hi Mohini ho beta.*'

'The girl from my office is a really good actor. She will do a good job,' I had explained to Gautam's mother.

'Why do you need to act? You can say you like him,' Gautam's mother had said.

For every mother, her son is their *raja beta* and if any woman is around him, it's to fall in love and father his babies. I convinced her eventually.

Rachita didn't agree straightaway. Through the week I kept pecking away at her.

When she gave in, she tried to make me believe that she was doing it to save my job, and not because she herself wanted to do it. She said, 'The only way you won't get fired for this is if I do this. Sarita can't let go of both of us.'

We are like two-thirds of the Powerpuff girls, I thought but I didn't say it out aloud.

She continued, 'And I'm doing this because you like him.'

'I don't like him.'

'Of course, you don't,' Rachita said.

On the day of shoot, it was a Sunday. We dragged Karunesh's lights to Gautam's house. Technically, it was theft because neither did we inform Karunesh nor made an official entry of borrowing the equipment. I had thought of asking Karishma and Arvind to join me for the shoot and then decided otherwise. It was best that we kept it uncluttered. Though I missed them being around. Of late, Arvind and Karishma had begun to spend quite some time at Gautam's house with me.

Things between Arvind–Karishma and Gautam's parents had now thawed but it had taken some work. His parents hadn't taken their abandonment of Gautam lightly and held an undying grudge against them. The first time I took the two of them to Gautam's house, his parents had refused to open the door for us.

'First ask the two of them to leave,' Gautam's mother had said.

'Let them enter,' we heard Gautam's father tell her.

'OVER MY DEAD BODY!' Gautam's mother had said to his father.

Even the donation of Rs 4 lakh hadn't moved her. It was only after they went to Gautam's house every day with me to apologize for a week that she cracked.

Now every second evening, Arvind, Karishma and I found ourselves around his bed, chatting. It was sometimes a bit irritating to have them there. It would eat into my time with Gautam's things, and my writing. But then, very often they would tell me more about how Gautam was.

On those evenings, sometimes we would forget that he was right there, and sometimes, we would assume that he was listening and would address him and talk to him and answer on his behalf.

'He would say Ganguly was the best captain.'

'He would say get a degree but also not let that degree define you.'

'He would say let's invite some random people to our drinking session.'

Unlike me, Rachita wasn't nervous about the shoot at all. We rolled in the equipment to his room. I introduced Gautam to Rachita like he was an actor playing his part—lying on the bed, half-dead—to perfection.

Rachita and I fixed everything in place and tested out the equipment. After a few rehearsals, we were ready to roll.

Rachita blew it out of the water.

The delivery, the tear peeking out of her eye, the gestures of her hand, the way she looked at Gautam—she landed everything perfectly. We took a bunch of takes so I could use the best parts when I edited them. I knew I would be spoilt for choice. Her modulation was just so believable.

Once I got back home, I transferred all the files to my laptop, downloaded a crack version of Premiere Pro, opened YouTube tutorials on editing, and got down to editing the clips. The first half chugged along. Then something felt amiss. The more I saw the clips, the more they seemed acted, over-produced, staged. It was all wrong. It was apparent that the girl in the video wasn't his girlfriend but a stand-in, an actor. The flaws stood out, magnified. This was too perfect. There was no way this would work.

I closed the project file, packed up the memory cards, the camera and went straight back to Gautam's house.

'Is there a problem?' asked Gautam's father, rubbing his eyes. It was 3 in the morning.

'I need to shoot it again,' I said.

'Where's Rachita?' asked Gautam's mother.

'She's not needed, I will do it,' I said. 'I will be Mohini.'

'But she did well? I saw the clips,' said Gautam's father.

'Let her do it, she will do much better. She knows my son,' countered Gautam's mother sternly.

Gautam's mother opened the door and led me inside. She switched on the light and placed the chair near Gautam's bed. She was leaving when she turned around and said, 'Let me know if you need tea.'

'I'm fine, Aunty.'

She nodded and said, 'You should always have been Mohini, beta. I knew it.'

I shot and re-shot through the night. It was 9 a.m. when I was woken by Gautam's father pacing around the room. I found him clicking through the footage that I'd shot the night before. He looked at me and then at the camera. Seldom have I seen him with a frown on his face.

'Is something wrong, Uncle?' I asked him.

He handed the camera to me, and said, 'Rachita's video was much better. Use that.'

Before I could string together a sentence, he stormed off.

I edited and uploaded my video later that afternoon.

Neelima Ji

Neelima ji reaches Mohini's house a couple of hours earlier than the time Mohini's mother had asked her to come. She knows one can always use some help, and more than that, company. It can be a lonely job caring for a comatose child. It's the last thing a parent expects, but it's also the first thing a parent fears. Fear is the foundation of any parent–child relationship and it starts even before the child is born. Being a parent means constantly cutting deals with god, promising more devotion for the child's welfare.

'You shouldn't have bothered,' says Mohini's mother and ushers her in.

'Can I see Mohini?' says Neelima ji straight off the bat.

'I was just about to—'

Neelima ji interrupts her and says, 'You make tea for us. I will do it.'

Mohini's mother nods and walks towards the kitchen.

Neelima ji enters Mohini's room. She has done this before, both for Ananth and for Mohini.

'Hello, beta. Good morning,' she says, 'I hope you don't mind that I will take care of you this morning.' She runs her fingers on her face. 'It's the least I can do for you.'

Her hearts brims with love for her, the girl who saved her son. Where would she be without her?

She notices the bed. She remembers every creak, every bend of this bed. It was the same bed her son lay on when he was sick. As she takes care of Mohini—empties her urine bag, changes the catheter, readies the water to wipe her down—she wonders how strong Mohini's mother would have to be to handle all what she has on her own.

Neelima ji looks around the room and sees stacks of books. Every time she comes here, Mohini's mother hands her a few books and insists she read them.

She would then call at odd times of the day and ask, 'Did you read it?' Mohini's mother would ask her piercing questions later.

As much as Neelima ji hates being dominated by someone who would be her *samdhan*, an in-law, she very often ends up getting bullied, just like her son.

Neelima ji is both scared and angry at Mohini's mother.

'You want to be like her,' her husband often told Neelima ji. Neelima ji knew it to be the truth.

Today Mohini's new bed is arriving. The old one will be sold to a scraps dealer. Neelima ji never gives away or throws away anything, and yet, she's happy that she would not have to see this bed again. She would have loved to give it away for free.

It takes an hour and half for Neelima ji to finish with Mohini. Mohini's mother had come to the room twice to check but Neelima ji had chased her away and asked her to rest.

Neelima ji had been shocked—and a little angry—when she got to know that Mohini's mother had a nurse that came over to take care of Mohini. She had come to the house and thrown a tantrum. But Mohini's mother had said sternly that this was her final decision.

'She's ours too,' Neelima ji had said.

'She's mine,' Mohini's mother had replied.

Mohini's mother makes another cup of tea when Neelima ji is done. They drink their tea and Mohini's mother tells

Neelima ji of all the new books she has read. She then checks if Neelima ji had read the books she had given to her the last time. Despite giving all the answers, Mohini's mother doesn't look impressed. She never looks impressed.

A little later, the hospital bed comes. It takes the two women and the delivery guys two hours to replace the old with the new. When they are done, Mohini's mother orders for food and they both sit on two sides of the sofa reading their books.

'They found the girl who's going to play Mohini,' says Neelima ji after a while.

'Rachita, I know. I like her. She's Anusha's friend,' says Mohini's mother without looking up.

Neelima ji often wishes her mother would open to her a little more but Mohini's mother always maintains a stoic demeanour. No matter how much Neelima ji tried to peel off the layers, find her pain and comfort her, it always ended in failure. It can't be easy for a woman to go through this alone, thinks Neelima ji.

Mohini's mother doesn't say anything for a while.

'*Main samajh sakti hu* (I can understand). I have been though it,' says Neelima ji.

Mohini's mother shakes her head.

'*Nahin* (no),' says Mohini's mother calmly. 'You can never understand what I'm going through.'

'My son too—'

Mohini's mother cuts Neelima ji. She looks at her, and says, 'Your son had a disease. It was his fate. No one but god could be blamed for it. But my daughter . . .' Her voice trails.

It was one of the rare moments Neelima ji saw Mohini's mother falter. She gets back to her book.

But Neelima ji knows she's not reading the book. There's something on her mind.

'If you want to say something, you can,' says Neelima ji. '*Aap mujhse keh sakti hain.*'

Mohini's mother looks up, tears in her eyes, anger in her voice, and she says what she doesn't want to say but can't keep herself from saying. It's something Ananth's mother has heard before and has prepared herself to hear over and over again if it lessens Mohini's mother's pain. Because it's the truth.

'My daughter is lying lifeless on the bed because of your son,' says Mohini's mother.

It brings tears to Neelima ji's eyes.

There is nothing she can say to that. This is the truth.

She watches Mohini's mother go back to her book.

Neelima ji says a little while later, 'Please don't hate my son.'

Mohini's mother smiles pitifully. 'How can I hate him, Neelima ji? Your son . . . he's my daughter's life's work. He's her crowning achievement. People know her because she saved a boy who couldn't be saved. Millions of people know her because of him. I can't hate him but I can wish that things were different. I wish my daughter wasn't lying lifeless in that bed because she met your son. I can wish that, can't I?'

Neelima ji nods and stares at her hands. Neelima ji knew it to be true. If the same had happened the other way around, she would have called Mohini a murderer.

Her son had almost killed his own saviour.

'You can,' says Neelima ji.

Mohini's mother continues, 'It's because of Ananth that my daughter is not here sitting with me. Your son was responsible. Nothing changes that. He put her in the bed he was once in. He destroyed her, Neelima ji. Ananth destroyed her.'

Amit Modi

A few weeks ago, Amit Modi had ordered vegetarian biryani to celebrate Gautam's death. His obsessive tracking of Gautam's profile had yielded results. He couldn't find the campaign. He couldn't believe his eyes. His prayers had come true.

He had died.

That bastard had died.

His happiness gave way to a strange emptiness. His hatred for Gautam had been his companion all this time. Now that he was dead, he started to feel a bit empty. But this emptiness, he could live with. He had thought once Gautam is dead, he would flush that madarchod, motherfucker, clean out of his life. And yet every day, he wondered about Gautam's death. How was it? Do people like him feel death? He found himself googling after-life theories.

Even now, out of habit and instinct, every day started and ended with him searching Gautam's name on WeDonate. Of late, tired of seeing 'no search results' he had been browsing through other fundraisers on the website, people who deserved the money they were getting. Sometimes he would even donate a couple of hundreds to one campaign or the other.

And then . . . he saw him.

Bhenchod, sisterfucker.

At first he thought he had gone a bit mad. He thought he had imagined Gautam. But then he was sure. He could recognize the face anywhere, with or without the hair.

The more he read, the more furious he got. The rage, the loneliness, it all returned in an instant.

They had changed the name: Gautam had become Ananth.

He had felt cheated; Gautam wasn't dead, and WeDonate was making further attempts to save the man who should have been dead a long ago.

He had mailed everyone at WeDonate in all capitals telling them that what they were doing was unethical and wrong. Only after he had pressed 'Send' did he realize that he'd put in a few more expletives than required. He got a reply from Sarita that it wasn't technically a lie and that he should mind his language.

That bitch.

But the rage settled down after he realized that there was only a minor inflow of funds. No matter what WeDonate does, Gautam would have to die. Apart from an anonymous donation of Rs 4 lakh, there hadn't been a huge contribution. If he knew who the donor was, he would have chased them down.

He had only started feeling a little better, sleeping a bit more, when in a couple of days, everything came crashing down.

A couple of mornings ago, Gautam's campaign had been given a complete overhaul. A new text, and a video. Video? He clicked the link to the video. It had made him lose his mind.

The video was a complete fucking lie! He knew the girl on screen. She wasn't Mohini; her name is Anusha Sardana and she was Gautam's case worker.

This was unfair.

It had been two days since he had slept.

Every few minutes, he refreshed the YouTube page and then the campaign page. The video was beginning to go viral. People were feverishly sharing it like their lives depended on it. Snippets of the video were being shared on Twitter and Instagram and being retweeted and reposted aggressively. Aggregator websites had started doing small articles on it. *REMEMBER THE TROLL? LOOK WHERE HE IS NOW!* The views were bumping up by thousands, there was no stopping it. There was some nonsense in the video about how Gautam, now Ananth, had been afflicted by a tumour that made him lose empathy, and hence he trolled people. That was fucking nonsense. What kind of a nonsense pretext is that? But the junta was buying into it. They were already forgiving him! When he scrolled through, the comments were all encouraging! People were lauding him, his love story . . .

Money was gushing in. Small donations, big ones, young and the old, everyone was rushing to save Gautam. Worse still, people were feeling bad about Gautam in the comments section. Hordes of people were praying for that bhenchod. Another couple of weeks and Gautam would have the money to get operated. That madarchod.

He couldn't let this happen. What kind of a man would he be if he let this happen?

He waited for two more days. Two more days for people to see that it was a lie. The girl's tears? A lie. What she said about the boy? A lie. He dropped in a barrage of comments saying the same thing but no one paid heed. There were replies to his comments asking him to fuck off. He was outnumbered by thousands. He put up screenshots in the comment sections and yet no one paid heed. They had glossed over his misdeeds. What is it about love that made everyone so weak? And it was all fake!

He hadn't felt this helpless before; this shouting into the void where no one heard him.

Today, he decided to revisit the WeDonate office. The video was touching half-a-million views and he had to be quick.

He rummaged around for the most indistinguishable, loose sweatshirt. He found a large cap too in his cupboard. Then he spray painted the number plate on his motorcycle. He drove around the building a few times and then entered the basement parking. He made sure he was not seen. He had done this before.

Once in the parking, he waited.

It's from here that both Rachita and Anusha exited the building. It was the closest exit to the metro station. He waited. He was positive one of them will see sense in what he had to say. How could they not? Gautam deserved to die! It's what life had decided for him.

He looked around. There were no cameras. There were never any cameras, just shells which gave a sense of vigilance but recorded nothing.

It was six and people from the other office had started to make their way out, get into cabs and cars and go back home to their families. How would the two girls not see that because of Gautam, he did not have a family to go back to?

By seven, the train of home-bound employees had thinned. Without fail, WeDonate's medical employees were always the last to leave. Amit Modi waited. The people from entertainment and tech support passed him by. He wondered if they knew what their colleagues were doing was wrong?

It was 8 p.m. when he saw Anusha. He would have liked it if Rachita would have been with her.

He reminded himself to be calm when he talked to her. Nothing had to blow out of proportion.

'Hi,' he said, blocking Anusha's way.

Anusha was startled. She regained composure and snapped, 'If you don't fuck off, I'm going to bite your face off!'

'WHORE. It's regarding Gautam,' he said.

'What about Gautam? If you want to help him—'

'You need to pull down the video. It's fake and he doesn't deserve what he's getting.'

He saw Anusha hesitate. He knew he was right. It was a lie.

'You need to get out of my way,' said Anusha and started to walk away.

'Listen—' he said.

'Stop following me!' said Anusha and quickened her pace.

He followed.

'He destroyed my life!'

'I don't care what he did. He deserves to live. That's my job,' she said.

He saw her take out of her phone and try to dial a number. Amit Modi knew she wouldn't get reception down there.

'He doesn't—'

The girl was already five paces ahead of him.

'THAT MADARCHOD DESTROYED MY LIFE—' he shouted but the girl didn't turn. She was still trying to make her call.

There was still no reception. Her fingers were trembling now.

'RUK TU SAALI! (Just you wait!)' shouted Amit Modi.

The girl was now beginning to run.

He ran after her and held her hand.

'LET GO!' screamed the girl. With the other hand, she was trying to text someone.

'YOU NEED TO STOP THE CAMPAIGN!'

'LET GO!' she shouted.

She tried to wrest her hand away from his grip. It was too tight. Amit Modi felt her hand get warmer in his grip. He saw the tears creep up in her eyes, the panic.

Good. She deserves it. *Haramzaadi* (bastard).

'GUARD!' she screamed.

'STOP KAR CAMPAIGN, *KUTTIYA WARNA KAAT DAALUNGA*! Bitch, I'll cut you up!'

Anusha was trying to wrest herself free when Amit kicked her, once and then again. She fell on the ground. She started to crawl away from him.

'*BOL KAREGI YA NAHI!* (Will you stop the campaign?)'

The girl was standing up now. She turned towards him, raised her hands, palms facing towards him in apology and said, '*Karu . . . karungi . . .* I will do it. I will do it tomorrow.'

She was crying now. Her words were garbled.

'RIGHT NOW, SAALI!' he screamed.

He saw her bleeding from the head. A thick stream of blood snaked it's way down from her face. He liked seeing her like that, on her knees, begging. She deserved another fucking kick. Why wouldn't she? He was sure she was amongst those who brought him down with glee when Gautam first tweeted about him. He was fucking sure of it.

'I will, please,' she said.

It was a lie. Amit Modi knew it. She wasn't going to.

'WHY WOULD YOU SAVE THAT MADARCHOD, HAAN!' he shouted. 'NO ONE LOVES HIM! NO ONE!'

She was now stepping away from him. 'I will do it . . . I will do it,' she mumbled.

'I don't believe you, WHORE!' he said.

'Please . . . I promise.'

He strode up to her and slapped her.

'SORRY BOL, HARAAMZADI!'

She stumbled backwards.

'Please . . . let me go . . . I will call my boss and tell her . . . it will be taken . . .'

He held her by her neck, choking her.

'*Tu bachaegi bhi to* I will kill him,' he said. '*JAAN SE MAAR DUNGA MADARCHOD KO!*'

'Leave . . . me . . .'

'MADARCHOD!'

He dragged her closer to the exit. The bars returned to his phone and hers. He saw her take her phone out.

'Call your boss,' he said.

Before she could do it, he took the phone away from.

'What . . .' she stammered.

'Wipe your face,' he ordered.

'What . . .'

'Just do what I say, *randi*, you slut!' he shouted.

He opened the camera app. She started wiping her face of the tears and the sweat and the blood.

'I will press play and you will confess that the video was fake and was made to save him. *Sun rahi hai, kuttiya*, are you listening bitch?' he shouted.

'But . . .'

'*KYA*, what!' he bellowed.

'This . . . this will destroy WeDonate's credibility,' she said in a small voice.

'*MADARCHOD, TUJHE LAGTA HAI MUJHE FARAK PADTA HAI?* (Do you think that bothers me?)'

The girl cowered but said, 'There are people who need the money—'

'*CHUP! CHUP!* Shut up!' he shouted. 'I'm switching it on.'

Amit Modi saw the minutest of hesitations. He saw it in her eyes. She didn't want him to die? She sympathized with Gautam! Rage coursed through his body. It was people like her who sided with Gautam's insidious posts. It was people like her who had fanned his tweets, made them explode, directed all the hate towards Amit Modi, destroyed him. He felt this was justice. She destroyed him. He held her tighter by the neck. The tighter his grip, the freer he felt. He felt all the anger come forth, he felt the strength, he felt power, for the first fucking time he felt in control. Everyone of them needed to die and he would kill all of them! He screamed out and then smashed her head against the parking pillar.

'FUCK YOU!' he shouted.

Her head split. Thick blood oozed out. She walked away from Amit. She was stumbling. There was a vacant look on Anusha's face. Her pupils rolled over and her eyes went white. She walked around in a circle and then slumped on the ground.

Amit Modi stood over her. The anger, the adrenaline still coursing through him.

The rage ran its course when Amit Modi saw Anusha's body tremble involuntarily.

Then rage gave way and fear crept in.

'OYE!' he said.

There was no response.

He was frightened now. He saw her stop moving. A little part of him wanted to help her. But . . . she looked dead.

He ran. He ran as fast as he could.

For a month after that incident, there wasn't a day Amit Modi didn't have a panic attack. There was no reportage of the incident. Every day he would buy all the newspapers and scour them for information. Apart from a little piece in *West Delhi Times* about an assault on a girl—robbery suspected—there was nothing. Every day he would wake up to the nightmare of someone banging on the door and dragging him through the streets.

A few days after the accident, Rachita Somani had added a footnote to the video about the assault on Anusha and her critical condition. She told the viewers that the only girl who saw good in Gautam was now dying. They changed the thumbnail and the title of the video.

The title was—DYING GIRL BEGS YOU TO SAVE HER DYING BOYFRIEND—and the thumbnail was of a split screen. There was a picture of Gautam on one bed, and Anusha on the other, both on ventilator support. The video garnered five million new views in a day.

The video's comment section had blown up. The comment section populated with people writing 'done', 'donated', 'breaks my heart', 'life's unfair, god bless', 'no money but best of luck to him'. Within three hours of the change, the campaign garnered another 84 lakh and WeDonate shut it down.

The rest of the money was diverted to the campaigns that were critically underfunded.

A couple of months later, Amit found out that the girl—Anusha Sardana—had slipped into a coma following extensive internal bleeding.

He had tracked her to a hospital in Connaught Place where she was admitted. He posed as a journalist interested in covering her story and her doctor told him there was no certainty as to when she would wake up.

Ananth Khatri

The hope Saraansh had showed me was swiftly snuffed out by Mohini's mother. She refused me access to Mohini's laptop. Now there were no tender looks, no outtakes to look at and make inferences of hidden love.

Things were at status quo. I wasn't going to go on the wild goose chase Saraansh was sending me on.

I was an interesting character to her and she committed herself to the cause. Wouldn't be the first writer who obsessed over someone. I have to admit that the little hope it gave me did make me feel fuzzy and I revelled in it till it lasted.

And as much as her mother's refusal had bummed me, I hadn't got time to think about it in the past week.

We gave the trailer shoot all that we had—twelve-hour shoots for seven straight days for a three-minute trailer. Saraansh bootstrapped the entire shoot and we did everything in-house. The first day was the weirdest of all. With the new haircut, and make-up, Rachita looked strikingly similar to Mohini. Saraansh had written a smart script which he kept fiddling with every day. It didn't require another actor but Rachita. There were backs, and hands and heads of people in the frame, roles that employees of WeDonate played. We shot and shot and shot. We only filmed at real locations—Saraansh insisted on it. It was all very new and quite disconcerting for me. I loved it though. The best parts of the shoots were the conversations about the framings of the scenes. We would stall the filming and figure out the best angles to shoot the scenes from. I loved doing that, and Saraansh let me operate the camera on more than a few occasions. I made a mental note of getting back to the camera someday.

What was even more of a learning experience was what happened on the edit table. We watched the same footage repeatedly till it stopped making sense. After the first day at the edit, I couldn't tell right from wrong and would doze off. Saraansh kept explaining to me why one shot was better than the other. It took up a lot of our time. Saraansh would work through the night, consuming ungodly amounts of coffee. When the trailer was finally ready, and Saraansh showed it to me, once with and once without music, I had lost all objectivity. I couldn't tell how good or bad it was.

It was only when Sarita saw it, and we saw in her expressions what could be best described as discomfort, we knew that it was good. I teared up a little. I think that's why we watch reaction videos—to confirm what we were already feeling.

'We need to show it to the office and then take their feedback. Schedule a screening,' said Sarita to me. 'Call Anusha's mother.'

More confident after Sarita's reaction, I showed it to Maa–Papa. They *bawled*. They watched it ten times in a row and only confirmed what I was feeling.

'It's her, it's her,' Maa kept saying.

She kissed her own fingers and then touched the screen as if it wasn't Rachita but Mohini.

'You did well,' said Papa later in the night.

I took the compliment and didn't share the credit.

They made me send the video to them over WhatsApp. I could hear them watch it a few times in the middle of the night and then again in the morning.

Today is the screening and Maa–Papa alternated between being nervous and arrogantly confident.

'How can people not like it?' they chimed.

I don't want to jinx it by saying anything.

While Maa–Papa discussed the two-minute long trailer like it's an entire movie, my mind went back to the video Mohini had created to save me.

Thanks to the last few days, I now understand the nitty-gritty of edits. I see Saraansh's point better. Rachita's video was heavily edited but Mohini's was one-shot. And now that I have seen people fumble with dialogues I know that unless Mohini was the greatest actor of all times it couldn't have been her first shot. So where did she store the other shots? How many shots were there?

A couple of days ago, I'd told Maa–Papa that I knew about Rachita's video. They always knew that Mohini's mother had told me that Mohini wasn't in love with me and the video was shot only to help me but they had never told me about the other video. They had conveniently skipped the part where Rachita had shot the same video in the room besides me.

I had watched them squirm when I told them I knew, although I held no malice towards them. They were just trying to protect me.

I ask my parents.

'How long did she take?' I ask them.

Papa says, 'She was there the entire night.'

'The entire night?' I ask. 'And you weren't there? Neither of you?'

They both shake their heads.

'But she took the entire night?' I ask again.

They nod.

'Did you see her shoot it?'

'We didn't,' says Papa. 'But I saw the video that went up before. I had asked her to put up Rachita's video.'

'What? Why would you do that?' I ask.

'You have seen Rachita's video. Hers was much better. That's what I felt,' says Papa. 'But she seemed adamant and she put up her own.'

'Hmmm.'

'Which one did you like?' I ask Maa.

Papa answers, 'You know what she thinks about Mohini! What do you think she will say? But yes, as much as I love Mohini, Rachita's was better I think and I told her that.'

Maa says, 'I am glad she didn't listen. She was always his Mohini.'

The words keep bouncing around in my head till I get to office. Saraansh, Rachita and a few interns have already set up the office for the screening. Everyone's working on the laptop, but I can see they are distracted.

'We are set,' says Saraansh pulling me to one side. 'Mohini's mother is about to reach soon.'

He looks nervous so I reassure him about the trailer. I tell him about my parents.

'I know, bro. Nimesh and Nikhat saw it and they were crying. Aunty will like it, I know, all—'

'I need to tell you something,' I interrupt.

I tell him about what Papa had said about Rachita's video being better than Mohini's, of him telling her and her still going ahead and uploading her own.

'So you're thinking . . .?' Saraansh leaves his sentence unfinished.

'What are you thinking?'

'You tell me first, bro,' says Saraansh.

'I don't want to be hopeful.'

Saraansh taps my shoulder. He's thinking what I'm thinking. We don't say it out aloud. We both think that maybe she wanted her name to be attached to mine and not Rachita's? We think that maybe she was a bit jealous? Maybe?

'Can you live with that? It's better than the last truth you knew,' says Saraansh.

'I can live with that,' I say.

Just then, Sarita walks in with Mohini's mother. She leads her to the only two chairs that are there for the screening. Everyone else is on the ground. The blinds are drawn. Saraansh walks to the front of the crowd. Everyone's looking at him. Will there be a speech?

'Please like it,' Saraansh says and walks away from the screen.

He points the clicker at the screen and presses Play.

The trailer fills up the screen. Everyone who has seen the trailer is looking at Mohini's mother. The two minutes seem to stretch out to an hour. In the darkness it's hard to make out what she thinks of it.

'What?' Saraansh nudges me.

I shake my head.

The trailer ends and the lights come on.

Vishwas ji flashes me a thumbs up.

We are all looking at Mohini's mother. That's what matters. Even though the sniffles, the wet eyes of people in the audience are testimony to Saraansh's effort, if Mohini's mother . . .

She looks at Saraansh and nods. She then gets up and walks out of the room. I see her hand coming up to her face. She's looking away from us when the first tears come.

Sarita walks up to Saraansh and says, 'She likes it. Go, talk to her.'

'Are you sure?'

'You brought her alive, go, bask in it,' says Sarita.

They shake hands and Saraansh trots behind Mohini's mother as they make for the balcony.

'Thanks,' says Sarita and turns away before I can acknowledge it.

For the next thirty minutes, I'm at my desk and people come over to congratulate me. They are all looking for Saraansh but he's outside with Mohini's mother. Which is something I don't like. I don't like that she likes him more than she likes me. In fact, she doesn't like me at all. Things have got better with time, but I can taste the unreasonable hostility in the air. It's not like Mohini stole a bit of the love she had for her mother and showered it on me, then why? What else do I have to do to earn her love? When will she truly like me?

Why doesn't she like me?

I get up and walk towards the balcony. I have not thought of how I will break their conversation or if it's even correct to do so.

I hear their voices now. I lean in because I hear my name.

'It's strange Ananth is making this,' she says begrudgingly.

'No one could have made this better,' offers Saraansh.

'If Ananth hadn't walked into her life, we wouldn't have had to make this. I would still have my daughter with me,' says Aunty.

I can hear her sniffle now.

'He loves her, Aunty. It's not his—'

'His fault? Is that what you're going to say?' I hear the desperation in her voice die out. She's now angry. 'Why don't you go ask Sarita how it's not his fault. Everyone keeps saying it's not his fault, it's not his fault. Of course it's his fault!'

'But—'

'It's because of him my daughter is on that bed today. Do you really believe for a moment that it was burglary?'

'I—'

'I have seen the video! For two hours that boy in the basement waited. Two hours! And then he . . .' her voice trails off. '. . . attacked my daughter. Go, ask Sarita what she thinks! No one wanted Gautam to be saved! No one!'

'I'm sure there must be an explanation.'

'There is. There's an explanation,' she says, her voice down to a whisper.

My heart pounds.

'Two months later I got a chit in my letter box.'

Her voice trails off.

'What chit? What was written on it?'

'. . .'

'Aunty?' asks Saraansh again.

'That . . .' Mohini's mother can't find the words to say it.

'Aunty, you can tell me,' says Saraansh.

'Just two lines. "I didn't want your daughter to be hurt but she shouldn't have helped Gautam. Sorry."'

'No.'

Her mother continues, 'There was a two-thousand rupee note with it. So tell me? Who is responsible?'

In that moment, my world turns dark.

Anusha's Mother

Anusha's mother has been happiest this week. Every few minutes she would open her daughter's e-mail and it would hang for a while. And then it would update all the new e-mails telling her how much they liked the trailer; how much they adore Mohini. The trailer already has 3.5 million hits.

The crowdfunding hasn't started yet. Sarita has told her they would first create a budget according to the response the trailer receives and then invite money.

Anusha's mother is happy thinking how many people will watch it.

And just like that, her happiness is punctured and muddled. It's been happening for the last few days. Sometimes she forgets why she suddenly gets sad and then the reason strikes her.

Gautam. Or Ananth as he calls himself.

His mother, Neelima ji, calls her every day to tell her that he hasn't been eating, hasn't been to work, and spends his time wandering around the locality. Sometimes Gautam's mother takes her by surprise by how hoarsely she can cry.

But what's she supposed to do?

She never meant to tell him. He heard it, it's his problem. This has always been his problem. He pokes his too much into everyone's business. And nothing he heard while eavesdropping was a lie. It was his fault. He should know that. Had he not tweeted those things, had he not made enemies out of so many people, her daughter wouldn't have gotten her head bashed in. What was her daughter's fault? Why is she in that bed?

Just then, the phone rings again and it's Gautam's mother. She cuts the call. She can't take another bout of crying from his mother.

Well, at least, Saraansh isn't calling anymore. He was calling her incessantly till she blocked his number. He had come home yesterday to talk to her. He had ended up crying and begging Anusha's mother to help his friend.

She had asked him to leave. He had done so obediently.

Anusha's mother unlocks her phone to check the comments below the video when she notices her battery is low. It has been happening quite frequently this week. Her time on YouTube is draining the battery.

She walks into Anusha's room to hook up the phone to the charger. She leans over to Anusha and kisses her cheek. She then turns to hook up her phone to recharge.

That's when she notices. The laptop is gone.

'Saraansh!' she mutters angrily under her breath.

Ananth Khatri

That's the reason why you shouldn't confide about yourself to anyone. When I see Saraansh walk towards me, I give running away a thought. He will eventually catch up. Let's just rip this off like a band-aid.

'No more hiding,' he says when he gets to me. 'Is this taken?' He points to the swing next to me.

'I don't want to see anything you have made,' I say.

He's carrying a laptop. I'm sure it's another edit. He has been mailing me for the last couple of days—media files. I have been deleting them without looking. I haven't got around to submitting my resignation but I will do that. Maybe that will keep Saraansh off my back. It is none of my business being there or being a part of this movie.

'It's not something I made,' he says. 'It's hers.'

And that's when it strikes me. Of course, it's not his laptop! I have seen this laptop a thousand times. It's Mohini's.

'There's something you might want to see,' he says.

I want to refuse him. No matter what he shows me, how will I undo what I have done to her. How will I ever be okay with the fact that it's because of me that she's on that bed.

He's opening the laptop. I can still refuse him.

I have gone through my timeline to find every insulting tweet I had sent out, trying to figure out who took out the anger meant for me, on her. There are dozens and dozens of accounts that are shut down. I have done this exercise before.

The first time I did it, it was to publicly apologize to everyone. It was painful but this . . . this is . . .

I'm not suicidal. But I want to shut down for a little while. Stop my brain from whirring incessantly. I'm not going to waste this life Mohini gifted me. But how am I going to live it well with the knowledge that I have now?

I don't refuse him. He takes a while to go through the folder where there are at least fifty-four videos.

The thumbnail is all the same. I squint.

It's her in front of my bed. Mohini and I. Now I know what the videos are.

They are the rejected versions of the one she had uploaded. He loads them all on to the media player.

'I don't want to watch them,' I say.

'You have to, there's something you need to see,' says Saraansh.

'After what I did to her?' I ask.

He looks at me, trying to fathom if I'm about to cry. I won't, I'm out of tears.

'You didn't do anything to her. The man was at fault,' says Saraansh.

I roll my eyes. *It's my fault.*

'You love her, and she doesn't believe anything you did was your fault,' says Saraansh.

'. . .'

'You have to see the video. If you love her, you have to see it, and you have to believe what she believes. That it wasn't your fault,' says Saraansh.

He holds my gaze.

'I—'

'Just watch them.'

The videos in the media player start to play.

One after another, each video plays. The script veers wildly.

There's one that's 138 minutes long.

'This is the video from where the final video was cut from,' says Saraansh. 'That one-shot was cut from this video.'

'Play it,' I say.

It plays.

'Hi . . . I'm Mohini and I'm a friend of Ananth, the boy you see behind me. You might know him as Gautam but that doesn't matter. The people who love him call him . . . fuck . . . Cut cut . . .'

She takes a pause.

'Hi . . . When I joined WeDonate I didn't think this would happen to me. We were . . . umm . . .

. . . fuck . . .'

Mohini gets up from the chair, takes a bunch of pages and reads the script. She takes her position again.

'Hi . . . When I joined WeDonate I didn't think this would happen to me. We were warned something like this could happen. I'm Mohini and I'm a friend of Ananth, the boy you see behind me. You might know him as Gautam but that doesn't matter. The people who love him call him . . . fuck . . . *aage kya tha!* . . . why am I stumbling so . . . fuck . . . Cut cut . . .'

Just then, there is a knock on the door and we hear a voice off-screen. I know it to be my mother.

'Do you need anything?' she asks.

'I'm fine,' says Mohini.

The door closes.

'Hi . . . When I joined WeDonate I didn't think this would happen to me. We were warned something like this could happen. I'm Mohini and I'm a friend of Ananth, the boy you see behind me. You might know him as Gautam but that doesn't matter. The people who love him call him Ananth.'

There's a pause. She takes a deep breath. She takes her phone out. She puts a video on play. I can hear what she's watching. It's Rachita. She puts a stop to it.

She turns towards me on the bed.

'Why on earth does this matter to me? Why? Why am I jealous? Fuck it. Okay, whatever, screw this. Let's start.'

She looks at the camera again.

'Hi . . . When I joined WeDonate I didn't think this would happen to me. We were warned something like this could happen. I'm Mohini and I'm a friend of Ananth, the boy you see behind me. You might know him as Gautam but that doesn't matter. The people who love him call him Ananth. His case came to me. I didn't want it. He wasn't worth saving, everyone around me told me that. He's not a good person, people kept repeating around me. His tweets told me that. But I was stuck so I dug in, tried to find more about him. And I did. Contrary to what people think, he's the most considerate person I have ever met.'

She cries a little. Then she shuffles through the pictures in her hands. She points them at the screen.

'He was a photographer. He spent his days clicking pictures of his friends, his family, his sister. He captured them in their most vulnerable, most beautiful, most human moments. To think that he would be a bad person, a person devoid of love or sympathy towards others—it didn't sit quite right. Every time I looked at those pictures, the love he has poured in every single frame, I couldn't believe he was capable of the hate people accuse him of. I will put a link in the description. You can see the photographs yourself.

'So I talked to his doctor, to other patients who had a similar condition as his. The doctor told me the tumour of his brain had robbed him of his empathy. He couldn't feel what words or gestures hurt other people. Now I can show you MRI reports and you can Google if it's true?

'But you have no tumour. You can feel, right? So try to feel this?'

She turns back and looks at me and then back at the camera.

'The boy behind me lost his sister in an accident. Three-year-old girl, a girl he had fed, bathed, raised not as a thirteen-year-old brother but as a father. She died in his arms in the middle of the road even as people like you and me walked past. She bled out in his arms. He had seen you. Watching. Recording on your phone. And yet not helping him. And this is the same YOU who reject him because he was rude? Unsympathetic? He had seen you at your worst. When you couldn't bother to take his sister's body to the hospital. And yet, even after losing his little sister . . . he didn't hate you. Not then. Instead, he sought to love you with all his heart, hoping he would change you one person at a time. He made friends and loved them with all his heart. I have met many of his friends to know that to be true.

'Could you have said that about yourself? Could you have had the courage to love the world as a fifteen-year-old whose dying sister was helped by no one?

'People laughed at me when I started off trying to save him. They now think I have lost it when I say that I love him.'

She places a sob at the correct moment. I have seen this before.

'There is an important distinction between me being in love versus we being in love with each other. Of course, he doesn't know me. But I know him and even with him lying there in a coma, I fell in love with him. I know, I know you're sneering.'

She shakes her head.

'. . . but in all probability I know more about him than you know about the person you love.'

She gets up and zooms out the lens.

'. . . there's the stack of everything he has ever photographed. Behind every picture is an inscription. So I have seen what he has, and I have seen things the way he saw things, which is more than you can say about anyone.'

She holds up a phone.

'I have read every text he has sent, every mail he has composed, every note he has written, every DM he has sent. I have also read every text he hasn't sent, every mail that's in his drafts, every note in his phone memory. I know everything about him that he hid from others. Have you? Can you claim that of the person you love?'

The tears return. She points to the stack of receipts.

'Thanks to his father's obsession, I have seen every single thing he has bought, and apart from camera equipment, he has hardly bought anything for himself. What I'm trying to . . .'

She cries dramatically now.

'He's a friend now. I know him, I know him more than I know myself. And I love every bit of him. All I want for him is to get up, be well, and hear from me that he's a nice person, that he's loved, that he deserves the best in life. He can't die . . .'

More tears come.

'He can't die with people hating him. He doesn't deserve it. He's not the person people have come to know. He's better, he needs to be loved. I will add the links to his photographs at the end of the video. Watch them and decide . . .'

She looks straight at the camera.

'Please save him. Please.'

That's the end of the video. That's where the links come up. But in this video, there's another sixty-eight minutes of footage left.

'Keep watching,' says Saraansh.

'Cut,' says Mohini in the video.

She sits there for a bit. She doesn't get up.

'She forgets to stop the recording,' says Saraansh.

Mohini then gets up. She looks at me on the bed.

She says to me, the one lying on the bed, 'I couldn't have let Rachita do it.'

Saraansh keeps his hand on mine.

I watch Mohini sit on the bed next to me.

'Can I?' she says. 'Of course, you don't mind.'

She then climbs next to me on the bed and faces the ceiling.

She says, 'Would you think I was being weird that I spent so much time staring at the ceiling? I felt like I was overstepping some boundary the first time I lay next to you, but fuck it. I'm not touching you. Well, except that one time I held your hand. I deserve that. I got a lot of money for you.'

She looks at me.

Saraansh says, 'She has done this before.'

'Just shut up,' I snap and try to stem my tears.

She says after a while, 'I'm going to be so wrecked if I get the money, you wake up and don't fall in love with me. I will be my mother then. A public relationship but private humiliation. Maybe that will be our thing, the Sardana women thing. I knew even while I was writing the script that I won't allow Rachita to play Mohini. And yet, I went ahead with it.'

She then starts to laugh.

'You . . . hehehe . . . all this time what I was thinking . . . that you and I, we are a fling. Can you believe that? That I had a passing liking for a . . . what are you . . . a corpse? I mean a living corpse. I mean . . . you have to agree it's a bit weird to sort of fall in love at first sight with a person in a coma.'

She then fixes my hair.

'It would have been even stranger if this were a one-sided fling. At least now that I have labelled this as love, there's some legitimacy, a little less weirdness to it. But that's what I thought of us. Every time I used to come here and steal glances at you, make my hand touch yours, sit here . . . pretending to work . . . in my head it was a fling. I mean, that's the best I could come up with.'

She then looks up at the ceiling again.

'Sometimes I think I fell in love because you are the perfect partner. One who listens and doesn't talk back. Confined to bed, you have little chance to go astray. I can control the length of your facial hair, your hairstyle so you look like the way I want you to and not go on a no-shave November. Beard's not for handsome boys like you; you have nothing to hide.'

She runs her hand over my face.

'You will be all right. It will be such a waste of a good life if you don't wake up.'

She shakes her head.

'You know what I'm looking forward to most? For you to wake up and photograph me. Naah, not for the 54 followers on Instagram. For myself. I want to know how you will see me. Will you hate me? Will you like me? I keep thinking about it every night, imagining various scenarios. In most, you're grateful to me because I saved your life but then you walk off with a *nice* girl.'

She turns towards me.

'You make me want to be *nice* again. Be good and kind. Isn't that something, Ananth? You make me want to believe in love . . . you . . . were supposed to be my story. Instead, you changed mine.'

She then puts her arm around me and closes her eyes. She whispers.

'I love you.'

'She stays like that for an hour,' says Saraansh and wants to forward to the end.

'No.'

She's next to me with her arm around me for the next hour. Then she gets up, fixes her hair and drinks water. It's now that she notices that the camera is on. She walks and switches it off. The video ends.

'She loved me.'

'She saved you,' says Saraansh. 'And in your own little way, you saved her.'